Chris Danes is a writer and broadcaster. He went to school in London and Chichester and then read Theology at Brasenose College, Oxford. Following research in New Testament studies, he was a schoolteacher for many years, becoming deputy headmaster at St Thomas More in Westcliff-on-Sea.

Chris was diagnosed with bi-polar disorder in 2001 and now undertakes a good deal of work for mental health groups, including Mind. He is a frequent speaker on mental health issues and has regularly contributed to *You and Yours* on Radio 4.

He has two grown up children and lives in Maldon with his wife Ruth, their dog, and five cats.

On Balance

Chris Danes

ST
MARK'S
PRESS

To Ruth, with love

And with grateful acknowledgement to
Alex Jeffries, Christine Ayers-Sach,
Andrew Jasper and Roy Chad

The corpse had been undisturbed in the boat's cabin for some days. A pair of bolt croppers lay beside it, sticky with coagulated blood and tissue. Flies had laid eggs in it, and these reproductive duties done were buzzing about feeding. They particularly gathered around bits of brain and the remains of the eyes. There were deep stabs in the abdominal wall where the material of the shirt had been driven hard into the organs by repeated blows, and these wounds were moving rhythmically in a ghastly parody of life as maggots went about their unpleasant but ecologically necessary business. This thing that had once carried around a man was naked from the waist down, and perhaps most disturbing was the area around the groin. A sustained attack had been made there, separating the penis and most of the scrotum from its parent body and lacerating the upper thighs. Insect life moved here also.

One

Samphire pierced the greasy mud near Mootborough's sea wall. Laura had asked a number of local people how to cook it, but kept forgetting. Something like asparagus, she seemed to remember. She rather fancied the picture of herself gathering the green knobbly spears and taking them home to serve to guests. They would be cautious at first and then delighted, and she would gobble up the compliments with melted butter. Maybe she could really be like that. She would keep bantams, giving the extra eggs away. She could make her own bread and gather sloes in the autumn for gin. She might wear a green waxed jacket instead of this too-thin frayed ancient denim, and tie her now unkempt and grubby hair, new washed with transforming fair trade and natural preparations, in pretty scarves. Paisley patterned, rustic and caring was the image, perhaps.

Before Dad died Laura had eaten samphire when they were all on holiday in France near St Valéry sur Somme. She had been about ten and it had been pickled: she could still remember the sharp surprising salt crunch of it. At her daydream, pine-tabled dinner party it would be like that again, only better because it would be fresh and without vinegar. She was pleased with herself, and on behalf of the soon-to-be-invited friends, that she had recognised the spikes in the mud. A few years ago she wouldn't have been able to. She would have been taken up with the daily drive into school, tricky parents and budgetary requirements, lesson planning and marking books and kids with insoluble problems. Briefly she liked herself for her new knowledge, just as she liked the relaxed conversations in the pub with people for whom samphire and sailing and ferrets and hens were to be taken for granted.

There were steps leading down from the sea wall onto the shingled foreshore where a litter of dinghies spread over the pebbles before the mud began, their painters overcrossing here and there in a deranged cat's cradle. Most of the boats were upturned as a precaution against rain: others, perhaps the property of more assiduous owners, sported tarpaulins and water-filled supermarket milk containers dangling over their sides to serve as fenders. Laura picked her way among them, admiring briefly and with half-conscious jealousy the simple ingenuity of people making do with what was to hand, their lack of concern for what looked right or was intended to impress.

The tufts of grass at the bottom of the wall were straining towards the town with the breeze. Laura left off her amblings, leaned against the concrete and closed her eyes against the climbing morning sun on the far side of the estuary. It warmed her cheeks and eyelids as she heard the noises about her, the slight hum of traffic from the High Street and its feeder roads, the cough and roar as somebody started an outboard motor before choking it back to catch the ebbing tide, the hiss of water running away over the mud and the birds chuckling and flapping on the salt flats from the far shore. When she looked again at the river the sun had left floating blobs of colour in her vision and she had to wait a few seconds before setting off towards the town. Slightly numbed by the breeze she quickened her pace, crunching the stones vigorously beneath her squeakily protesting and scuffed trainers.

It would be break time at school now. The children would be playing football or hanging around in groups, chased from their form rooms into the sunshine by the prefects, for indoor break was only allowed on wet weather days. Colleagues would be on duty with their hands cupped around mugs of tea or instant coffee from the Staff Room, waiting for Laura or one of the other deputy heads to come and spend some time with them before blowing the whistle to start the reluctant shuffle back into class. Except, of course, it would no longer be Laura. Her exile made her want to drink alcohol again. Cooking brandy in coffee would warm her up and give her an excuse when she got home.

The foreshore was covered with detritus. A dead seagull, its beak open and with a milky rotting eye, stared at Laura from a mass of filthy blown feathers and sand flies. She shuddered and walked on. A tangle of discarded fishing net held a plastic coke bottle and dead crabs captive. Some slut too idle to find the bins the Council provided perfectly obviously along the Prom had thrown a dirty nappy down. Laura lifted it by its corner, carried it up to the path and disposed of it. A great glob of snot squatted glistening on the path, which might have led her to believe that Mootborough was suffering from an outbreak of tuberculosis had she not been familiar with the hawking habits of the more unruly of the Upper School pupils at John Rigby's. With a spasm of anger she remembered that her own Lizzie was bound there next year and would be followed by Davie the year after. She thought of her children, of Lizzie's shampoo-fresh hair

11

snuggled against her own cardigan and Davie's soft shy desperate end-of-the-weekend goodbye kiss, and quickened her pace again as a precaution against the tightening of her jaw and the grittiness around her eyes which presaged another angry weeping fit.

She wanted to get home quickly now, past where the former council houses had their anally retentive flower beds and marigolds standing like soldiers in a row, firing squads for her own talent's failure and a reproach for the Spring and Winter indolence which had left her garden weedily overgrown and, she was certain, a cause of much tutting among her hateful immediate neighbours whose gnome-guarded swards were their main weekend activity. Last year, she told herself savagely, she had been mad about gardening. She had cleared and weeded, planted and shaped, planned and plotted on graph paper for the best that ingenuity, nature and hard work could devise. She had gone to the pub with broken fingernails and socks that were gritty with soil. More than once she had laughed with some bloke as afterwards, when they undressed, garden dirt had tumbled from her hair and the crevices of her sweat-weary flesh, and they had resorted to a giggling shower before sex. Now the garden fork stuck in the flowerbed since the Autumn and the remainder of the tools thrown haphazardly in the once minutely arranged shed were yet another of her enthusiasms discarded as quickly as begun, like the half-finished novel on the computer and the expensive teach-yourself-course in Italian from the days when she idiotically thought, until reality and responsibility had reasserted themselves, that she might just possibly escape to become an English guide in Florence.

Dad, she thought, would not have approved, any more than he would have approved of her enforced retirement.

He had been a committed gardener, keen on fair days after work to exchange his soap smelling surgery clothes for old ones before dead-heading the roses or inspecting the underside of leaves for signs of incipient death, the finding of which would lead to much clipping out and spraying before the pubs opened at half past six. Heavier work was left for weekend mornings, when beds were forked over, lawns mown and bushes planted. She guessed he had gone about it all with the same determination that had driven him against all the odds from his background among the back-to-back housing of pre-war East London to a national service commission and then to medical school.

To ward off despair and obeying what she had been taught, Laura reminded herself that Dad was not there to approve or disapprove any more, and that in any case it was demonstrably hypocritical of him to have set impossible standards which she would always fail. After all, she was not the one who had overturned the car pissed while on call to a patient. But the memories persisted and took an unhelpful direction. The headline from the Mootborough Standard, 'Local Doctor in Drunken Death Crash' thoughtfully sellotaped to her desk in school the Tuesday before the funeral. Her attempts to bite back tears in the laburnum filled churchyard. Her mother crying for a month afterwards.

Laura had responded with hatred. She had hated Dad, hated her mother's constant sniffling, hated her younger sister's grasping, needy affection and her elder one's sensible attempts at cheerfulness, and most of all she had hated herself for having felt safe and doing nothing to prevent it all, as though somehow she could, by force of her young will, have turned the steering wheel the other way or stopped him having a drink or made the telephone not ring.   Later, reading History at Cambridge and collecting the series of academic prizes which were eventually to lead to her First, she knew that she had been trying to break away from Dad's memory and to assuage it at the same time.

By the time she reached the front door Laura was crying heavily. She was used to this. At first, four or five years ago during her last days in work and the divorce from Jack it had been very embarrassing, but now somehow it did not seem to bother her so much. Rather than attract unwanted attention from the ignorantly sympathetic she had acquired the technique of silent weeping, only wiping the tears away when it became impossible to see or in order to remove smudged makeup on the rare occasions she wore mascara. In this way she could wait for the moment when it became possible to cry without inhibition in noisy solitude. Of course this did not work all the time. Still too frequently she found herself caught out when alcohol and the need for companionship had loosened her tongue, and she had seen the embarrassed turning away of heads among the tables round about her, the sudden concentration of people on their pints which she would remember in a hungover morning with the cold self-knowledge of practice that once more she had made a fool of herself.

Vaguely aware that the paint on the door was blistering Laura let herself into the nineteenth-century two-up, two-down cottage she had bought with her share of the money from when Jack and she had split up. The terrace was an attractive one, with some fancy red brickwork arching over the doorframes giving contrast to the sandy stocks of the rest of the walls. The front walls of the houses ran directly onto the pavement, and as Laura was fond of telling herself in her happier times and pointing out to others, 'this had preserved the integrity of their original design as working people's houses: for, thank God, there was no room for additional bay windows with all their attendant horrors of fake lead lights and mock carriage lamps, nor could box-like porches be placed in front of the building line to affront the eye as was the case among the bigger houses of, for instance, the Saltbridge Road.' And whispering back that inner voice: *bollocks: you are just apologising for not living in a posh house any more, you hypocritical dissembling bitch.*

Inside the cottage was the usual muddle of ashtrays, coffee cups and old copies of newspaper supplements. Laura grabbed a handful on her way into the kitchen at the back of the house and put them on the worktop to be dealt with later, then leant heavily against the sink as she filled the kettle and a glass of water for her half-forgotten morning tablet. She swallowed the little green and white torpedo without much faith, pinning her hopes instead on the contents of the half-bottle of Three Barrels that she unscrewed and slugged on top of the bitter-smelling coffee granules before adding hot water, milk and sugar. She carried the mug to the sofa, and tucking her legs up underneath herself gave way to great, heaving noisy sobs made worse by the knowledge that they were about everything and nothing.

Two

Saltbridge Medical Surgery
Mootborough

21 June 1999

Dear Doctor,

I wonder if you wouldn't mind taking a look at a patient and friend of mine, Mrs. Laura Morton, the daughter of the late Dr. John O'Higgins who used to be senior partner here. Laura was brought to me today by her husband and I am certain she is clinically depressed. We have all agreed here that in the circumstances costs will be borne by our practice under fund-holding arrangements. Laura is one of the deputies at St John Rigby School and I think that things may rather have got on top of her, so I have signed her off work for the next two weeks *pro tem*. I have also started her on 20mg of fluoxetine p.d.

Yours sincerely,

Christopher Andrews, M.B.,Ch.B.

Dr. R. Lewis
Consultant Psychiatrist
Earl's Friary Hospital
Amblehurst.

MEMO

From: Ronald Lewis, M.B., Ch.B., F.R.C.Psych.
To: Jean Tomlinson
Date: 30.6.99

Jean:

I've got another depressed senior teacher for you. Laura Morton: 35, married, deceased doctor's daughter (knew him vaguely I think,) works at a (guess) Catholic school. Intelligence ++ but 0 insight into her own condition. Uses conversation as a blood sport: hard work but you may enjoy it. Drinks. On 20mg Prozac but I may up it. Not up to work this term, maybe longer – you tell her: she seems to hate me. Not suicidal I think. Put you down for 1 x 14 days with her. I'm seeing her every 6 wks.

Ronnie.

Three

The pub was evening-alive with smoke and beer. At some point in the week she now found it difficult to pinpoint, Laura's despair had broken. To her delight, along her route a squirrel had chuckled and run ahead of her along the churchyard wall before jumping his farewell into a walnut tree. For a couple of days she had been thinking about a number of plans for a happiness she was eager to share. She would apply to the Open University to become a tutor again, finish her book, and buy a swimming-pooled property in France with the proceeds where she could invite all her friends. Only yesterday Libby Purves had been interviewing a woman author on Radio 4, and since hearing their conversation over the washing-up – it was good she was not being so lazy any more about housework – Laura had rehearsed in her mind what she would say to Libby, as she had begun to think of her, after the inevitable success she would herself enjoy post-publication. After all, other people did it who didn't seem any brighter than her, and seldom had she felt more alive or witty or more capable of applying her intelligence to renewed efforts which would make up for the past few years and send her spinning into a new life which would carry with it the best of the old and redeem it. She would certainly succeed, and tonight she was determined to celebrate her decisions and to grasp happiness by the balls.

Les was behind the bar. She liked Les very much, she suddenly decided. She liked the Glaswegian accent he had never lost, his ancient cardigans, his unashamed habit of rolling his cigarettes in a machine rather than by hand, the nicotine stains on his hands and old man's moustache, his straightforwardness and sudden surprising bursts of knowledge. She waited as he finished serving a round, taking in the hugely enjoyable sensations around her: the sparkle of the light on polished brass, the incense curls of tobacco smoke, the burr and rumble of conversation split by laughter. Les turned to her.

'And will you be partaking of a wee drinkie with us this evening, young missy?' Always the same. It made her giggle.

'I will, Les, if you would be so kind. In fact I think I shall have rather more than is good for me tonight. A pint of Adnams, please.'

'Just you go steady, young Laura. I'm too bloody old to go putting you to bed at the end of the evening.'

'Oh, go on, Les, just this once. You promised.'

He handed over her pint. 'Feeling a bit like that tonight are we darling? Away with you. Go and pester someone your own size.' She laughed and waited for Les to say, as she knew he would, 'How are you doin' anyway?'

Laura handed him the money. 'OK thanks. In fact I feel really good. What about you?'

'Musn't grumble. Nae bugger listens when I do anyhow.'

Laura's friend Andrea's voice came from behind: 'That's because you're such a miserable complaining old Scots git,' and then to Laura: 'Hello, babes.'

'Och, piss off, the pair of ye. I've got better things to do serving these gentlemen here than listening to your nonsense.' The laughter included the two strangers who had approached the bar. Andrea touched Laura's arm, slopping a small amount of cider from the glass she was holding in her other hand. 'Come on, sit with me.'

They carried their pints back to the benches around the walls. The upholstery reminded Laura of furry seat covers on coach trips from her primary school, when she would scramble for the back row and sit with the backs of her knees prickling against the material and giggle with her friends, waving at the cars behind them. She smiled at the memory.

'Cheers.' Andrea supped greedily at her cider and Laura gulped the beer. She had long ago decided she liked beer a lot.

'So you all right?' Andrea was dressed in jeans and a T-shirt that had seen better days and which Laura guessed belonged to her boyfriend. She had no makeup on and had clearly already drunk at least a pint or two. Nonetheless Laura had noticed how her black shoulder-length wavy hair, comfortable waist and blue eyes, together with a fine pair of boobs bobbing against her top had caused the men at the bar to cast looks at her in admiration. She certainly had it, she thought. Good for her. Not that she looked that bad herself, she reckoned, after her shower and change of clothes, and she leant forward slightly so that her own breasts strained against the material of her shirt. She was pleased to feel one of the bloke's eyes on her.

'Yes, thanks. I am really good. I think I may be really going places. What about you?'

'Just fine, babes.'

Over the years since Laura had left work and despite the differences in their backgrounds and education Andrea and she had grown close in that casual way that pub acquaintances will. This evening Laura felt especially fond of her, and by half way down her second pint they were on a roller coaster of hilarity, eagerly swapping salacious small town gossip.

'...I don't believe it. In the greenhouse? At the kid's birthday party?'

'No, honestly it's true. They've been at it for ages apparently. Janice at the Queen's told me.'

'My God, do you think he knows? She'd have a bit of a job explaining away a ginger baby. Terrifying. Science should wake up to our ginger problem.'

Laura knew that this was an old enough and rather unkind joke, but never mind any of that. To her immense satisfaction and delight Andrea screamed with laughter, tucking her legs up and rolling sideways almost into the next table where one of the old boys from the barges was enjoying his drink, his Breton cap perched on his head as though it had grown there.

'Ooops, sorry Bob.'

The older man regarded them with good humour. 'Looks like you two are having a fine time.'

'Yeah, we are,' said Andrea. 'I'm ever so sorry. Can we get you anything?'

'No, darling, I am fine thanks, it's kind of you to ask.'

Laura loved all this, she thought. She loved the closeness of pub life where everybody knew everybody, the mixing of age and class, the egalitarianism of alcohol and conversation and the implied friendship in buying one another drinks, and above all she loved her own ability to make people laugh. All of them made her feel warm and at home. She went to the bar and leaned against it with Andrea for another round. The two men from earlier had moved away to a table in the corner and she nudged her.

'Who are those two over there?'

'Them two? Don't you know Pete? He's the one with

the greasy hair and leather jacket. He's been working in the Philippines and comes back here for part of the summer. He was in the year above me at John Rigby's. The other one's his brother, Mark. They're both arseholes.' Mark had his back turned so she waved at the one called Pete: 'Hello, darlin'. You OK?'

Laura laughed. 'Andrea, you shock me profoundly. Such hypocrisy. Same again please, Les.'

'Wait your turn, lassie. I've nae got three pairs of hands.' Laura thought quickly: she must make Les laugh. She had it.

'So not one for me, one for Andy, and one to pull the pints? That's shame. It sounds nice.'

Les gave a mock lascivious grin. 'I bludy wish.'

Andrea giggled. Turning towards Laura she swallowed some cider and nodded towards the brothers. 'Still, arseholes or not, d'you fancy them then – since you was asking about them?'

Laura giggled and considered this. Decidedly not, she reckoned, but who cared.

'Does a starving woman refuse a crust of bread?' Andrea sloshed cider into renewed laughter, and Les chuckled and shook his head as he overheard. Laura felt the pleasure glow in her face and fingertips, and drew deeply on her cigarette. She really was in good form tonight.

'Good evening, ladies.' George Brightly was one of the pub regulars, and hugely popular. Fifty-something, he was nattily dressed in blazer, polo shirt, deck shoes and canvas sailing slacks, and was one of those people who seem to know everybody and everybody seems to know. Among other things Laura knew him to be a freemason, a supposedly Independent district councillor, a bachelor, an inveterate do-gooder, a fanatical sailor, a company director of something-or-other, and a regular Mass-goer at the Catholic church which she had more or less abandoned. He was drinking his habitual pink gin, although she knew too that this was before moving on later in the evening to beer. He flapped his pinkly large hands at them and homed in on Andrea for a kiss.

'George darling. Mmmmmmmm, you're so snuggly.'

'You too, my dear.'

God, she must be pissed, thought Laura.

'Hi George,' she said as she turned her cheek towards him. His face was smooth and smelt slightly of cologne.

'So how are Mootborough's most elegant creatures?'

It wasn't so much that Laura disliked George. In fact she found his carefully polished manners and BBC vowels rather quaint, and his anecdotes were very good. What made her feel rather uneasy in his company was that when she had been a deputy at St. John Rigby's he had been on the board of Governors there as a County Council appointee. He had never been unkind to her face about it of course, and indeed was so scrupulous in avoiding any mention of the school that Laura no longer even knew if he were still a Governor. Yet while he was careful to include himself as the target of many of his stories, enough of them were directed at the failings and ridiculous qualities of others to make Laura wonder if she too had not at some point been the subject of some. For this reason she felt slightly irritated by Andrea's fulsome welcome before dismissing the thought as unworthy, possibly evidence of mild paranoia, and threatening to a pleasant evening. Besides which, she reminded herself, Andrea was deliciously and notoriously two-faced with occasional friends. Maybe there would be some fun in this conversation despite its unpromising beginnings. But for more time than was necessary Andrea and George talked about boats, and Laura began to be bored.

'So have you got *Stella Maris* out of the water yet, darlin', or what?' said Andrea, to Laura's growing irritation.

'A couple of weeks should see me finished. I've got a bit of work to do on the rudder and then I have to slap on some antifouling. I hope to be craned in for the start of April.'

'Cool, honey. Anything special planned?'

'One or two things perhaps. It's rather difficult to say at the moment what with one thing and another, but I was hoping to nip over to Holland sometime, and maybe go along the north coast of France for a bit.'

'On your own, George?' Laura asked, in order to keep herself in the conversation so that she could undermine it and be funny.

George drew on his Café Crème. 'Probably not. In fact I was possibly thinking of taking one or two of the lads from this Galilee Lads' Mission thing with me. A couple of them are coming on really rather well, and they are kind of fun to have around. That's not to say that you two wouldn't be most welcome to come out yourselves for a sail if you fancy a day on the Estuary.'

Andrea laughed her cigarette-smoky laugh. 'You gotta be joking! I'd just get pissed and fall in. Ask Laura.'

'Well, Laura? A day's sailing?'

'Maybe, George. We'll have to see. But tell me about this Mission-thingy. What is it? It sounds adorably old-fashioned.'

'The Galilee Lads' Mission? Oh, that's a new thing I found last season. I thought I had told you about it, dear. It's very good work, and ecumenical of course. Run out of Amblehurst by the Anglican Rector of St. Cyprian's there, Father Jackson. The aim is to get underprivileged youngsters out on the water, you know, all that sort of stuff. They really love it.'

'Sounds great,' said Laura, hating what she could not help but think of as a nauseating display of religiosity and experiencing some other, less sharply defined inward shudder.

'I think it's good too,' George was saying. 'Of course there's an awful lot of nonsense to go through with criminal records checks and insurance and so on, but that's sadly necessary these days I suppose. Oh, I say, excuse me, there's a chap over there I must see.'

Andrea and Laura said their 'see you laters' and watched George as he retreated into the other bar with its tourist views over the River.

'Pouf,' said Andrea, succinctly. Laura was relieved immediately: Andrea did not like George that much either, apparently, and was being homophobic to boot. Now she could afford to be magnanimous and show how nice she was.

'Do you really think so? I always thought he was more, well, asexual, really. You know, not interested. Hardly a raving queen, is he? And we shouldn't be nasty about gays anyway.'

'Oh, come on. Everybody knows he's one of them. And he left us as soon as some leather boy turned up, anyway, which makes him queer so far as I'm concerned.'

Laura giggled. 'Bollocks. How do you know he was a leather boy?'

'I'm making a guess based on past whatsitsnames. And anyway, what about taking little boys out in his boat?'

Laura pulled a face. 'I think you have a very nasty mind, Andy. Let's have lots and lots more to drink. You can tell me more about the famous birthday party and I will tell you about how I am about to write the great English novel and make loads of delicious money. Another cider for Andy, please, Les, and I think I'll have a Jack Daniels and Coke.'

The brothers had moved over to stand beside Andrea at the bar.

'Hiya,' she said to them. 'You've seen Laura around, haven't you? This is Pete and Mark.'

Laura was closest to the one called Pete, and turned to greet him. 'Hi. I hear you've just got back from the Philippines.'

'Yeah, that's right. Flew in last week for a couple of months, see my kid, that sort of thing. He lives with his mother here. He's a star, great kid. Adores me. Can't say the same for her either way, hurgh hurgh.'

Unease prickled Laura's scalp. Between the end of one of the man's sentences and the beginning of another, a number of very quick thoughts had come to her all at once. His hair was dirty and needed cutting, but apparently he liked it flapping over his eyes, perhaps so that he could draw attention to himself by repeatedly flicking it back with his hand as he was doing now. His skin was oily, so that standing close to him she could see grime clinging in his five-o-clock shadow and under his eyes, blackheads on his nose and one in the folds of his right ear. He was leaning too close to her and smelt of beer and dirty clothing. He had given away too much information all at once and thus assumed an intimacy that did not exist. His son was great but apparently he rarely saw him, a condition that Laura had seen all too frequently among the families of disturbed children at work. He had been discourteous about the boy's mother, so daring Laura to be drawn into his conspiracy or to differ from his values and risk an argument. He was looking at her too closely, his laugh was full of catarrh and self-confidence, and it had a contemptuous edge. She had to swallow and draw back before asking him, 'So what do you do abroad? Are you engaged in some charity work or something like that?'

Pete drew wetly on his roll-up. 'Hurgh, you've got to be fucking joking. I've got my own business. It's brilliant out there. Only place to go to make money. They'll work for nothing, no problems with the fucking EU like you've got over here and the fucking Unions. They know they are lucky to be in work and don't whinge. It's cheap as fuck, plenty of booze, sand and sun. It's fucking excellent if you know how to work the ropes. You should try it, come and see for yourself. What do you do? You said to Andrea you was a writer or something?'

Laura now had the excuse to try to catch Andrea's eye for rescue, but she and Mark were talking and she couldn't.

'Sort of. I was a teacher before then.'

'A teacher? What of?'

'History. And a bit of French.'

'Hurgh.' There was no doubt the laugh was contemptuous now. 'Good job you got out if it then. What's the point of teaching a dying language like French? The Internet is where it's at. Everybody will be using English in a few years' time. I'm doing a website for my business. It's great: if I had my laptop I could show it to you. And history just produces other history teachers. They were all a bunch of wankers at my school.'

Laura's mind was racing with a dislike that was close to real anger, just as before and on the way to the pub it had raced with her happy plans.

'Let me get you another JD,' Pete was insisting.

'No, honestly. I would rather you didn't.'

'Come on, I'm having another one anyway.' He turned to the bar as though she had given her consent. 'A JD and coke, Les, and a pint for me. See what Andy and Mark want.' Back to Laura, leaning over her again. 'So what are you meant to be writing? I've never met a writer before. Come to think of it, it is a long time since I've had a white woman.'

In the screaming matches which had preceded her split from Jack and which they now carried on intermittently over the telephone, Laura experienced rage as a white cold loss of control which her mind was powerless to direct and which despite herself, engaged her intellect as a weapon. Typically this would happen when she felt really good; buoyed up by hope and optimism, she would be thwarted in some plan or made some horrible discovery which would send her running beyond the tree-line of reason onto the dangerous scree slopes above, her wits slipping from under her. As she considered what had been said to her all that happened again. She put her glass down very deliberately on the bar.

'What did you say?' she asked.

Pete looked away from her, shrugged and laughed.

'I asked you what the fuck you said, you miserable piece of shit.' Silence again as Pete filled his lungs with smoke.

'How the bloody hell dare you talk like that?' Laura asked.

Andrea had overheard and was casting anxious glances in her direction. Good. Let them all hear: it was time somebody stood up to people like this. Laura was right to be angry. There were profound principles at stake here, more important than her own happiness or reputation. She was shouting furiously now, and the bar had fallen silent.

'You don't just insult me. You are a moron. You talk

about your workforce as though they were shit, you are contemptuous of the teachers who taught you to read – supposing you can in fact read, of course – and you speak about women as though they were pieces of meat. You are completely and unbelievably racist and awful and embody in your morally execrable and, incidentally, physically repulsive person everything I hate about exploitation and sexism. You are a fuck.'

Andrea was at her side now. 'Come on, babes, don't go into one again. Let's go. Come on. Let's leave. He's not worth it.'

Les had come from serving in the other bar: 'Come on, Laura, darling, that's way enough now.'

Andrea was pulling her towards the door. She could feel herself shaking with anger.

Pete's voice from the bar: 'Yeah, hurgh, get lost. Nobody would want you anyway.'

Laura shook her arm free of Andrea's hand and launched herself towards Pete, seizing his three-quarters full pint and throwing it in his face before heading with Andrea to the door in confusion and a peculiar pride commingled with terror.

Four

The corpse had been undisturbed in the boat's cabin for some days. A pair of bolt croppers lay beside it, sticky with coagulated blood and tissue. Flies had laid eggs in it, and these reproductive duties done were buzzing about feeding. They particularly gathered around bits of brain and the remains of the eyes. There were deep stabs in the abdominal wall where the material of the shirt had been driven hard into the organs by repeated blows, and these wounds were moving rhythmically in a ghastly parody of life as maggots went about their unpleasant but ecologically necessary business. This thing that had once carried around a man was naked from the waist down, and perhaps most disturbing was the area around the groin. A sustained attack had been made there, separating the penis and most of the scrotum from its parent body and lacerating the upper thighs. Insect life moved here also.

The police photographer had been copiously sick into the water of the moorings, and Inspector Dom McGahan thought better of uttering the automatic 'Jesus Christ' which sprang to his mind. Now that the boat had been opened the smell of death in the police tent was so strong as to be almost a taste, and already his mouth was filling with the sweet saliva that over indulgence in whiskey had long led him to recognise as the herald of vomiting.

Speaking would mean breathing in, and he had no wish to do so. He retreated to where Uniform stood by the tapes, swallowing hard and doing his best to keep his eyes steady just as a seasick man searches for a still point. Beyond the blue and white stripes he could see a moderately large crowd assembled by the pub, a pretty woman in young middle age standing slightly to one side with an elderly man, and he forced himself to concentrate on them. His nausea subsided and as it did so the woman began to look the more attractive still, and he noticed how the old bloke was one of a succession of such who had stood around the pubs in Mootborough ever since he was born there. He wondered whether they knocked them out like garden gnomes, and then surprised himself by catching the inappropriateness of the thought. Strange how the mind can flip under pressure. Was that the etymology of *flippancy*, he wondered? No, obviously not. Then he felt sick again.

Five

Before she had gone to see Dr Lewis, Laura had never been inside a private hospital of any kind. She had broken down at Dot's party and Jack had taken her in that resignedly compassionate way of his to see Chris Andrews, and Chris had referred her under some new and probably highly ideologically unsound scheme. Laura did not like to think about this. She knew that Chris's practice were paying her fees out of deference to her father's memory and that without her family connections she would be with everybody else under the local NHS Mental Health Team. This was ironic of course, because what was making her feel uneasy was precisely the sense of social justice that she had inherited from Dad. He'd been a staunch NHS man who regarded deals and back-scratching with contempt. And there was this other thing, that in the field of her treatment she felt an outsider and disempowered recipient, so when she had once tried to voice them to Jack her concerns had washed and broken against the wall of his lawyer's pragmatism.

'Don't be silly, darling. We may not like things the way they are, but that's how it works in the NHS now. I am sure Chris is a good doctor and is trying to do the best for you, and that your dad would have done the same. For goodness sake don't start jeopardising things for theoretical reasons you can do nothing about.'

So Laura had shelved her misgivings, which in any case were merely a background noise behind her other concerns. Chief among which was to try somehow to get well, if she really was ill, for the children's sake; she was already frightened that her relationship with them might be slipping from her grasp.

The large, luxurious and squeakily clean reception area was empty of other patients as Laura presented herself at the desk. A vase of beautifully arranged yellow roses stood here, their buds so perfect that only a sense of what would be *de rigueur* in such an establishment prevented Laura from assuming them to be silk. The girl on duty was similarly faultless, a Barbie-doll of careful make-up, nail polish and caring efficiency. Laura, struck by the contrast with her own bitten nails and thousand-wash-grey underwear, felt immediately inadequate. She did her best to return the girl's vacuous smile.

'How nice to see you, Mrs Morton.' The girl's name was apparently Trudy. It said so in bright red on a white plastic badge. 'Please take a seat and Jean will be with you soon, I'm sure. Help yourself to coffee and biscuits.' Laura murmured her thanks and went to sit on one of the Chesterfield sofas which were scattered over a blue carpeting whose pile was far deeper than anything she had known in any of her own homes. The room reminded her of a lounge in one of those expensive hotels that, just occasionally, she and Jack stayed in overnight as a special treat on their way home from Continental motoring holidays, or of the Senior Common Room of her College in Cambridge, where a few times in her abortive research career she had been invited by a friendly or perhaps lustful don. There were copies of broadsheet newspapers on highly polished occasional tables, and the aroma of posh coffee came from a machine next to which china cups and saucers had been placed. No lipstick-traced plastic cups or tabloid press here, she reflected; no dog-eared and out-of-date copies of *Hello* magazine and *Woman's Own*. Near the window the only other occupant of the waiting area, an elegantly dressed middle-aged woman adorned by a string of pearls, sat crying behind *The Times*. Laura picked up a copy of *The Guardian* and gazed listlessly at the latest iniquity of the Government.

After some minutes her half-hearted attempt to read was interrupted by Jean Tomlinson's soft appearance at her side and quietly spoken invitation to come along to the consulting room. Jean was Laura's psychotherapist, a title that frightened and upset Laura and made her feel ashamed. It had, she felt, too many discredited Freudian overtones, too much of the American *shrink*, too many resonances of white coats and ridiculous bearded men asking prurient questions of the damaged and despairing. Jack knew how she felt, and it annoyed her that he would use the term freely in front of their friends as though he were trying to exorcise his own fear and shame while punishing her with a display of his own liberalism.

'Laura has got the most marvellous psychotherapist...' Or an even bigger boast: 'The people at Earl's Friary are really splendid, you know. Do you know it? It's opposite St Michael's Church. Lovely grounds, and really very discreet.' And Laura would respond with some mild rebuke: 'Come on, Jack, they don't want to hear all that,' which inevitably drew the public response that she shouldn't feel ashamed, that it was an illness like any other. But Laura did feel very ashamed, and was beginning to be uneasily aware that behind her husband's apparent solicitude there was now showing a more brittle edge as her treatment progressed without her apparently getting any better. On such occasions she usually buried herself in her wine glass.

Jean's consulting room was as well furnished as the reception area. This time long-stemmed red roses instead of yellow ones stood on a well-executed reproduction of a Georgian desk, and the comfortable armchairs on which she and Laura now sat were separated by a low table on which a plain box of tissues sat in solitary testament to the distress of however many well-heeled patients were on the lists. This was Laura's fifth visit. The first had been spent with Dr. Lewis, an hour of answering questions about her family background, personal history and present feelings while the consultant, a youngish middle-aged man in an expensive suit, turned his version of the tissue box over and over in his hands, failed to meet her eyes, confirmed Chris's diagnosis of clinical depression and told her she should continue to take her Prozac. Since then she had seen Jean every fortnight, to talk, apparently incessantly, about her upbringing, relationships and professional career. Sometimes she wondered if this did any good at all, for although she supposed these sessions were helpful to Jean and Dr Lewis from a diagnostic point of view, they made her think of herself too much and risked the dangers of boredom of self-obsession. And at times she was indeed bored and self-obsessed seeking refuge in her misery at home and hugging the yawning sadness as she had hugged Mum and Dad when she was young.

Nevertheless, she had to admit that some of what she had learned from Jean had been useful. In particular Jean had taught her to challenge her own darkest thoughts by the use of intellect, and since Laura had always had a pretty high view of her own intelligence, this approach to her illness both appealed to her vanity and had been met with some measure of success. So for instance, if faced with the overwhelming feeling that she was a bad mother or had no friends, Jean had taught her to challenge the underlying assumptions these ideas contained by looking at the evidence, to see the thoughts even as she was suffering from them as symptoms, much as at Cambridge she had learned to question the underlying assumptions of a supposedly objective historical narrative while reading it. In this way, even as she hated herself in comparison to other parents, she had learned to count up in her mind all the good things she had done for her children and the fun they had together and to ask herself why, if she were such a bad mother, Liz and Davie so clearly loved her. And faced with the idea that she had no friends, she carefully counted the number of people who accepted her invitations to drinks or dinner and recalled their shared laughter together. In doing all this she was learning too to discount the seductive voice of an atavistic and distorted religiosity that told her that it was spiritual pride to feel good about herself. But it was hard work to stand back thus from herself and to subject herself, when she felt least like doing so, to an intellectual mind-game, and hard not to feel anger and self-pity that others were apparently spared the process, which Jean called Cognitive Behavioural Therapy, or CBT.

Each session with Jean began with a résumé of the previous fortnight's work, and Laura and she were now discussing the helpfulness of the progress they had made together. It was always expressed in terms of teamwork and co-operation as though the counsellor were a fellow traveller.

'I am glad you are finding the CBT helpful,' Jean was saying now. 'A lot of people do. It is a bit difficult to get used to at first but most of our clients find that the more they practise at it the more it becomes second nature. I think that you may have made a step forward there.'

'Oh, I think it is very helpful.' There was a laburnum tree outside the window behind Jean, its flowers poisonously yellow in their attractiveness. Laura felt desperately anxious to please the woman, as though she were a primary school child showing her teacher a latest drawing or story. She needed to say something intelligent in order to prove that she was fully engaged in the process of her treatment, that she was on Jean's side and keeping up with, and perhaps even exceeding expectations as she had so often done at school.

'I don't think CBT really helps with the underlying causes of distress though,' Laura said.

For a moment Jean looked wrong-footed. 'How do you mean?' she asked, and Laura felt a *frisson* of intellectual excitement.

'Well, what I mean is that it is more of a pain management system than anything else. It is like people who have repeated migraines taking codeine or something. It offers symptomatic relief at the time and helps you to think through things, but it does nothing to address the underlying causes of the condition. That is what I think anyway.'

'That is very interesting, Laura. So are you saying that there are things which we ought to talk about more, perhaps ones we have touched on in the past, which you feel are at the root of your distress, and which CBT helps you to cope with…'

'Exactly,' Laura broke in, excited by their sudden mutual insight. 'But it doesn't make them go away.'

'OK. So maybe we should spend some time exploring those issues today, which kind of ties up with what I had planned for us anyway. Do you feel up to that?'

Laura nodded. Now suddenly she felt very small and

tense, a little girl asked to account for her possession of illicit and secret chocolate. There was a long silence.

Laura knew about this, knew that Jean was waiting for her to find the unaccustomed stillness socially unbearable and make her fill it with words that would open herself out and give away the things she had been holding back. Part of her was furious with such a cheap trick, while the rest was performing a calculation as to whether it might in fact be worth going along with it. She gazed at the laburnum again. Eventually it was too much for her. The whole rigmarole was like one of those staring contests she and her friends had gone in for at school, and Jean was much more practised. She gave in.

'I think there are two things really. Of course I could be totally wrong.'

'Go on. There are no wrongs and rights here. What you feel and what you say are important.'

'OK then.' Laura took a deep breath and felt it waver in the back of her throat with the first sign of the tears that she knew would come at some point this morning.

'I think the first thing is my father and the way he died. The second is something that happened at work.'

More silence. The sun was catching the yellow blossoms outside the window, which now moved slightly in a breeze. Laura had seen Jean making some unusually flowing notes in her file and began to feel trapped, as though she had said too much and had committed herself to a course of action about which she was not entirely sure, as when perhaps she had on occasions flirted rather too heavily and found herself pinned against the wall at a party. Jean seemed to sense this and was ready to take pity on her.

'It's OK, Laura. I think you have done really well in identifying a couple of things. If you don't feel strong enough to talk about them now that's fine. We can look at them in some future session.'

Laura shook her head.

'No, it's OK. Thanks. I might as well get on with it.' With the sense that at first the words were being dragged from her and then with increasing confidence, she started to talk about the car crash which killed her father, noticing how the other woman occasionally raised an eyebrow despite her professional calm as she continued to listen and make occasional notes. Laura began to be lost in her history, time suspending itself on the coat-hanger of her words as once it had suspended itself for her in Latin translations and the recovery of social conditions among the long-dead poor. When she finished she realised that the laburnum outside the window was moving more briskly in a stiffening wind and that she needed the tissue box which Jean pushed towards her.

'I just wish he hadn't killed himself.' Silence for a while.

'OK. Is that what you think he did?'

'I don't know. Of course in one way it is obvious he did: he was alone in the car and nobody else was on the road…'

Jean made another note and said, 'Nonetheless, it is an interesting choice of words you used.' More silence again: the laburnum was really moving about now, and the absurd thought entered Laura's head that, had she wanted to go sailing today, it would be unpleasantly hard work despite the sunshine. She wiped her nose.

'Do you want to go on?' Jean asked. Laura gave a little half-laugh, an indication to both of them that although she was distressed she was in control of herself.

'I might as well now I have come this far. I don't think Dad really killed himself deliberately, you know. But it's obvious he was drinking very heavily, and that is very self-destructive behaviour, isn't it? It used to frighten me when I was a kid, and I thought that if he really loved me then he would stop, so there must be something wrong with me. After he died I blamed myself terribly. In some ways it seems like all my life – working hard at school, getting into Cambridge, working for my degree and then climbing up the career ladder, that I have been trying to show him how much I loved him even though he was dead, to give him something back even though I hated him for dying and leaving us alone all at the same time. As though anything I did would make any difference anyway. And in any case it always goes wrong because just as things seem to be OK and I start to succeed at anything I have this stupid self-destruct button. Like this business just before I left work. I haven't really told anyone about it much.'

'Do you want to tell me now?'

'Yes. I think so. It is a bit messy but I'll try. I may cry again.' Another little half laugh.

'That doesn't matter. It's what we're here for, you know that.'

'OK. Well, it happened a few months ago, when I was the Pastoral Deputy Head at St John Rigby. I had done curriculum work before but the Head Man believed in moving us senior staff around different responsibilities, and when the last pastoral bloke retired the Headmaster told me it would be an excellent opportunity to get new experience in a field I hadn't done much work in until then. Of course I had been a form teacher, but apart from that I hadn't done any real pastoral stuff at all, and frankly I wasn't a terribly good form teacher either. I had crawled up the ladder by improving academic results as Head of History and taking on lots of extra responsibilities when it came to things like OFSTED inspections and so on. We had a couple of very weak deputies in those days and the Head and I did a lot of work together that really needed doing. I think he had come to rely on me and we got on extremely well personally, and maybe he felt guilty that I was taking on so much of what should have been the deputies' jobs. Anyway it put me in a good position to apply for promotion. First I got the curriculum deputy's post and did it for a couple of years. I think I was pretty good at it, redesigning the timetable and challenging under-performance in some lousy departments who were failing the kids. Perhaps you can imagine the sort of thing. When I made the move over to Pastoral Deputy it was very challenging. I did some good stuff like organizing weekly pastoral meetings and so forth, but really much of what I did was very administrative and I wasn't terribly good at one-to-one contact. Some of the children had really big problems, confidential stuff which I had never been privy to before, and although I went on some ridiculous one- to three-day training courses and so on, I was really out of my depth. I kept thinking, these kids need a properly trained counsellor and family advisor, not some bloody failed historian who took teaching on out of the need to earn a living. And of course I was still on a half teaching load, and the Head kept disappearing out of school for meetings so that I was left running the show, so there was very little time to catch up. It was all very sub-optimal, hand to mouth kind of stuff. I couldn't keep up with my marking and was continually called away from lessons, so it ended up that the one thing I knew I was really good at – teaching – was compromised as well, and I knew that the other staff were noticing it, even when I had been the one to criticize them for not being on top of things earlier. And it's never easy being promoted in a school where you have been a junior teacher. It was especially hard when Elizabeth and David came along.'

Laura paused, surprised at herself that she had been able to be so eloquent about something which she had hitherto been unwilling to admit to anybody except, miserably, herself when wrapped under the duvet covers.

'You are being really strong, Laura. Go on.'

'Well anyway, one day the Head of P.E. came to see me in my office. He had brought a boy in Year Eight with him and made him stand outside the door. I suppose the boy, whose name was Jon, must have been about thirteen. Kevin, this P.E. teacher, was really furious and very frightened as well. I already knew that the boy had previously been in trouble a great deal and found it very difficult to get on with the other kids, fighting with the boys, and making really inappropriate sexual remarks towards the girls, far beyond what you would expect from a lad of his age. He had already been on report card a number of times, which I had to review at the end of each week. Anyway, what made Kevin so angry was that this Jon had been told to play badminton in his P.E. lesson, but instead had taken the racquet and smashed it to pieces on the gym floor. When Kevin had told him to stop Jon had shouted at him, telling him to fuck off and all that sort of thing, and swung a punch at him. Of course Kevin had given him a bit of a tap back, and Kevin was absolutely shitting himself that whatever happened to Jon he would get into trouble for hitting a kid, because of course you aren't allowed to do any of that kind of stuff any more.'

'So what happened?'

'Obviously I tried to calm Kevin down as much as possible. I told him that we could cover his backside by claiming reasonable restraint on the boy – you are allowed to do that. I think Kevin was reassured so I sent him off to teach his next class, and sat the boy outside my office with a flea in his ear and the promise of several more. Then I got the Head of Lower School to come and see me. He was a really lovely man who had been at the school for years and had an encyclopaedic memory and real kindness for the kids, but he did have problems about sharing information, as though somehow he needed to feel the children belonged to him. Anyway, this chap Graham reminded me – actually I hadn't the foggiest idea – that Jon had an older brother who was in our GCSE year and another one who had already left. The word on the streets from Governors and Staff who knew the family was that the father was a very strange man. Graham told me that there had been problems with both older boys, and in particular that there was a repeated pattern of sexually inappropriate behaviour in all three. I was more than a bit put out that Graham had not told me this before – after all, the boy had been on report card to me several times on his say-so as Head of Lower School, and it particularly annoyed me when he told me that he had discussed the whole business with a Sister Benedict some months ago. She had been the boys' primary school headmistress, who had also indicated that she had reasons for having considerable suspicions about their father, who lived alone with them.'

'What happened then, Laura?'

'Well I was pretty furious with Graham so I made an appointment with Sister Benedict and insisted that he went to see her with me. We talked about all three boys, and she agreed that they had been very difficult at St. Ignatius's. She said again their father was a pretty weird guy, but she wouldn't go any further. Typical bloody modern nun, covering her own sacred and liberated arse.

We went back to St John Rigby and I looked in all of Jon's exercise books. The rest were OK, but his Rough Book was appalling and believe me I am not easily shocked. There were pictures of sodomy and fellatio with boys, and violent sexual fantasies about girls and female members of staff as well.

'I guess I went on a crusade then. I couldn't think about anything else. I'd been on a course recently about child sex abuse and I was absolutely certain that something was deeply dodgy in the family and that it was almost certainly to do with the father. I knew that at some point I should call Social Services, but before then I wanted to be really sure of my ground. I think I saw myself as some sort of saviour for this boy. So I called Jon into my office and spent a long time interviewing him, going over and over why he thought he might be behaving as he was, showing him his rough book drawings and so on. He wasn't a very bright lad and I got pissed off with him, so I asked him straight out, is your father abusing you?'

There was a bit of a silence now in which Laura felt extremely ashamed of herself and could not bear to look at Jean, who she knew would never have made such a foolish mistake.

'I know it was stupid of me,' she said.

'You don't need me to tell you that. I think you are punishing yourself enough already.'

Laura drew a deep breath. 'Well, as you can imagine, the shit really hit the fan then. The boy completely clammed up and refused to talk any more, except apparently to his father, so I started to get telephone calls from his Dad, first at school and then on my mobile. God knows where he got the number from, perhaps from some lazy bloody secretary. Sometimes he was drunk and he threatened to kill me. I felt that I deserved it and was too ashamed to tell anybody. Eventually I asked the Headmaster for help, but he said that if I could not stand the heat I should stay out of the kitchen. Then I found myself going to pieces and ended up here.'

There was silence in the room again, which Laura felt as disapproval.

'So how do you feel about it all now?' asked Jean at length.

'I failed everybody and drink to make it all go away,' said Laura, and wept. When she had finished she noticed that the laburnum tree had ceased to move. Behind it the sky was graphite grey, with low and slanting sun rays catching the splashes of yellow and green before disappearing under the bank of cumulonimbus as it moved over Amblehurst and the hospital. Jean had sat quietly feeding her tissues.

'Are you OK?' she asked. Laura wiped her nose again and nodded.

'I am so sorry.'

'Don't be. Look, I think that there are some possibly quite important issues here, which we might consider exploring further. I think there's quite probably a connection between your feelings about your father's death and your perceived failure with the boy at your school – his name was Jon, wasn't it?'

'Yes, that's right. What do you mean?'

'Well, it seems to me like you feel you have been trying to somehow make up for what happened to your Dad all those years ago, and that you have some very ambivalent feelings about him. On the one hand his memory has driven you to achieve some marvellous things but on the other you have some strong negative stuff there as well. I think that it is quite possible that in Jon you saw an image of yourself, because in many ways what happened to you – the drinking, the apparent lack of care your father had about his family when he went out to drive that night – was a form of child abuse. You wanted to rescue Jon from what had happened to you, and this led you to make mistakes which you would otherwise not have made and for which you now blame yourself.'

'But I failed him.'

'There are always going to be other teachers, Laura.'

Suddenly Laura felt anger build inside her and a buzzing in her ears. She had not been prepared for this slick reconstruction of her life, this reduction of her love and concern to a symptom, and felt humiliated to have them presented to her in all their terrifying likelihood. For so many years she had clung to the image of herself as a good teacher, had thought that she had found something at which she could at last succeed and contribute despite everything. Jean's professional and objective concern had uprooted all of it, as though it were some final punishment for what she had done to Jon and his family. Ridiculously, childishly, she could only spit out her words: 'That doesn't help me, does it?'

Silence again, this time in which Laura felt rage and fear pulsing at her temples. She was ready at any moment to run away, or to fight this woman with the most devastating means that politeness would allow.

'Possibly not at this stage,' Jean was saying in that infuriating bloody oh-so-calm counsellor's voice, 'and I think we need to do some more work together on these issues. It's nearly the end of our time now and I really think you have done well in this session, but there is something I want to say. On a number of occasions you have mentioned that you have been self-medicating on alcohol. I have to tell you, and Dr Lewis will tell you as well, that for you especially, drinking is a very bad idea, and I think we are going to have to investigate that very seriously, because not only is alcohol itself a depressant, but also because it will stop your Prozac from being able to work for you. You are still taking them I suppose?'

Laura nodded sullenly. This was all she needed.

'OK, good. Now, you are with Dr Lewis for his review next week, and then I shall see you the week after.'

Jean stood. They must have been to the same self-assertiveness classes, Laura thought wryly: how to get rid of parents or patients who threaten to stay too long in your room by standing up and making them feel uncomfortable.

'See you then.'

'Yes. OK. Thanks, Jean.'

The Barbie Doll in reception waved goodbye as she left, but Laura wasn't concentrating and didn't see her.

Six

The first drops of rain were falling as Laura left the hospital, splashing onto the tarmac of the car park in big summer blobs some inches apart before they coalesced into a uniform grey. By the time she had started the engine and was pulling out of the hospital entrance they were exploding on the road and bouncing back upwards. She put her headlights on at the junction, taking extra care with the right turn. Some ten minutes afterwards, as she negotiated the outskirts of Amblehurst and joined the Mootborough Road, the traffic eased and gave her time for thinking, the route and even gear changes becoming automatic in their familiarity. She was shell-shocked and angry from her conversation with Jean, but in the meantime there were things to do, responsibilities to be lived out. Supper had to be made for one thing, and Poppy thanked with some flowers and a bottle of wine for looking after David and Elizabeth. Then she tried to remember the contents of the fridge and couldn't, although she was sure there were some fish fingers and oven chips in the freezer which would do for the kids' tea. But for the wine and Jack's dinner with her she would have to go to the supermarket: maybe Jack would forgive her if they had one of those pre-prepared gourmet meals. She pulled into the out-of-town trading park, hearing for the first time as she stepped from the car the thunder that had been masked by engine noise.

Once inside the shop and equipped with wire-and-plastic shopping basket Laura saw that there were people milling about her, and their closeness suddenly frightened her. This feeling became more intense so that, ridiculously, it seemed to her that each of them could see into her mounting distress and judge her for it. She became dizzy, and this brought on a new fear that she might fall or shout out and make a fool of herself. She could feel her breathing starting to shake and become shallow. Her chest was heaving, there were quick hard thumps under her breastbone and she began to panic, gulping great draughts of air as she fought for oxygen that her rational mind told her was freely available. Sweat on her scalp was wetting her hair, and as she hyperventilated pins and needles appeared in her hands and feet. Her fingers cramped inwards in response to the shifting acid-base levels in her blood, making it difficult for her to hold the basket. She had to sit down or she really would make a fool of herself. She stumbled across to where plastic chairs had been placed by the wall opposite the check-out desks and perched on one of them, discarding her basket at her feet, and placing her head in her shaking hands. Two grubby children were romping nearby, laughing out their boredom as they waited in food-stained clothing for their mother, the girl in glasses with one lens broken, the boy grossly overweight with piggy eyes and punching his sister in the arm as she screamed at him to stop. In desperation Laura suddenly wanted to shout at them, to yell, 'Stop it, you little bastards, for fuck's sake stopitstopitstopitstopit,' and was horrified that she might actually do so, just as when sometimes while waiting for a train she had been inexplicably terrified that she would leap onto the tracks as an express approached. She clasped her rebellious hands tightly together and, although she was hardly aware of this, moaned softly and rocked back and forth. Somewhere she realised that she badly needed a pee, but she was unable to move.

'What's wrong with her? Look, she's weird. She's a weirdo.' The boy pointed, his sister following his finger and beginning to whisper in his ear, laughing, until they both began a ritual of pointing and giggling. Finished at the checkout, their mother heaved into view, an image of her son writ large in tattoos and enormous bosom. 'Jordan, you come away. You too Chantelle. Come away now.' She loomed over Laura.

'You orta be ashamed of yerself comin' in here in that state. My kids are good kids. You're frightenin' 'em. Look at you: you're not fit to be out.' She turned to her children. 'Come on you two.' And as she retreated, 'Bleedin' 'ell, it's bad enough goin' bloody shoppin' without all o' this.'

Oh God, the woman thought she was drunk. Over their shoulders the children were laughing at Laura, sticking out their tongues and dragging their feet.

'Fuckin' well come on, will ya?' The woman was yelling at them now. 'Leave 'er alone. She ain't nothink to do with you.' The children reluctantly peeled away, the boy raising his right index finger towards her behind his mother's back. Laura felt sick.

Gradually normality began to reassert itself. Laura felt the thumping in her chest subside and realised that she was breathing without effort again. The cramps and then the tingling in her hands had retreated, the people around her were only going about their normal business. She headed for the ladies, where after emptying her sore bladder and a quick check on hair and general appearance in the mirror she felt at least passably human. She knew that she had experienced what people called a Panic Attack and was surprised both by its intensity and by her own hitherto rather insensitive reaction to accounts of its manifestation in others. Nothing like a dose of first-hand experience to quicken the sympathy, she thought wryly. She bet bloody Jean had never had a panic attack in her life. And somewhere too she was pleased that here was a definite symptom, a physical proof, that she was ill and not merely bad or weak. With renewed energy she left the loo and retrieved her basket. She moved up and down the aisles, finding with increasing confidence a rather super looking *Breast of Duck with Caramelised Onions* for herself and Jack, and for Poppy a bottle of expensive-looking (but rather cheap) Australian Sauvignon blanc and some limp-looking freesias. Then she remembered that there was only a smallish amount of gin left at home and maybe not enough tonic, and it would be nice to have the excuse to have a drink with Poppy, so she retraced her steps and picked up those as well, and a lemon just in case. Bollocks to Jean, and bollocks to the tattooed bitch and her dreadful children: she might as well be hanged for a sheep as for a lamb, and in any case after everything that she had been through today she deserved a drink. Tomorrow would be time enough. Some lines of Byron from her far-away A Level classes came into her mind: *'Let us have wine and women, mirth and laughter, / Sermons and soda-water the day after.'* She paid with her credit card, having no idea of its balance and caring less. She would tell Jack about it all and would be able to get through to him this time, the capable, intelligent Jack whom she had married and who would be like he used to be and he would listen and believe her and come up with some bad taste joke about it all and let her shower and maybe make love to her and everything would seem all right for a while.

Seven

Dom McGahan was not some hardened actor and television policeman used to seeing the most grisly make-ups of human remains. And actors didn't have to suffer the smell, so murders were common on TV. Fictional cops were as happy and familiar with murder as doctors are with an outbreak of the flu, but the substance of his life was more to do with things like his carefully prepared speech to the Town Council tonight. He had actually rather been looking forward to that, because there were some really very interesting plans about CCTV for the lower end of the High Street, and he had something he badly wanted to say. Damn. His nausea had gone off properly now and he ached for a cigarette but did not dare have one with the uniformed PCs standing about. Instead he inspected his scuffed brown leather shoes, and shoved his hands deep inside his baggily comfortable trouser pockets. He was tangentially aware of the noise of some gulls, the smell of the river, and a warm breeze lifting his thinning hair and ruffling the sleeves of his blue cotton rolled-up shirt. This garment flapped open at the midriff and hung over a growing paunch about which he cared little. Dom had always regarded the physical training and compulsory fitness of the early part of his career as his weakest area. He had delighted as each new promotion brought him an increasingly sedentary position, enabling him to do what he was really good at, which was thinking and working things out. Now with both the excuse of his increasing age and his seniority in rank, he had not had to do more than break into a concerned trot for several years. As far as he could remember it was when a woman police constable had tripped and sprained her ankle in the car park.

Dom privately knew that much of his promotion had been due to his gift for what the management speak people called *prioritising*, or what his mother would have called, 'Making a list, for Jaysus' sake,' mimicking her own mother's broad Irish. He supposed 'prioritising' would do, although his grandmother would certainly have hated the perversion of the beautiful language of the Oppressor. 'No country, however evil or heathen' he could hear her say, 'could be wholly forgetful of God and produce Shakespeare.' If you can make a list you can get over the raw shock of seeing intestines splayed over a cockpit sole like paint. Making a list makes people think that you are in control when they are looking to you for support. Making a list makes order out of chaos, God the eternal Word speaking mathematics into the waters of Creation. He sat on one of the pub benches and began to work one out.

Eight

As Laura let herself into the house the children came running towards her. She placed the shopping down and swept them both up into her arms, kissing their cheeks and lips and jiggling them as they laughed in delight and greeted her, Lizzie with her almost-grown-up talking and Davie with his 'Mummeee, Mummee.' God, but they were getting heavy now. She put them down again and they ran after her into the breakfast room adjoining the open-plan kitchen with its Aga. 'Twack,' Davie was saying, 'Twack.'

'What did you say, darling?' asked Laura.

Poppy was in the kitchen. She looked pretty stunning in well-cut jeans and top, her hair tied back sensibly to prevent the children from pulling on it. Laura embraced her. Slightly older than Laura, Poppy was a friend of hers and Jack's whose divorced status and absence of young children made her a useful dinner party guest when bachelors were invited, and whose sense of humour and willingness to muck in assured her of a place at the table even when they were not.

'Poppy darling, I can't thank you enough.' Laura rummaged around in her carrier bag, placing the ready meal and tonic water in the fridge and the gin on the large breakfast table by the flowers which Mrs. Hill, the daily woman, had cut from the garden and arranged that morning. Producing the wine and the freesias, which were now mangled by their contact with the clinking bottles in the car as well as wilting as before, she handed them over to Poppy. 'Look, I got you these. Oh God, I am sorry about the flowers. Just look at them.'

'Laura, don't be so silly. It's really sweet of you. Thanks. Let's put them in some water and see if they recover.' She went over to the sink with its view through the conservatory to the garden and filled a glass. Laura and she sat at the table.

'Twack, twack.' Davie was shouting now, running in and out of the sitting room and doing knee-bends at the breakfast room door to attract his mother's attention as Lizzie wandered in, thumb in mouth and Jemima Puddle-Duck held to the crook of her neck. Seemingly oblivious to the presence of her younger brother, she knocked him as she passed, and he sat down heavily on the floor. 'Twack,' he said again, this time his lip trembling.

'Lizzie. Darling,' said Poppy, 'mind Davie. He's only two, remember, and you're a big girl now.' Laura went to pick the little boy up and sat him on her lap. 'What's a twack, darling?'

Lizzie removed the thumb from her mouth. Although the dawn of Davie's language had hardly reached the stage of intelligibility for adults, his sister had an uncanny way of understanding him.

'He's got a new tractor,' she said, and waved Jemima's beak at her brother.

'Ooooooh, a new tractor? Where did you get that from, Davie?'

'Poppy bought it for him. We went shopping. It was nice. I got a new bracelet. Then it rained. Look.' She held up her arm and showed off a string of brightly coloured beads on elastic. Davie wriggled from Laura's lap and started trying to pull her towards the sitting room.

'You go and fetch it, darling,' she said to him. 'Show Mummy in here. And those are lovely beads, Lizzie.' Laura felt a moment's social unease as Davie reappeared, the bright green plastic toy held tightly in his closed fist. 'Oh, Poppy, it's really very sweet of you, you really shouldn't have… look, let me pay…' but Poppy cut her off.

'Don't be silly. We had a lovely time, didn't we guys?' Lizzie nodded and snuggled closer to her mother. Davie was running the tractor up and down the floor on its cabin roof, making 'Brrrrm, brrrrm' noises interspersed with the occasional 'Twack.'

'I know what,' said Laura, 'let's all have a drink. Would you like some juice, kids? And Poppy, what about you? I'm going to have one, I have had a hell of an afternoon. G and T?'

Poppy glanced quickly at the kitchen clock. 'Why not? It's only twenty minutes to kick-off time anyway.'

Laura busied herself with the drinks, filling Tommee-Tippee cups and finding ice and lemon and a cold bottle of tonic from the back of the fridge. Forgetting the unfinished Gordon's in the cupboard she removed the gin from the table and carried it to the work surface, only half conscious that in doing so she was hiding from Poppy the very large measure she poured into her own glass in comparison with the merely normally generous one she handed to her friend, who was in truth no slouch in alcohol consumption. The children sucked noisily on their drinks as the adults attacked theirs, the first glow of alcohol burning its relief into Laura's mouth.

'So how did it go?' asked Poppy.

Laura lit a cigarette and went to open a window to let in the still sticky after-air of the storm and, conscious of her children's health, blew smoke out into the garden. 'I don't know. Pretty upsetting actually. Never mind, let's not talk about it.'

'I'm sorry. So it wasn't helpful?'

Laura shrugged. She had hoped that had shaken off the afternoon for the while, putting it aside for her conference with Jack. 'Well I suppose it's all part of what they call The Process.'

'Like in a food processor?'

This was better. Lightening up. 'Exactly. Or maybe a sausage machine. Depressives in one end, well-rounded and stable individuals out the other.'

Poppy had caught the mood now. 'Well I could do with a sausage machine of my own,' she said. 'Sausage has been very hard to come by recently, even with Frankie away with his Dad.' Poppy and Laura laughed, and Lizzie, disconcerted as children will be by the confusing world of adults, tried to pull the conversation back to herself.

'I like sausages. Can we have sausages tonight? Can Poppy stay? Can she have one of ours?' The grown-ups caught one another's eyes and laughed again.

'It's fish fingers tonight, darling. You like them, don't you? And I think Poppy may have things of her own to do this evening...' But Poppy interrupted her.

'I tell you what, Lizzie. Suppose I help Mummy get your tea and give you two your baths tonight, then you will be all nice and ready to see Daddy when he comes home. Is that OK, Laura?' But Lizzie was already waving Jemima up and down and laughing, 'Yes, yes,' and for a moment Laura was angry at being managed, the apparent criticism of her evening routine, and her daughter's fickleness. Then she reflected that Poppy was probably lonely and that she was perhaps being over-sensitive and it would certainly make the evening less fraught to have some help. She poured some more gin into each of their now near-empty glasses, smiling at Poppy in silent atonement for her thoughts and questioning as she did so why it should be this particular drink which so many of her friends used as the default relaxant.

For the next hour or so Laura and Poppy fed and bathed the children, happily maternal in one another's company. Small everyday tasks that Laura had recently found almost impossible to do on her own became suddenly easy with Poppy, and she felt sad that they had seemed so difficult. By seven o'clock the children were fed, bathed and in their night things, their tea things cleared away and washed up, the kitchen surfaces wiped, and there was, blissfully, nothing more to do but have another drink in celebration and wait for Jack to join them.

There had never been anybody else but Jack, really. They had been together since they were eighteen and undergraduates and making love in her ridiculously small bed in College, discovering one another's bodies and how to make one another orgasm as they explored with delight one another's minds, talking about C.S. Lewis and music and social justice and whether Waugh's *Brideshead Revisited* was about finding grace or merely a snobbish hymn to a world better lost as they lay smelling of one another's bodies before sleep overtook them. They had kept their affair a secret for at least half a term, Laura remembered, amusing themselves by being wittily brutal to one another in public to put others off the scent. In this way they had kept themselves aloof from those other undergraduate couples, usually poorly dressed and disengaged from College life, who made a great show of their affairs to the general embarrassment of others. In some way the secrecy also helped to salve their consciences, for both were Christians who had met through singing in the chapel choir, Jack with his muscular public school Anglicanism and Laura with her Catholicism which, however liberal and post-Vatican II, was too intellectually honest to pretend that premarital sex and condoms were the highest expression of human love. Later as their relationship grew and they became more woven up with one another they had begun to exchange home visits during the vacations. This made it more difficult to sustain an aura of secrecy, but the habit of mutual sharpness combined with sex, of picking up on minor faults and weaving hilariously argued character assassinations on each other had by that time become a permanent game they were never to lose, an integral part of what it was to be the couple Jack-and-Laura, a double act in which they both delighted even as each new insight wounded. In it they exchanging tenderness for a harshly expressed hilarity-knowledge of the other which apparently suited them both and which Laura told herself bound them together more closely than any traditional love story ever could. They had planned that it would end in a well-thought-out marriage that would take away and redeem whatever errant bits were in their relationship, sanctifying and redeeming them. Not that they were dewy-eyed about marriage in general. Jack was too conversant with matrimonial law, Laura too knowledgeable about history, and both too well read in novels and the bleaker of the modern poets not to include a good deal of cynicism about matrimony in their game as well. Very occasionally Laura was uneasily aware that all this contained a certain intellectual snobbery, a belief that she and Jack were somehow different from normal couples and were more capable of taking whatever each dealt out to the other, and that this could be potentially damaging. But she had never talked to Jack about it, for somehow that would be to break the rules and maybe lose the game forever, which was habitual and delicious.

The element of mock-hostility in Jack and Laura's relationship had been encouraged by the attitude of Jack's mother, a woman who, sitting against a backdrop of cats, bad biographies and Regency Stripe, terrified them both. She had made it clear that she regarded sex and marriage as items in a list of Ladies' Tiresome Duties to be Performed on the same level as dispensing small amounts of money to Worthy Causes (mainly to do with animals and old soldiers), making sure that the various casual staff she engaged were kept on their toes, and that what she called and was successful in making 'A Ghastly Christmas Party' was arranged each year for the circle of acquaintances she considered to be worthy of her attention. She thought any display of affection as being in the sort of extreme bad taste best left to the Lower Orders, and enjoyed looking down on her lawyer husband for being what she regarded as *Trade*. She did this with a ferocity she fancied was still to be found among the landed stock with whom she identified herself, because while her own family had once been wealthy farmers, his people had been grocers and even now his practice involved a good deal of work for small businesses. Thus he represented a great disappointment to what her own adored mother would have dreamt for her, which was a suitable match to a well-off landowner's son. As one of six daughters in wartime, however, and her sole suitable lover having screamed his life out over occupied France in the burning rear turret of a Lancaster, Beatrice had remained forgotten and on the shelf. Her father's small fortune had been wiped out in turn by the depression, some foolish investments, and according to Beatrice, the iniquity of Attlee's Government. Forced into a brief period of having to work for a living, she had finally married Jack's father in '54 for a swiftly disappearing lust, his money and fertility. Her disappointment and anger at all of this had boiled down to a point and focussed as a fiercely disordered love for Jack, her only child. She was determined therefore that he was to succeed where she had failed and marry in a manner which she regarded as suitable and advantageous, however peculiar such values might have seemed to a casual observer in the 1980s. Thus on Laura's visits, once the original politeness had worn off and it was apparent that she was threatening to be a permanent part of Jack's life, Beatrice had made it clear that she was both surprised by and viciously opposed to the nature of Laura's relationship with her son and regarded it as merely a temporary foolishness from which she would wrench Jack back into her own control. Looking back on it all later, Laura always believed that Beatrice's best moment came after the occasion when, after each had qualified, Jack and she had summoned up enough courage to announce their intention to marry. Beatrice had at once countered that, by Christ, she would always keep Jack's bedroom as it was, so when they got divorced and he was waiting to marry some heavenly creature who wasn't a teacher or a bloody Catholic he could come back home while he sorted himself out. Laura had been so shocked that she did not at first apprehend the meaning of the words, and when she and Jack had been in the pub alone afterwards and she had actually worked out what had been said, she was too flabbergasted to cry. Jack himself had seemed permanently defeated and resigned to his mother's behaviour, and she knew he felt he had no way of fighting back because it was his parents' money that had paid for his school and University fees. Only Jack's father, whose pharmacological flights from his wife with the aid of a bottle of whisky reminded her of her own Dad's drinking, offered some comfort. 'Don't listen to what that bloody bitch says,' he had said to Laura once while they were alone before the drinks cupboard. 'She has made my life a fucking misery.' A few months later he had died suddenly of a stroke. Laura had never really been allowed to get to know him.

Beatrice had eventually mellowed to the extent of allowing Laura to stop calling her 'Mrs Morton' on the day before the wedding, and seemed positively pleased, with Jack at least, when they had told her the news that Laura was pregnant with Lizzie a couple of years afterwards. She had even allowed Laura to kiss her, something that Laura was never again to do until Beatrice was dead and she pressed her lips to her corpse in the cold hospital ward. Jack remained dry-eyed at both his parents' funerals, but strangely at Beatrice's Laura had found herself unable to hold back her tears. When she asked herself why she came up with the answer that it had been all so unnecessary and such a waste of time and life. Eventually Jack had told her as much as he knew of his mother's story and she had endeavoured to understand how she had become as she had been. Only occasionally did she ask herself what damage Beatrice may have done to Jack, but she never made any connections.

After the necessary muddle and unpleasantness of the funeral Jack had inherited what seemed to Laura to be a very substantial amount of money, and they had continued to play their game with one another, right through the children's births. She struggled to keep up with her own career with baby minders and disposable nappies and an almost pathological desire to show Jack, with his large lawyer's income and disappointing degree results, that she with her First and smaller teacher's salary could still pull him down, and could still make him look ridiculous when he was being a fart. And he would play the game and get her back and they would make love and be ready for the next round.

Or at least that is how it used to work until very recently. The children getting a bit older had of course taken some of the fun of it out. You couldn't, after all, really go at it together with them watching. It was necessary to present a united front. But there was something more than that. It was as though now that she had really failed she hardly had the self-confidence to play at all any more. She had repeatedly put off telling Jack about the extent of her professional disaster, while dreaming that maybe if she were finally to confess to him about the whole Jon business she could admit defeat in one round and they could laugh it off and start another one. But up until her conversation with Jean this afternoon the potential price had seemed almost unthinkable. Such an admission of total misjudgement might be to risk finally losing the game altogether, and she wasn't capable of facing that. She was pretty certain that Jack would hate it too, for she had a shrewd belief that he needed her to keep on playing with his mind to keep him up to intellectual scratch at work, and for that he needed to respect her.

Sitting on the sofa with Poppy opposite her, however, Laura knew that the game was stalled. Jack was bored with her now, bored by her long silences and weeping, bored and embarrassed by her drinking, bored by excuses of illness, and bored by the sex. She knew she was letting him down there too. Every day she told herself that she would stay sober and surprise him, let him do whatever he liked. She had searched his computer for what he supposed to be his secret collection of porn and had a pretty good idea both of his fantasies and her own ability to live up to them. It usually aroused her to think like this and that made her think it would be no problem by the evening. But by then she would have had the children all day and was feeling pretty miserable about herself too, so she would have a few drinks to cheer herself up. She had to pretend to Jack all the time in the evenings that she wasn't as drunk as she was because she knew that his worry and despair at his own inability to stop her sent him into a rage which could fly at her suddenly before he remembered that she was supposed to be ill and then he tried so very hard, bless him, not to be angry. So she would think how much he deserved sex and would really, really try, but very often she couldn't get aroused even when he went down on her so he would just fuck her and have his own orgasm. Once she had heard him mutter, 'Christ, I might as well have a wank' in his *petit mort* after ejaculating inside her shamefully unresponsive body. And twice over the past few weeks he had seemed to be living out some rape fantasy, perhaps as a punishment, perhaps in a final, desperate and misplaced attempt to arouse her. She had no choice but to let him, and he had hurt her. And of course there was a third possibility about that, that he had reached the end of his tether with her, which she richly deserved, was beginning to hate her, and had hurt her deliberately. Yet immediately she dismissed this idea because she knew their lives were inextricably bound up with one another's. They had the game. They belonged together, always brutally honest, *semper contra mundum*.

Laura watched the children watching TV with half an eye, and observed Jack talking to Poppy about his work.

He was being a fart even now, lounging there with his well-cut sports jacket, flannels and silk tie and boasting quite shamelessly about how he had apparently single-handedly preserved the ethical work of the practice against the evil machinations of his partners who wanted to cut back on legal aid, *pro bono* and matrimonial cases. Laura knew perfectly well that he did all this stuff because he felt he ought to be socially responsible and caring and liked to think of himself as such, but wasn't actually caring or ethical enough actually to put himself out very much or do anything which would reduce his salary. He would never have considered going to work in a really poor area or doing VSO when he was younger, for instance. This would have made her want to laugh a few months ago, but now she found it merely irksome. She wanted the children in bed and Poppy to go, so that she could talk to Jack seriously about what had happened in the supermarket and maybe even all the rest of the stuff. But Poppy showed no signs of going and appeared to be lapping up all of his bullshit, giving out little exclamations of interest and urging him on, her eyes fixed on him as though Laura were no longer in the room. Laura wanted to slap her, knowing for a fact that she was a Tory whereas even though he wasn't much good at it, Jack was motivated by the socialism which they shared and which he had adopted as a defence against his mother. Jack rose from the expensively covered Edwardian armchair with the amusing brocade camels he had chosen and which she knew he thought spoke so much about his good taste and carefully studied sense of humour. He offered more drinks and Laura of course took some, allowing him to fill her glass lest she be left out of a round. But she had already decided that for a while she would duck out of a conversation in which she was apparently an unnecessary accessory. The children were leaning together half asleep, Davie's head of curly hair propped against Lizzie's shoulder and Jemima run aground and half-forgotten on the sofa. Laura took a sip of gin.

'Time for these sleepy-heads to get upstairs, I think.' She picked up Davie, easing Lizzie back down on the sofa so that she did not fall now that his body weight had been removed. Davie stirred in that delightful way of his and hung his arms tight round her neck, pressing his lips to her cheek as though he wanted to squeeze out the tears of love she immediately felt forming in her eyes. She bent him over Jack, who offered a peremptory 'Good-night Davie' and a five-o'clock shadowed cheek-peck while Poppy, without rising from her chair, asked to help in one of those ways which one knew, despite her earlier enthusiasm to help Laura during the afternoon, was now not intended seriously to be taken up.

'Oh, no,' said Laura. 'I'll only be a minute.'

Laura could hear the rise and fall of the conversation downstairs as she eased David beneath his duvet and knelt beside his bed to stroke his forehead until his breathing became regular and full sleep had overtaken him. She looked at his face and wondered again at the miracle that can produce a fully functioning human being from love in only nine months' time, so perfect in his intricacy and terrifying in his fragility. A former colleague of Jack's was on dialysis, and she thought how it would take a huge and not very efficient machine to mimic the behaviour of just one of Davie's little kidneys, which was very like something you might see in a butcher's shop but here inside him was alive and doing something so mysterious and wonderful to her that the limits of her mind were bent outwards with the effort to understand it. She had felt a bit the same when she had read about string theory and quantum mechanics in Stephen Hawkins and Bill Bryson's pop science books, but now much more so, for here it was before her, in this warm, breathing, heat-pumping eating and excreting thing of love which had been made by sex. And then there was the miracle of mind itself, the overlapping intricacies of the brain as it raced to incorporate and make sense of Davie's world for him, weaving the language he was learning without apparent effort in no way any adult ever could learn, shaping his emotions and intellect and moral sensibility, bringing him to experience more and more of the love she had for him and which would be only the beginning of many loves and which she hoped would end with the Love that lasts forever.

For a moment as she leant over Davie Laura was overcome by terror, imaging the drunk on the road who could smash her son's body and of the paedophile or the drugs and disease which could wreck his brain and leave his mind to grow up damaged in ways too horrible to contemplate. Such things happened. At once as though a switch had been thrown she began to beg the Blessed Virgin for protection for them both, the icon of suffering motherhood who had seen her Son die, and she clung onto the childhood words in desperation: *'Hail, Holy Queen, Hail our life, our sweetness and our hope...'* and then stopped in shame and self-ridicule, knowing that God simply could not work like that or he would never have left six million Jews to die in the death camps, and that Jack would laugh at her for her sentimentality and addiction to bad nineteenth century translations of what he called 'medieval Catholic tat.' And of course he would accuse her of having had too much to drink, although that was a lot of balls because a lot of people had produced their best work when they were drunk half the time: look at Hemingway.

As she returned downstairs to pick up Lizzie, Laura was aware that there was less noise of conversation coming from the sitting room than there had been previously and was embarrassed to think that perhaps Jack and Poppy had overheard her prayers. Ever since becoming ill Laura had been prey to what she described to herself, and very occasionally to Jack, as 'Bad Thoughts.' These were sudden remembrances of past embarrassments which played unbidden through her consciousness in vivid and horrifying detail, of times when she had made a fool of herself or hurt somebody else, as she thought unforgivably. Sometimes they were accompanied or drifted into a morbid fear of death itself, when the sum total of her awful, shameful worthlessness would come crashing in on her and she would be overcome with a horror-filled certainty that there was simply nothing other than this physical life and that she had ballsed it up. On such occasions she would often compare herself to her friends who she thought had succeeded so well and whose good opinion she valued, and this or some other emotional trigger about her failures would lead to involuntary exclamations which escaped her mouth before she had been given time to think, as though her body and part of her mind were rebelling against her terror, distracting her like an animal with the beginnings of a flight or fight response. Frequently she had been forced to sit up in bed, her senses heightened and saying 'Oh dear God, no' and Jack asking over and over again, 'Are you OK?' when of course, humiliatingly, there was nothing really wrong except in a place that nobody could ever reach. At first Jack had seemed sympathetic, then frustrated by his own inability to make these moments stop, and now he sought refuge in laying a hand on her in a resigned sort of way. She was pretty certain that he connected it with her drinking and was losing sympathy, and maybe he was right. Her prayer about Davie had been very like one of these, and though she thought she had been whispering, perhaps she had not been conscious how loudly she had been speaking and Jack and Poppy had overheard, and that too could be added to the list of things to make her cringe and shout to God about.

She had not dared to talk to her counsellors about the Bad Thoughts. There was so much God language involved that she was pretty certain she could not trust them. Their ignorance of the history of ideas and uncritical relativism was certain to make them dismiss all such talk as being delusional. Dr Lewis had been downright sniffy about St John Rigby's at Earl's Friary, and her experiences with Jean and conversations with casual acquaintances in the field had made her pretty certain that psychotherapists do not do spirituality. Even those who had some sympathy for the language of faith were made to hide it in professional situations. At what she thought of as her best times when the Bad Thoughts came, Laura thought about Jesus on the Cross, *'My God, My God, Why have you forsaken me?'* And this gave her comfort and some relief from the horrors, but not always. The terrors of the grave still surrounded her.

Jack was standing fiddling with something on the chimney piece as Laura came into the sitting room to pick up Lizzie, and Poppy too seemed distracted and flushed, although this was a bit difficult to see as she was holding Lizzie in her arms and had her face buried in the little girl's hair. Laura felt the confirmation of her despair creep over her: she really would have to talk to Jack this evening, it was all so hopeless and things simply could not be allowed to go on like this. She took Lizzie to bed and once again was aware of a lowering of voices downstairs that made her face burn with self-hatred. When she returned to the sitting room she grasped her gin and cigarettes and tried to apply her mind to the conversation, which had now turned, perhaps as her feet were heard on the stairs, to Poppy's new hobby of collecting and making things out of driftwood she found on the estuary foreshore. Laura could not really concentrate and found it irritating that Jack was showing such enthusiasm for a subject which she thought frivolous at a time when she was desperate to have him alone to talk to, even though she knew that this was irrational since after all, he could not be expected to have a crystal ball to tell him what was going on in her mind. After ten minutes or so she was unable to stand it any longer and, finally remembering the unfinished bottle of gin there, made the excuse of checking on the supper things to go into the kitchen. There she fixed herself an illicit and extremely strong drink, read the microwave instructions on the duck, and hoped fervently that Poppy would take the hint and bugger off.

For a moment it occurred to Laura to wonder whether Poppy and Jack's changes in conversational mood and pitch during the evening had actually been nothing at all to do with her, but rather caused by them flirting with one another in a way which, she being absent for some of the time, stepped beyond the boundaries of normal banter between very close friends whose partners one also knows well. She finished her drink as she contemplated this, looking out across the rain-soaked garden to where hydrangea leaves dripped wetly onto the sodden lawn. She reached the conclusion that it was probably not worth bothering about mid-way through her final gulp for several reasons. First among these was the fact that

Poppy had really always been her friend first and Jack's only second, so that she and Poppy spent a great deal of time together. That would surely be pretty difficult for Poppy to do if she were making any kind of real play for Jack. Poppy had always been extremely kind and loyal to her too, not falling away as other more casual acquaintances and colleagues had done when she became ill, and Laura could not really imagine her being able to mess about. And finally it had to be admitted that while Poppy was extremely pretty and could be great fun, she was hardly Brain of Britain and Laura knew enough of Jack to think that he would pretty soon tire of somebody whose education had stopped at a list of crummy grades at A Level and who cooked for a living, even if she was senior chef in a minor public school. With this uncharitable and horribly snobbish thought she choked slightly, which she told herself was instant retribution, and giggled. Then the slightly darker reflection entered her head, that if Jack and Poppy were having a bit of a flirt then it was really no great surprise because she had been so awful to Jack recently, and she was hardly in a position to complain. She hid the gin things and placed the glass in the sink before returning to the sitting room.

'So that is the extent of your whittling endeavour at present?' Jack was asking, leaning forward in his seat and grinning at Poppy.

'It is indeed. But by Christmas I shall have made things for all my friends that they won't dare hide in case I come round.'

Laura laughed. 'That's a really excellent idea. Putting art to the practical use of pissing off one's friends. I am looking forward to seeing what we are going to have.'

'Oh yes, I shall have to find something really excellent for you two,' replied Poppy. 'Something huge and unwieldy I think.' They laughed. 'Look, I think I had better get myself on my way and let you have your supper.'

Laura relaxed into her seat in the knowledge that at last they were on the home straight, so that when Jack asked Poppy, as she knew he would because he always did, 'You'll have another drink before you go?' and Poppy accepted as she always did, she did not mind at all. Laura was beginning to feel the warming and comforting fuzziness of the first level of serious intoxication, a stage which she enjoyed and which she often wished she could preserve as a steady state and during which she could be charming and funny, sexy and volubly relaxed. When finally they had finished their drinks and said their thank yous Jack showed Poppy to the door, where there was, Laura registered but decided not to pursue, a bit more whispering and a shade more time spent than was strictly necessary.

As he returned Jack pinched one of Laura's cigarettes and lit it, then slightly surprised her by asking peremptorily, 'I suppose you'd like another drink as usual? I'm having one.'

The rain outside was beginning again now, this time in gusts that whipped the top of the gum-tree in the garden they had allowed to grow too tall. 'You and Poppy seemed to be having a good time. Did you have a nice afternoon?' Jack asked.

'Oh, Poppy was fine. It was very kind of her to look after the kids. But listen, Jack, no I didn't have a nice afternoon.' She was determined to talk seriously to him now she had the chance. She had the feeling that if she left the opportunity aside she might not summon up the necessary resolve again.

'Really? Why ever not? It looks to me like you have

been having some fun attacking the gin bottle.'

'Well OK, we had a few drinks. It's not like you never do anything reprehensible. And anyway, I didn't mean while Poppy was here, I meant before then.'

'I didn't say it was reprehensible. It's absolutely up to you what you do with your time.'

'But you were implying it.'

'No I'm not. I wish very much that I could afford the time to sit around drinking gin at all hours of the day.' She couldn't work out whether Jack was playing games or not. In any case it wasn't going to work like this.

'Please, darling,' she said, 'don't be like that. I really can't take it today, OK?'

'But Laura, you never can take it. There's always some bloody excuse…'

'What do you mean?'

'There's always some excuse for you to drink. And another one to stop you from facing up to stuff.'

This wasn't a game. Laura felt as though she had been slapped. This was not the way she had planned the conversation and she was shocked that Jack could have so suddenly moved onto the attack. Something must have really rattled his cage. She fell silent for a moment and drew on her cigarette as she calculated how in spite of her hurt and his anger she might yet rescue the situation. Even with the alcohol her mind began to race efficiently, flicking through possible replies like somebody using a card index and discarding them for astute reasons that took only fractions of a second to calculate.

'Jack, I know I drink too much, but I don't think it's fair to say I haven't been trying to face up to stuff.'

'Really? It seems to me that it's absolutely fair.' Not normally a chain smoker or even a heavy one, Jack found a new cigarette from his own packet and lit it from the end of the one he had stolen from Laura.

'For Christ's sake, Jack…'

'What? What do you mean, Laura?'

'Please let me talk to you. Please.'

'What the fuck do you think we're doing? Playing hopscotch? Planting a herbaceous border? Starring in an amateur dramatic production of *Iolanthe*?'

'You know very well what I mean.'

'No I don't. I know you're drunk as usual and Poppy had to stay with you to make sure that kids were OK…'

'That's not fair.'

'Oh, for pity's sake open your eyes, Laura. Take a good look at yourself.' He was really angry now, his voice and hands trembling, eyes cast away from her as he struggled to keep control, but he'd started and would have to carry on with what he and Poppy had agreed. Laura's mind was racing again.

'It's not like that, Jack, it really isn't. I had an extremely distressing time in the hospital today with Jean and then I had some sort of horrible attack in Tesco's.' Jack made a sort of snorting noise in the back of his throat.

'Look Laura, I am getting to the point of past fucking caring, to be honest with you. I am sick to death of it, sick of you being drunk all the bloody time and embarrassing me in front of people, sick of listening on and on about your sodding illness and sick to death of you making no fucking effort for anybody because you're so bloody self-obsessed. For Christ's sake, you've got the best bloody treatment anybody could ask for, and you're behaving like some stupid washed-up lush. Do you know that's what people are beginning to think of you now? And do you know, I am not fucking surprised. You wouldn't believe the looks of pity I get about being married to you, and now I can hardly trust you to be with

74

the kids on your own. If you feel so terrible about yourself why don't you do us all a favour and find somewhere to fuck off to and drink yourself to death or hang yourself or something, you miserable ungrateful bitch.'

Laura was going to lob the heavy glass ashtray at Jack's head, but didn't because she very quickly saw that he was right. She saw too her own absurdity in believing that it had been she who had been trying to make him see things head on. Of course it was the other way around. Look at her reaction to what Jean had said when she had challenged her to make an effort about her drinking, look at her own failure to get better over all these months. What had happened in the supermarket was nothing more than a selfish reaction to being confronted with the truth about her failure and illness, which was that they were her own fault. With the clarity of an epiphany she knew that she was indeed entirely responsible for her own situation. The heart of the reality from which she had been running away was essentially a moral one in which alcohol misuse played a large part, but she could not get away from it as easily as that because her moral turpitude predated her drinking and she used drink precisely as a means of escape from the sheer awfulness of herself. She took a great gulp from her gin and heard Jack tut, saw his anger distorted through the side of her glass, and her imaginative and critical intelligence was caught up and quickened, her synapses whirring into making connections with everything that Jack had said and all the terrible things she had done, the Bad Thoughts and her failure and Jon at school and the end of her career which she had deserved and her stupid hanging on to worthless rubbish like her snobbish sense of pride about her degree which she just gripped on to so tightly to make herself feel better when she was really so useless and she realised that Jack was really right and that she was really a terrible parent and she had never done anything for anybody and the girls had sellotaped that headline to her desk and Dad had died and she had thought she was a good teacher but she obviously wasn't and she drank too much and wasn't even fanciable any more not like Poppy and she had thought that she could talk to Jack but that was stupid because she hurt him so much all the time and the game was stalled and nothing was going anywhere and there was only nothing really left except the children and they would be better off without her if she was like this all the time because she was bad all through like Jack was saying and whatever suffering she was experiencing now she deserved.

Without speaking Laura got up, went to the kitchen and pressed her hands hard on the work surface, her head hanging down and hair brushing her cheeks, which had what people had told her in another world were fine bones. She was surprised to see how there were tears falling out of her and forming in little salt pools near the bread bin. She had not even been aware that she was weeping and wondered vaguely when she had started. Crying would make things a bit more difficult because it was important not to disturb the children and to make things worse for them after they had already been through so much through her own stupid fault, so she would have to do it all quietly. She knew where her degree and freshman's photographs were, hanging on the wall of the little room which they called the Study and Sewing Room. She would begin there, and oh, yes, she remembered, her lecture notes were there in files too, occasionally looked at over the years to construct A level courses and to help her in teaching her OU students. What a laugh, what stupid iconography of a worthless life. She took the gin bottle from the cupboard, unscrewed the top and held it upturned to her mouth like Pepsi. She had never drunk neat gin before and her critical faculties registered that it was actually pretty disgusting, like drinking scent. Screwing the top back on the bottle she found some black bin bags and a tack hammer in the kitchen drawer and crept past the sitting room, vaguely wondering at one point why Jack was so quiet but then rapidly assimilating his silence and lack of intervention as part of the Revelation which had begun to overtake her mind.

In the sewing room she took down her university and school photographs, those awful studio portraits in cap and gown and grinning lined up staff rooms, and placed them in the bin bags together with her lecture notes and lesson plans, which she unclipped from their retaining rings. They scattered in irrecoverable disorder into the shiny blackness, and Laura nudged the bags with her feet to give them a good shake up. By the time she had finished they were pretty heavy, but not really much more so than a couple of holiday hold-alls, so she was able to manoeuvre them down the stairs and out of the front door into the warm evening rain quite easily, the water making little percussive noises on the plastic crinkles and, she saw, already beginning to blot and smear the ink of her handwriting. Back inside the house she collected her handbag, keys and the tack hammer. She slipped on the red wet tiles outside and in her half-fall before she recovered herself, saw in the cloud-started light of the single streetlamp the spinning raindrops above her head as things of sudden unbearable beauty and poignancy, sacraments of the vastness of a universe. They which would go on whatever she did and whenever she died, and could perhaps offer still to the kids the chance of what she had wrecked in the stupidity and weakness she must end by destroying the hateful person about whom Jack had spoken so that she could begin again.

The light was reflected briefly on the side of the tack hammer as Laura raised it and she thought of the story of Abraham and Isaac picked out as she had once seen it in the sunshone pinks and browns of a mediaeval wall painting in an Italian church, the Patriarch with his hand raised to kill his son in sacrifice, the Ram who adumbrates Christ forever thorn-stuck by some obscure fresco artist's hand, unless it wasn't really fresco but that other thing you did with the plaster dry, it would be clever to know its name when other people didn't, but for God's sake who cared, and how ironic that this was exactly the sort of thinking that she so hated about herself, the old self-satisfied intellectual snob bitch Laura who she was going to destroy now by bringing the hammer down. Gosh, what a noise it made. She had not expected such a racket. Good job the kids' bedrooms were at the back of the house. Now, and now and now and now smashing the glass of those stupid fucking photographs and herself grinning like an idiot, so full of self-importance and smug cleverness and wasted hope and greedy for an ambition which would end in tears and disaster. She reversed the hammer and broke into the raw cardboard of the photographs with the claw, tearing the image of her own old, younger self with a huge sense of relief and freedom as each blow brought its absolution and her tears dried. Provoked by the Abraham story a line from the Gospels came into her head: *Unless a man be born again, he cannot enter the Kingdom of God* and she gasped at the realisation that she now not only knew exactly what Christ had meant, but that she here was living out his teaching as she had never done before, and that this was a grace-filled moment. The Holy Spirit had brought her to do what she was doing and was filling her now with His strength and glory of sacrifice. Her hatred of her old self was the righteousness of God at work.

Eventually Laura's hands were smarting and her wrists aching too much to carry on, and she threw the hammer into one of the bags and walked away from the house. She wasn't much of a one for walking in the evening on her own, still less in the rain, although occasionally on fine days she and Jack used to go for a wander around before the kids were born, looking at people's gardens and possibly ending up at one of the pubs for a couple of drinks on their own. But she could not possibly return to the house yet, she needed to walk and think, to allow the epinephrine levels in her body to subside and stop making so much fuel available to her and so at least to get her breathing down.

There weren't many people on the road. A few dog walkers who Laura knew by sight nodded at her as she passed them, and she returned their greetings. One of them she thought was called Joe, a short, old man with a sweet, funny face straight from a Breugel painting. He had a wire haired Jack Russell and was a frequent sight about the town. As he passed Laura he remarked, 'Bit wet to be out without a coat, love.' Laura's mind clicked into a response, a childish white lie straight from childhood: 'Oh, it's OK thanks, I am only just going to the corner shop and back,' and she found herself surprised to flicker a smile easily as they both walked on, a smile which became some indefinable switch in her mind. She wondered what it was, but put the thought off with the more pressing worry that it was going to look odd wandering around without a coat, although at least she had jeans and a top on and not a summer frock. Then, passing next to a buddleia overhanging the pavement she recognised the nature of the switch her mind had made, and realised that she was suddenly and overwhelmingly happy. She relished the actions that she had taken. She understood the attempt at meaning behind the lyrics of songs that hitherto she had sniggered at for being sentimental and spiritual rubbish, and they began to play their tunes in her mind. The Hills were Alive with the Sound of Music. Somewhere Over the Rainbow Skies were Blue for her. She believed, indeed she knew that a Flower Grew for every drop of Rain that Fell, at least in the sense of the wonderful mystery of the ecological balance, to whose maintenance as God's creation she now dedicated her life. And she could see trees of green and skies of, well, grey and rainy but she laughed because it really was a Wonderful World and everything would be all right. She thought of John Newton and how he had turned from being a slave trader to writing *Amazing Grace* and wondered if he had felt as happy as she did in the snappy surprise of his conversion. Above her as she passed, a horse chestnut tree shuddered in the breeze like an enormous cat, sending raindrops scattering onto her shoulders and arms, and one went down the back of her neck and she giggled and turned her face upwards and laughed aloud at the extraordinariness of all things, feeling that she had grasped the Theory of Everything and it remained only for her to do the sums one day to express it to others and astonish the world.

Laura neared the corner shop. It had a yellow, brightly illuminated board and was incongruously perched on the end of the self-consciously protected Conservation Area. Post-card sized signs containing ill-written messages advertising Ironing Taken In and second-hand Hoovers were posted in its windows along with occasional admonitions from the management in the punctilious politeness of the Asian shopkeepers. Laura always said she adored them, was always careful to be nice to them and had learned all their names. She had told Joe and his dog she was going to the shop, so she might as well go there. And since she couldn't possibly go home yet she might as well buy herself something to drink. Then she could think what to do best about Jack somewhere, because he would obviously have to be told about the change in her and all the marvellous things she now knew about, but he was too angry and sad to take it in at the moment.

Mr Patel Senior was behind the counter, his face as large and jolly as an one of the aubergines he sold, smiling his 'Good evening, Missus' at Laura. She could see herself in the convex mirror set high above the counter, her foreshortened and distorted frame contrasting strangely with the man before her as in a hall of mirrors. It was as though, nonsensically, something had happened to her sense of perception and the world was different from the messages her mind was perceiving and which formed the basis of her actions. What a creepy thought, she mused before grabbing again at her happiness and the matter in hand. 'Can I have two of those miniatures of vodka, please?' she asked, pointing them out where they stood by the cigarettes as though Mr Patel might not know where he had put them, but really of course because she didn't buy miniatures usually and was a bit nervous. 'Oh, and twenty Silk Cut. Thanks.' She felt as though she were fourteen again, buying a packet of ten Number Six without her mother's knowledge on a girlfriends' day out shopping in Amblehurst, and she laughed a little. Mr Patel raised an eyebrow as he handed her goods over and grinned.

'You won't get very far at a party with those, Missus.'

'Ah, but actually I am going to a bring-a-bottle do for very small people. Your supplies are exactly the right size.' Mr Patel roared with laughter and shook his head.

'Gulliver's Travels with vodka, then,' he said. 'Alas that I cannot join you.'

'I am sorry too, Mr Patel. Say hello to Ayisha and the boys for me.'

How nice everyone was, Laura thought as she left. How dense she had been not to see it before. The rain was stopping now. Laura put one of the little bottles in her handbag and, crooking the other to hide it as much as possible in her right hand, broke the seal and unscrewed it with her left. She hated to throw litter so put the snaggly bottle top in her handbag for later disposal. Thus armed she tried to remember whether wandering about drinking in the street, while certainly not socially acceptable, was actually a criminal offence, but couldn't. But she didn't want people to be upset with her anyway, so she walked down Dogshit Alley and came out at the park, where she leant up against the churchyard wall and swigged at the vodka, which was much better neat than the gin had been.

Right, now, what was she to do about Jack? She looked out over the river, taking occasional sips of her drink, at the way the estuary snaked out into the blur of the wet evening and the salt flat islands, the small yachts aground on the mud with their lines dripping onto their mooring buoys. The children would be fine, they were fast asleep. But getting back to Jack and getting through to him once she got there was going to be a real problem. Crikey, they didn't call these things miniatures for nothing, did they? There was nobody much about. Laura walked over to one of the bins and threw the bottle away together with its top, cracking open the new one as she walked back to take up her place again by the wall. If she went home now there would be the most terrible row, which would be pointless because Jack would think he was talking to the old her and would be too angry to listen to anything different. Better to leave it for at least an hour or so and then he would have had time to calm down. With luck she would be able to sneak the bin bags round to that skip she had seen across the road, except then she wondered if part of her did not want Jack to have found them already.

Laura finished the vodka. It was colder now. The obvious thing was to go to the Anchor and wait for a bit. The lights from the windows looked invitingly warm, there was an R. *Whites* litter bin by the side door she could flip her bottle into. Vaguely Laura wondered if she were drunk, but she wasn't staggering about or anything and her elation seemed to be masking her sense of everything else.

She had quite a nice time in the pub. There was a bubbly, funny girl called Andrea she got talking to. And oh, Christ, there was George Brightly, but thank God he hadn't seen her and seemed to be just leaving. There was a Scottish barman who combined just the right amounts of amiability and reserve that Laura always considered his work to need. And at some point Laura realized that she was very drunk, which was a bit of a shame because something terribly important had happened this evening and she needed to talk to Jack about it. She was surprised when Poppy arrived with a kind of 'I am doing my compassionate and concerned bit' look on her face, but she thought it was probably a reasonable enough idea to let her take her back home, where Poppy put her to bed in the spare room and for days Laura slept and got up and had a pee and went back to bed again and got up and wandered about and went back to bed again, turning down meals and eating secret yoghurts and crying and wondering how Mrs Hill and Jack were coping with the children, who came in occasionally and bounced on her bed, but that set her off weeping again and made Jack angry.

Nine

Earl's Friary Hospital
St David's Road
Amblehurst
'Help When It's Needed'

26 July 2000

Dear Laura,

I am very sorry that you have not felt able to attend your last three appointments here. I think we made some good progress in our previous sessions but in the circumstances I am sure that you will understand that we do not feel able to keep charging Dr Andrews's practice for your treatment. Do keep in touch with your G.P. and should Dr Andrews feel that you need further help from us we will of course be available to you here.

I think it is very important that you keep taking your Prozac and I wish you well for your continued recovery.

With all good wishes,

Yours sincerely,
Jean Tomlinson.

Ten

After the evening of Pete and the pint-throwing Laura kept her head down for a while. It wasn't one of her really Bad Weeks. Rather she just wanted to avoid the hassle of reintroducing herself to the pub and felt unsure of how she would be received. It was, she reckoned, strategically better to let the next bit of gossip take over and leave her own indiscretion half forgotten in the glory of the latest novelty. Part of her was afraid too of seeing Pete again, but she told herself she was damned if that was going to stop her seeing Andrea, Les and the rest of the crowd indefinitely. So as a distraction technique she set about clearing up the house, wrestling with the hateful vacuum cleaner on the stairs and washing the floors, arranging her bookshelves into some sort of order and finally even dusting. Dusting was a seldom-accomplished task about which she felt pretty proud even after her mother pointed out to her on the telephone that it is more efficient to dust before hoovering. During the evenings she talked to Liz and Davie on the Messenger program on her computer, their faces appearing grainy and slightly time-lagged on the screen. She enjoyed this, though. More than the telephone it enabled her to have private time with them and it meant that she did not have to telephone Jack's house, where there was the danger of getting Poppy answering and she would have to spend the rest of the evening asking for the grace not to be angry, bitter and destructive.

Laura had only recently learned to ask for this. At first when Jack had moved Poppy in and it became apparent to Laura that her former friend's solicitude to her children had been part of a well-constructed plan of adultery, she had been filled with an anger and a sense of betrayal so intense that for the first time in her life she found herself prey to violent fantasies. These feelings were made the more intense by a distressed conversation with Lizzie about Secrets which had led on to the discovery that Jack and Poppy had, early on in the separation, talked about their plans to both of the kids and told them that they were on no account to talk Mummy about it all. Laura had found herself furiously dwelling on how even in her child-like ways Lizzie was worried about dual loyalties. Thus Laura dreamt of Poppy's face smashed against some pavement by a runaway lorry, she wished cancer would make her frigid and cause her oh-so-pretty hair to drop out and kill her. In her half dreams before sleeping when she imagined Jack's cock in Poppy's mouth or her legs wrapped around his back in the act of sex she had more than once wondered how much it would cost to hire someone to get rid of her for good, this woman who had betrayed her and engaged in a deliberate campaign of seduction towards her husband and the children she loved so much.

On another occasion, at a drunken evening with one of the more idly malicious of the secretaries from Jack's work whom she had met by chance in the Anchor, she had found out that Jack and Poppy's aims had long predated her own final weeks of illness at home and that Jack had been meticulous in his planning for breaking with her even as early as her first appointments at Earl's Friary.

According to Maureen, Poppy's affair with Jack had been pretty common gossip at the firm ages before Laura had twigged it. Maureen told her that he had discussed his options with at least one of the partners to her certain knowledge. She had overheard them.

For all these reasons Laura's idea that there was a game, an indissoluble bond between her and Jack which would last forever had been revealed for what it was, a humiliating fantasy. With the coldness of certainty she realised that Jack's legal training and his knowledge of her unstable mental state had enabled him to play mind games with her while making it easy for him to manipulate matters so that he had got exactly what he wanted. At the time of their divorce he had been civilised to the point of unbearable courtesy, as though they were perhaps discussing the purchase of a new car, with much 'darling this' and 'darling that' thrown in. She had even then trusted him, had been certain in her depression that he knew best and that she had brought much of the disaster on herself. It was only many months afterwards that she had vaguely admitted to herself that in agreeing not to contest the divorce she had allowed him to persuade her to accept a financial settlement and contact agreements for the children that were most advantageous to him and disadvantageous to her. Even now the contemplation of this could leave her chokingly angry with Jack and Poppy, who could apparently use somebody else's sickness to pursue their own lusts and financial agenda to the detriment of everyone around them, including the children.

And yet Laura knew enough to realise that this was only one way of telling the story. At university she had learned that in modern historiography each version of the truth was held to be inextricably bound up with the writer's own preconceptions and life experience, so that when she read the Marxist E. P. Thompson about the Industrial Revolution she should expect a very different narrative from Trevor-Roper's or Trevelyan's. And hadn't she been told that in the same way the biblical critics of the twentieth century thought that understanding the life situations of the early Christian communities that produced the texts was essential for understanding the Gospels? Laura knew very well that events do not merely exist in the past, but in the way they are retold, often for polemical purposes unconnected with the bare historical facts. She was too honest a scholar and had now been made too forcibly self-aware not to apprehend that in the same way the prism of her own story with Jack could in theory be turned to face the light in different ways and that to her former husband, to Poppy and the children, very different aspects might be visible. In her prayers she acknowledged her need to grasp this, but she was as yet still too astonished by the hurt to be able to get beyond the blame and bitterness and rotate the glass. If she were able to she guessed it would part of what Andrea would call 'moving on' and maybe even 'getting a sodding life.' But it all hurt too much. Very occasionally Laura felt bad enough about this inability that she wondered if it would be worthwhile making an appointment at her GP surgery. It had been getting on for five years that she last had been to Earl's Friary, and the only times she talked to a medic since then were when she had to go for the statutory five minute reviews of her prescriptions for Prozac. Ashamed of her failure to keep up the commitment to the hospital and worried that she might once more be attacked for her drinking, Laura was deeply reluctant to ask for help. In any case, she told herself, she was usually very much better and more able to cope than she had been in the past.

There had been very few repetitions of the terrible tack hammer and photograph time. Her life since then had been one of idle friendships, job applications mysteriously turned down although she had been completely honest about her illness, and squeezing as much love out of the time allowed to her with the kids as she could.

Laura sighed and looked out through the open sash window of the sitting room to the warmth of the street beyond. She wasn't really sure what to do with herself now that she had run out of energy cleaning the house for the day, although she lit a cigarette in celebration of the end of her labours and sat on the sofa contemplating the half-read books she had piled neatly on the coffee table. They were, she decided, the normal jumble of stuff. Rubbishy thrillers, most of them unwanted gifts, rubbed covers with weightier historical and scientific material she had felt she ought to read but had weakly set aside at various points 'just for a break', their pages spiking out a hedgehog of old bills, envelopes and postcards which served as bookmarks. What she really liked were the modern women novelists, whose works she devoured and passed on to the charity table in the pub because there wasn't enough room for them in the cottage. She supposed that her addiction would be more cheaply catered for if she could be bothered to go to the public library, but she disliked the idea of her choice being limited and having to order stuff. Besides, she thought, she would never get it together enough to return them by their due dates. She had suffered before at the hands of pursed lipped librarians dispensing fines, she thought, and laughed at herself. Anyway, paperbacks weren't all that expensive and the Hospice could do with the money. Vaguely she wondered how much it cost her, but decided it was too vulgar to work it out.

Laura was just reaching out for a grimly salacious-looking black volume with a dagger and a pair of French knickers on its cover when her computer bonged at her from the desk in the dining room. This was the signal that one of her few Internet contacts had come online and wanted to talk to her. At first when she had got her broadband connection and was agog at the speed and technology now available to her, she had been rather too liberal with handing out her email and Messenger addresses, a mistake which she was quickly to rectify after being bombarded with any number of sexual solicitations, many of them vividly illustrated with photographs whose frankness did nothing to add to the appeal of their senders. After a week of this she had changed her account details and was now very careful to limit access to the children and a few close friends. There were now fewer penises in her life but she felt much better for it and was less liable to be interrupted, while discussing homework with Davie or Liz, by enquiries as to what kind of panties she had on. So sitting at the computer, she was pleased to see:

Davie is online and has just sent you a Nudge.

Laura:	Wotcha. U OK?
Davie:	fine thx.
Laura:	Good day at school?
Davie:	yeah it was OK but I hate hate hate hate maths!
Laura:	Aw c'mon

Davie:	I was top last term and now Stuart is :(
Laura:	OK where did you come?
Davie:	Second but Stuart is a bum head
Laura:	LOL you have done brilliantly to be 2nd. BTW why don't you turn yr cam and mic on?
Davie:	I'm talking to Jenny at same time, too hard to do both
Laura:	Oh OK don't let me see you then LOL you love her more than me LMAO
Davie:	MUM!!! OK LOL…HEY HEY hey Mum hey have you heard about the body?
Laura:	No. What do you mean?
Davie:	they have found a body on one of the boats there are police everywhere down by the Prom it is really COOOL.
Laura:	Are you sure about this? Today?
Davie:	yup. We heard about it at lunchtime :)
Laura:	WOW! Tell me.
Davie:	well Mark went home for lunch and he

came back and told us.

Laura:	Are you sure he isn't having you on?
Davie:	NO no honestly it's on Essex Radio and everything it is SO COOL they think he has been done in WHACK WHACK WHACK. Everybody is talking about it.
Laura:	LOL OK but I don't think we should be taking such delight in these things.
Davie:	eh? don't understand.
Laura:	You are being bloodthirsty. A person is dead after all if what you say is true.
Davie:	Oh I no that is terrible but it IS exciting isn't it?
Laura:	I suppose...are you sure it's true? Mark isn't winding everyone up?
Davie:	honest it is. We saw loads of police cars and everything walking home too.
Laura:	Gosh.
Davie:	MUM, can we...? Can we, can we...?
Laura:	Oh God I suppose you want to go and take a look at what is going on.
Davie:	YAY!!!!! Can we, can we can

we????????????????????????????

Laura:	Hang on. Let me think. Where is Lizzie?
Davie:	just come in.
Laura:	And Poppy?
Davie:	in kitchen doing stuff.
Laura:	OK well I suppose it wouldn't hurt if we took a stroll down the Prom just to see the police cars.
Davie:	YAY MUM! Thx thx thx.
Laura:	OK ask Lizzie if she wants to come and tell Poppy what you are doing. I will meet you at the corner of Amblehurst Road in ten minutes. DON'T cross the road on your own.
Davie:	gr8! See ya in 10 then
Laura:	OK.

Your conversation with Davie has ended.

Well at least it was something to do, was extra time with the children, and she might even enjoy the walk. Laura told herself these things as she gathered together her bag and keys and checked her hair briefly, and of course it was all true, but ruefully she had to admit that she was just as grimly titillated by Davie's story as he had been. Maybe the only thing different about adults and children in things like this, she thought, was that adults learn to control their more gleefully macabre instincts, sanctifying them by dressing them up as serious news items on the BBC and in the newspapers and only rarely letting them out to play. Perhaps that was what BDSM was all about. She had never been bothered to think about it before and had always regarded those who were into it with mildly salacious amusement. For a moment she wondered if all that might turn her on, and as quickly decided that it would not. No gimp masks for Laura, thank you very much. This she found slightly surprising considering she was up for most things, but there you go.

Outside the air was warm with the smell of hot tarmac. Wallflowers gripping precarious lodgings in crumbling masonry reflected back the warmth of the sun with the colours of old stained glass, and tubbed geraniums were as dusty as hymn books against the red bricked walls. Laura was transported back to her primary school playground by the smell of the road, to the seemingly endless hours of playtimes spent sitting playing jacks cross-legged on the tarmac. Jacks was less hurty than running games because if you banged into one of the big kids and fell you could graze your knees really badly and one of the dinner ladies would take you in and put iodine on the wound while you cried. She could still remember the sharp redemption of the plaster, the transition from wailing to snotty sniffs. It wasn't all bad, though, she mused, because as far as she could remember if you had a really big plaster, preferably one through which the blood seeped, you could be pretty sure that your mates would be gruesomely solicitous and that for the rest of the afternoon you would be in some way a minor goddess. Actually those wallflowers were almost the same colour as what you get when blood oozes through an old fashioned fabric elastoplast. She supposed that the guy in the boat would have his burst of glory too, she reflected, only there wouldn't be any kindly old bag with iodine for him, poor bastard.

Half consciously Laura began to take notice of her feet in her peripheral vision, to be jerked out of her lazy daydream by Davie's laughter:

'Mum, what are you doing?'

Laura's mind snapped to attention and as she bent down to him it pushed giggles of self consciousness out of her mouth. 'Minding the bears, darling.'

'You're weird.'

Laura laughed again. 'No, it's true. Everybody knows that if you tread on the cracks in the pavement the bears will get you.' Davie took her hand and they walked together, elation at one another's company slippery between their palms as they played together. Laura told herself that she hadn't really expected Lizzie to come anyway.

'Yeah, right, I used to do that when I was like…four. You're forty-four.'

'Forty-three, thanks very much. And anyway, you can never be too careful. How do you know that this bloke we are going to see didn't tread on a crack in the pavement?'

Davie laughed. 'Mum, that's just sick.'

But it wasn't sick really. Avoiding the cracks, saying the rosary; trying to live a decent life, were they any different from minding the bears of Judgement? And why wasn't Lizzie there? She couldn't ask Davie because he hated talking about Poppy so much in front of her. They walked down the shallow slope away from the castle escarpment and towards the estuary. Laura noticed the preponderance of yellow blossoms everywhere, stealing their deceitful lethal beauty from the sunshine and the warmth.

Davie was straining ahead to catch his first glimpse of the anticipated activity on the Prom. As they rounded the park corner and with a whoop of delight he pointed with his finger quivering at the blue and white plastic tape and the police cars and white vans beyond. 'Look, Mum, look, this is well cool, look.'

Laura tried again to temper his ghoulish enthusiasm. 'OK, OK darling, I am looking.' But despite herself she was very impressed. The images were so familiar from television that for a moment she half expected David Jason to appear from somewhere behind a police car. She felt confused that her own town was being used as theatre, and then at the suddenness of knowing that the scene in front of her was, shockingly, happening. She found herself holding Davie's hand tightly and felt him pull away, too young and too full of the self-centeredness of childhood to find the prospect of reality frightening.

'Ow. Mum, let go, I want to see.'

There was a small crowd of people gathered as there always is on such occasions, dog walkers who just happen to develop a sudden enthusiasm for an unusual route, neighbours from several streets away deprived of a ringside view from behind their curtains, and a gaggle of children escorted by more or less shamefaced parents. Laura joined the representatives of this last group, feeling protected by their joint possession of a more or less plausible excuse for rubber-necking. In their small town way they mostly knew one another by sight or better, and nodded greetings were exchanged as they talked banalities in hushed voices as one might at a funeral.

'A lot of cars.'

'Yes, a lot.'

'I've never seen so many.'

'There's a big white van there. Wonder what that is.'

For hot dogs, maybe, Laura thought, but did not dare say it. Across the narrow road and just in front of the police tapes the doors of the Anchor stood open. Its regular afternoon drinkers had peeled themselves away from the bar to stand in tipsy appreciation of the tantalising distraction before them. Among them was the ghastly Pete, who thank God had not seen Laura. He was busy in a noisy extemporisation that was audible from several yards away on the theme of his wide knowledge of different countries' police procedures on the unexpected discovery of 'stiffs'. Laura noted with spiteful amusement the many backs turned on him and the trapped look on the faces of his immediate interlocutors. Only Barges Bob, leaning on his stick near the wall, seemed to be paying him any attention. The Breton-capped face, which had greeted exhausted soldiers as they were boarding *Nitrogen* at Dunkirk, was anciently still. Laura looked away to do a quick check on where Davie was, there still by the tape talking excitedly to one of his schoolmates, and from the corner of her eye saw Bob push himself upright and walk slowly to where Pete stood. Laura watched him wait in patient dignity before speaking in his beery old fashioned Essex, quietly tobacco-burred voice.

'Excuse me mate, but I don't think you should be talking like that. Mouthin' off and trying to draw attention to yusself all the time. A man is dead juss down there. Now I didn't know 'im that well, mind, but we knew 'im, see. Juss you try and remember that, and have a bit o' respect.'

As Bob continued to stare at the younger, much taller man, Laura's mind clicked into delighted action. There were two wonderful possibilities here. First was to see a public defeat for her enemy for which she was not responsible. This would assuage any lingering feelings of guilt she had for her own recent behaviour, vindicate her judgement, and provide her with a new ally and friend in old Bob. Less immediate but nonetheless delicious was the revelation that Bob thought he had information about what was going on, and apparently knew to whom the discovered body belonged. She knew that she could take advantage of her mild acquaintance with him in the pub to lever what he thought he knew out of him, for despite his advancing years he had a keen interest in bosoms and beer. In this way she could be one step ahead of the game.

'I'm sorry, mate,' Pete said to Bob after a long silence during which he appeared to have developed a twitch in his face and his immediate companions a fascination for the ground at their feet. 'I didn't mean to give no offence.'

'Well, don't bloody offer it then,' said Bob. 'Most of us round here take what we're given for free.'

After this there was a bit of what Laura always thought of as an *Adlestrop* moment, when everything goes quiet except for a couple of significant sounds, and you know that you will probably remember it for the rest of your life. For Edward Thomas it had been somebody coughing on a train and the birdsong outside. For Laura it was the sound of sudden laughter around her and the bang of the Anchor's side door. Soon there were thumps and jangles from inside as Pete smashed out his fury, humiliation and self-hatred on the fruit machine. Somebody she vaguely recognised as a moderately dishy male nurse called Alex said 'Wanker,' and Laura was flushed with relief and delight. She was, she decided, absolutely in love with Bob.

She walked over to him.

'Hello Bob. I thought that was rather well done.'

'Hello, Laura. Yuss, well he was rather making a nuisance of hisself.'

'How is your glass? Let me get you a beer. I think you deserve one, and I want one anyway.'

'That's very kind of you Laura, I'll have a pint with you, ta.' Bob was grinning.

Laura ascertained that Davie and his companion would like coke and crisps (one plain, one cheese and onion) and went to the bar. She was slightly disappointed that Les the barman was not there to witness her triumph. Nonetheless as she ordered she made sure that she raised her voice to a level which would carry above the furious plinky-plonking of the one armed bandit. Then she turned and stared at Pete's back, fully aware that he could see her in the mirror above his face. She let out what she hoped was a snort of amused contempt before heading back outside to dispense the drinks and snacks to the children. Bob was leaning against the wall and they both drank quietly for a while. They reckoned they each knew what they were going to talk about, and that neither had any desire to rush the conversation in the Turkish-Delight richness of its novelty. Laura judged that about half way down her pint would do, so when she reached it she asked:

'So, Bob, who is it? I mean, whose boat was it?'

'*Stella Maris* she's called. She's under that police boom tent thing there. Nice boat I suppose for one of those big Tupperware yachty things. Not my sort of thing though, more for your weekend gentleman sailor. Still, poor bugger's dead now.' The sweetness went as she heard Bob say, 'That bloke George. That's who it was. George Brightly,' and something like a serpent uncoiled itself in

Laura's mind.

'Holy Mother of Christ, Bob, I mean, I knew George well from teaching, not just here.' The pious blasphemy, which had started as an affectation to annoy Jack and then stuck, sounded strange in Laura's Cambridge voice and struck a false note even to her own ears. She sneaked a look at the old man, whom she was pleased to see looked neither shocked nor surprised.

'I'm sorry, love,' he said, looking out over the crowd of children and remaining adults near the police tapes. He took a sip of his beer and nodded towards them. 'I see your David is growing up. These young 'uns do love a bit of drama, eh?'

Laura felt put down, seeing in the remark a mild rebuke for her excitement, but not one yet so severe as to put an end to her soliciting of information. She gave a smile.

'Yes, of course they do. Mind you I suppose it's not every day even we see something like this. Do we know what is really going on?'

'I don't know no more than I've been told, love. Guess we'll all have to wait for the news to get round. It will. It'll be in the *Standard,* and even if it's not then everybody in the pub will still talk a lot of bollocks about it.'

No more help from there, then. Despite her disappointment Laura smiled and they finished their drinks companionably, the beer copper-striking through their sunlit glasses in the silence and sending from each a splosh of colour onto the wooden table at which they sat.

'Come on Davie, it's time to go home.' He was looking bored now anyway, scuffing his shoes against the ground and only addressing occasional remarks to his friends. Laura hated describing Jack and Poppy's house as 'home' to the children. Each time she did so she had to push down the lump of anger in her throat and her mind filled up so that other thoughts were pushed aside. Her hand trembled as she took Davie's, and she saw him sneak a glance of concern at her, a glance she recognised and told herself no boy of his age should have to give. Despite her previous excitement the fat larva of self hatred began eating again at her mind all the way back along the paths which were now humming with the news of death.

Eleven

Darren and Mick found it dead easy making the arrest. The boy had done a runner as soon as he had seen their uniforms through the front window, some weedy kid who thought he was hard. Darren laughed inwardly at the memory of the short pursuit, the boy all gangly legs and arms against his own worked-out body, the feel of the thin wrists and ribs as he had pushed him up against the wall and cuffed him outside the council house with its grimy carpets and smell of dog and cigarette smoke. As soon he had pinioned the boy's arms in that sharp snap of the modern handcuffs they never expected Darren felt triumphant and excited, like when you put your hand under a new girl's skirt for the first time and feel her part her legs. The kid had started crying and blubbering on about his mother and wriggling about as they got him through the house. There had been greasy postcards and foreign-looking religious pictures on the wall, some bloke pointing to his heart Darren thought might be Jesus, and Darren told the little shit to shut up and stop struggling because one way or another he was going to get hurt. He grinned at the memory. The carpet had been tacky with dirt underfoot. It was one of those houses where if you are in the Job the joke was to say you have to wipe your feet on your way out. Darren felt a sudden spurt of anger. He'd always hated people who lived like that. They let everybody down, the low lifes his dad had said didn't have any pride in being British, potheads and habitual drunks and nutters who lived in crap and spread it around in crime and stuff. There were a lot of Pikies round here, of course, and it had a lot to do with that, the way they interbred and infected decent people.

It was a good feeling driving back in the car, the adrenalin still pumping in his self-consciously honed muscles. This is what he had joined the Force for, that rush of knowing that he had got some little turd banged up. He had done a few chases before but nothing like this, never in a murder. He turned this over in his mind, the idea that he was the arresting officer in a Big Case creeping slowly over him as he grasped the knowledge that this was even better still. This was real police work he had done. He had always wanted this, ever since he was a kid watching *The Bill* and first forming the idea that being a copper might be great. All that shit they had gone on and on about at college with the old boys telling them that police work wasn't like what you saw on the telly and it's about paperwork and community consciousness and that was just a load of bollocks. It was years since any of them had been near a bloody criminal. They'd always sneered at him and put him down because he wasn't so good at the school work as the physical stuff. Well, now he had shown them: he had nicked a murderer in a one-to-one struggle. Even the Guv'nor would have to show him some respect now. He was a right laugh with his good relations with councillors and community policing awareness policies. He made them all listen to a talk about multidisciplinary co-operation with social services last month, for fuck's sake.

Dad would have been well proud. It was a real shame he wasn't around to see it. Darren felt a new spurt of anger against the lung cancer that had got his father last year. The wiry, hard seventy-five year old body had finally given out against all those army cigarettes in the sharp laugh of an indestructible, immutable icon swearing that it was off for the knacker's yard before disappearing forever into the yawning blackness. Real men like his dad, and Darren himself, knew that was all there was and looked it in the face. Darren didn't have any time for religion and life after death and all that stuff, it was all balls as far as he could see, although his dad had always taken him to the War Memorial service on Remembrance Day and he still liked marching in best uniform at funerals and stuff. Vicars were a joke though. They were all piss and wind. Darren tried to imagine that poufter vicar at St Barnabas running after some low life, the idea making him snort with laughter.

'Yeah, good piece of work, eh?' Darren knew what Mick was trying to do by saying that. He thought he was laughing about the arrest again, was trying to carve out a slice of Darren's property. Well, tough shit, Darren had been first on scene and Mick hadn't.

'Didn't see you doin' much, Mick. Thought you'd stayed behind to change a tyre.' He said it with a laugh in his voice, like you do in the pub, but he knew it would sting. Mick had broad enough shoulders to take it. They were kind of mates. Not anything homo, just mates. He'd found out that Mick was a good laugh in the pub and didn't take any bullshit. At first they had been careful what to say to one another, because there were a lot of wankers in the Job who would do anything for promotion. They were the ones who went along with all the community responsibility and anti-racist crap, so you had to be very careful what you said. Darren hated all that, people who couldn't use common sense and coppers who grassed one another up.   Everyone knew it was all bollocks.   Like when Darren did his tests at College. When he had decided just to bullshit and write down anything his lecturers said without caring, his marks had shot up.   He had gone on to the Job with no trouble, which showed what a lot of crap everyone knew it was. He hadn't changed at all but they still let him in, because the truth was they knew they wanted coppers like him and Mick.   Real coppers who nicked murderers and who weren't afraid to tell the truth quietly among themselves about immigrant crime and low-lifes.   It made him feel angry that blokes like him and Mick did the hard graft on the streets but got passed over while assorted arselickers, lesbians and blackies climbed up the ladder using their political correctness.   Mick had given him an England Flag for the World Cup and they had hung it from the upstairs window of Darren's house.   It looked just like what everyone else was doing of course, but both of them knew it stood for something even more important than football, and for once they had the excuse to express it.   It was about preserving tradition and identity against the low lifes and Pakis who had taken over East London and had forced his dad and Mick's parents to move away from their roots, because as they said, you felt like a foreigner in your own land in Forest Gate nowadays.   Darren thanked the God he didn't believe in that he didn't work for the Met.   He knew decent coppers who were really pissed off with all the trash they were getting into the Force there. Mick and he sometimes talked about this over a pint or two.   They reckoned that some day people would wake up to what was going on around them, maybe after things had started to get even worse.   Then they would have to turn to common sense, the social workers and pen pushers would be put back where they belonged, and coppers like him and Mick would be on the front line. Darren slowly turned over the idea of himself as the riot-clad enforcer of white English decency in his delighted mind. All sorts of childhood images came to him: of St George and the Dragon in the stained glass window at Church Parade when he was in the cubs, Captain Kirk in *Star Trek* outwitting the ugly Klingons, and of Judge Dredd with his unlimited violence and legal powers. All that would be much more fun than having a go at this snivelling little shite beside him, and he looked forward to it as much as he longed for a victorious season for West Ham. He had never understood the Arsenal thing with Mick. But say what you like about that, both of them were sticking up for what they believed in as much as they could, doing a bit of dodging and diving maybe but nothing too stupid and like today, getting stuck in and bringing home the right result.

The boy had started whimpering again in the car, saying over and over again, 'What's happening? What will happen now, please?' and Mick glanced backwards from the wheel: 'The other officer told you to shut up, so shut up.' He caught Darren's eye as the boy subsided, and grinned.

Darren felt more relaxed now. It was OK to let Mick have a bit of the fun. He watched the roof line of the shabby housing association estate pass above the boys' comically quivering head. The little bastard was crying again now and sort of wriggling to move his handcuffed arms from behind his back, Darren realised, in a stupid attempt to wipe away the tears. Darren watched him for a couple of seconds. It was like something in a Tom and Jerry cartoon and he laughed aloud. Mick asked what was up, and he said 'Tell you later.' Later. That would be a great. This weak piece of filth would spew up a confession inside a couple of hours. Then it would be congratulations and back slappings all round, and off down the pub in Amblehurst with Mick in the evening to go on the screaming piss and tell one another about it all over again.

Twelve

Laura spun the dial on the microwave to blast some left-over Bolognese sauce, put a piece of bread on to toast and grated some supermarket super-finest parmesan to put on top. With a shudder she remembered the old toenail Parmesan of her childhood that had hung around in the back of larder cupboards in round green tubs, smelling of sick and old socks. This began an interior and uncomfortable ideological dialogue about the benefits of consumer choice versus her belief in the iniquity and general un-greenness of the major retail food suppliers. She could only settle her mind over about it by a postponement and a quick prayer for the Poor, adding onto the end on one for herself, her habitual intercession for acceptance and peace. As she pulled out the steaming bowl of sauce she had to move quickly to place it onto the worktop before it burnt her hand. And she had to leave off the praying quickly too, otherwise the niggling would start again, that she should really try to go to Mass this week, that she was better now and could not forever put it off by pleading illness.

The telly was the thing to escape from these uncomfortable thoughts, and maybe there would be something after all about the day's events on the otherwise lamentably bad *Look East* programme provided by the BBC in the apparent belief that the inhabitants of East

Anglia were total morons. Laura placed her Bolognese-on-toast with its knife and fork on the coffee table and took up the remote control to watch as she ate. The national evening news was coming to an end with Huw Griffiths soft-lilting his way through the headlines, the beauty of his voice contrasting oddly to Laura with the murderous absurdities of American foreign policy, the rape of children in Africa and yet another accusation that the police had shot an innocent man, this time in some noisome suburb of Liverpool. But she enjoyed the compulsory jolly story at the end about the brave and patriotic battling granny who had parachuted for the Prince of Wales, enabling her as it did to snort with disgusted self-righteousness and elevated amusement.

'And here in the East Tonight...' Here we go, thought Laura, I bet there will be nothing except the usual news of a cardboard box blowing down Luton High Street or some other piece of earth shattering bollocks. But as she relaxed back onto the cushions she was astonished to see the tower of St. Peter's and a shot of the Anchor and, as in a mirror, herself, Bob and Davie in a crowd of people. Her astonishment gave way to an intense excitement and she briefly hoped Davie was watching, although she couldn't ring because of Poppy and anyway she didn't want to miss anything. In such a state she hardly heard the spoken headline, but as the screen flicked over to other stories before returning to the studio and the grave face of Peter Walters, the male half of the presentation team, her racing brain allowed her to watch.

Camera on Walters, close up, grave and sad face.

Walters: Police today confirmed the finding of the body of a man on board a sailing yacht in Mootborough, one of Essex's best-loved and ancient maritime towns. They have said that foul play is indicated but that the victim cannot be named until a formal identification has been made. We go over to *Look East's* Chris Wade in Mootborough.

Outside broadcast from outside the Anchor. Camera shot over pub, river and police tent. Cuts to Wade with microphone.

Wade: Yes, Pete, today Mootborough has been shocked to hear of what appears to have been the particularly vicious and nasty murder of one of their own, a man who as you say, police cannot name, but who is widely believed to have been one of the town's close sailing fraternity. This is a terrible and tragic event here. I can tell you, Pete, that there have been further developments in the last few minutes and it would appear that the police have made an arrest in connection with the incident and that a youth, who also cannot be named, is being held in police custody. I have here with me Inspector Dominic McGahan, who is handling the investigation locally.

Camera pans out to reveal Dom McGahan standing beside Wade, and Wade half-turns towards him.

Inspector, what can you tell us about these tragic train of events?

Laura winced and for a moment thought that she saw a similar look of pain pass over the face of the policeman's face in the TV screen.

Close up of Insp. McGahan

McGahan: Well, as you say for various reasons we can't say who the victim was at the moment, but it was certainly a very unpleasant crime. Today – this afternoon in fact – a couple of our local policemen arrested a young lad. You'll understand that we can't tell you who he is, but we aren't looking for anybody else. I am sorry that I can't go into any more details for you now, but I hope to be able to keep everybody up to date through the Press as we go along. Thanks very much.

Camera pans out to include Wade, briefly revealing the camera of a rival TV crew.

Wade: Thank you, Inspector.

Close up on Wade obscuring the errant camera.

So there it is Pete, a grim day for Mootborough.

Long shot of river with St Peter's tower then return to studio, Walters still looking grave.

Walters: Thank you Chris. And now here is Sue with the rest of the day's news, and (*brightening demeanour*) I believe there is something about a donkey weighing competition in Suffolk, isn't there, Sue?

Laura was slightly bemused as she pushed the 'off' button on the remote control. She realised now that she had seen the Inspector around in the town a few times, but had never spoken to him. Certainly it had never occurred to her that he was a policeman. If she had thought about him at all, she decided, it would have been as an amiable senior architect or suchlike with a strong penchant for doing his allotment. He didn't sound like a copper either. For these reasons Laura decided that she probably rather liked him, and so briefly wondered how he had ended up where he was.

Hugo jumped without warning on her shoulder from behind, and as she started in alarm he dug his claws into her and scrabbled with his back feet to gain a purchase on his favourite place, which was snuggling his face in the crook of her neck while using her bosom as a platform for his bum. Laura had got him when he was ten weeks old, a ginger kitten with blue eyes. He had been so adorably handsome that she knew not even Lizzie would be able to resist him. For some blissful weeks it had worked. Lizzie had come round every day and they had all played together, rolling cotton reels along the floor and doing those leapy-leapy games with bits of wool. But now that Hugo was a couple of years old none of this happened any more, and while in general Laura was still fond of him she felt at the moment that there were limits to the number of times she was willing to put up with his assaults. 'Piss off, you bastard,' she said to him, and prised him off his perch, his reluctant paws snagging the material of her shirt. As the cat freed his claws he suddenly panicked, struggled and scratched her, leaving a thin line of blood on her arm that stung more than she was happy with. 'Hell,' she said abruptly, and went into the kitchen to wash. Her father had always been on about something called Cat Scratch Fever, which, while she had never heard of anybody actually getting it, was enough to make her cautious about such injuries. She ran her arm under the tap and dried it on a Souvenir of York Minster, her mother's gift after one of her innumerable sightseeing trips. As she applied antiseptic cream and a plaster, the Cat began rubbing himself against her ankles and doing that silent mewing thing that meant he was hungry, which was why of course it was her fault that he had jumped on her in the first place. She felt a surge of amusement. 'OK, you idiot,' she said, and forked out some evil-smelling cat food, cheaply full of visible and nameless anatomical horrors, onto his plate. It always made her want to gag but she was buggered if she was going to start buying the expensive stuff when her limited money could be better spent in the pub and on a few clothes.

These duties done and dismissing to the back of her mind some sad thoughts about Lizzie, Laura returned to the sitting room and lit a cigarette. So they had arrested someone, and probably locally if so quickly. The only possible and entertaining course of action was therefore to return to the Anchor this evening to have a drink or two and find out if anybody had any news as to what was going on. Andrea would be bound to be there: she was as big a gossip as Laura knew herself to be, but even so it might be best to make sure just in case. Laura dug around for her mobile, eventually finding it in the midst of an unsavoury mixture of cat hair and biscuit crumbs down the side of the sofa. Lizzie and Davie could do the text thing really fast using fingers and thumbs, but she was still learning. She didn't like doing it very much because she realised that when she and Jack were splitting up, Jack's sudden ability to use the text abbreviations he had previously scorned had been a symptom of his playing away that she had missed. Nevertheless she did not want to appear old-fashioned or snotty among friends to whom texting was a normal form of communication, so laboriously picked out the symbols one by one: 'C U i n p u b 2 n i t e a t 8?' and pushed the 'Send' button for Andrea's number. By the time Laura had ground out her cigarette on an ashtray of the Basilica at Lourdes the phone had emitted a heart stopping 'Beep-beep' and Laura was able to read the comforting message, 'S u r e b a b e s.' It all seemed very time-consuming to Laura. She had no idea how much or how little it cost.

As though in order to demonstrate the efficiency of an older technology the landline rang and she answered, 'Hello?'

'Hi Mum, it's me. Did you see us?' Davie's voice, alive and hardly distorted by the wires.

'I most certainly did. What do you think?'

'Well, I was really excited before but now I like, feel really different, because you know, it sounds horrible really.' Laura knew that Davie was not trying to curry favour. His nature was one of complicated tenderness and childishness all at once, the two clashing together and contradicting themselves just as they do, she thought, in so many adults. Yet it was a pity he had been made to be like this so early. As Laura saw it his childhood had been smashed around a bit, and she felt the need to reassure as strong as lust.

'Oh, darling,' she said, "don't feel like that. I was excited too; you're bound to be excited. And yes of course it is horrible as well. I guess things can be both at once. We all feel sad about the man who was killed. The way you can help him now is to say a prayer for him tonight before you go to bed. But did you see us two at the beginning?'

'Yes, that was cool. I thought it was really fun, and then I like thought, Whoa, I shouldn't be feeling like this when I saw the rest. There were some good shots of the Town though, weren't there? I know that policeman too. He came in to school last week or sometime to talk to us in PSE. He was funny. I liked him.'

'Really? What did he talk to you about? Was he nice?'

Laura asked.

'Dead nice. Really nice. Something about drugs and stuff I think, and families and that. But he was like, you know, not like a teacher or anything. He was just dead cool. He made us laugh and, like, got his point across really well. Not like Father Malcolm does buggering on about nothing.'

'That's great.' Laura felt an explosion of happiness inside her head, hearing her own satirical wit echoing in Davie's growing maturity, mangled though she was afraid his early years had been. 'What's Lizzie up to?' she asked, the habitual question she must ask out of conscience but the one that both she and Davie knew was a kind of self-reflexive lie, an attempt to assert her motherhood over someone who appeared to be drifting away from her on the tides of adolescence.

'Oh, she's been out. She and Poppy have just come back from Amblehurst.' He sounded embarrassed, as though trying to protect her, and Laura was only able to respond with an 'Uhuh' and a pause.

'Will you be around tomorrow, Mum?' asked Davie, breaking in on the awkwardness he could not hug away on the 'phone and tearing her thoughts back to him to try to make her smile again.

'Sure. I don't know what I will be doing though, so ring me or whatever. And you know, be careful what you say about Father Malcolm, you know? It's OK for me, but some people might get all upset about it, and he's a nice bloke in lots and lots of ways, even if he can't teach PSE for toffee…'

'Mum, I'm not an idiot.' No, thought Laura, you aren't, and laughed as they said their goodbyes.

Thirteen

Drew was thirsty. He had kept asking for a drink and they had given him a plastic beaker of water but it wasn't enough and he was very hot. The policemen frightened him and he didn't like to ask for any more because they seemed very rude and rough and he didn't know what they could do to him. One of them had called him a 'little shit'. He didn't know if this was allowed and it had surprised him. Although he thought he had changed and washed all the blood and stuff off they had taken all his clothes away and made him wear a white suit thing like you see on the telly, which made him feel kind of important but scared him as well. His mouth felt croaky and he was having difficulty thinking much about anything except he was thirsty, so he sat on the bench and stared at the wall. Sometimes he wondered what Mum was doing, if they had told her yet. She would be upset and angry. He didn't want to think about that. He had not meant to upset her. But she would be very upset. It wouldn't be so bad if he had just hit him hard once, but Mum would find it really hard to take the way he had smashed him around afterwards, especially his Thing. Mum didn't like to talk about things like that. He wished somebody would come and give him some water and let him know what was going on. He stretched out on the bench and tried to sleep, his lips drying and cracking as he breathed, and wished someone would come and talk to him.

Fourteen

Laura took a lengthy shower and changed into clean jeans, a top and a linen jacket for her trip to the pub. As she showered she had tried to concentrate on being happy about Davie's uncomplicated friendship for her and let the water wash away her anxiety and jealousy. She really had to stop flying off the handle at the news that the Bitch had been spoiling Lizzie with Jack's money. She had to rise above it, it was sad but inevitable, all girls broke away from their mothers, it was just the Poppy thing that made it so much worse. The water had splashed over her face as she raised it to the shower head and she had a flash memory of herself screaming scatological curses down the telephone when she had learned that Jack was intending to take the children away with Poppy on a holiday last year, a holiday she could no longer contemplate being able to afford. 'You stupid, stupid woman,' she told herself aloud, suddenly seeing in her own feelings for Lizzie a possible model for understanding Jack's mother's fierce jealousy, and knowing too that in creating scenes she was only pushing Lizzie away towards Poppy further. The sound of her own voice speaking in the tiny bathroom had unnerved her, and as the water ran over her face and hands for a moment she wished she could wash away her failings with the shampoo lather. *Lavabo inter innocentes manus meas et circumdabo altare tuum, Domine.* The Bad Thought came and went and though her mind staggered it stayed spinning properly, perhaps this time because of the insight it had given her into Beatrice.

Fifteen

'Did you see them videos what Scene of Crime bought in?' Mick came into the room while he'd been working on his account of Andrew Halloran's arrest, and for a moment Darren experienced a spasm of irritation. He always got like that when people interrupted him when he was writing because he would forget what he wanted to say, and then have to read everything he had done, again and again, before he could think himself back into it. He held his hand up. 'Hang on, mate,' he said, and finished his picked-out sentence laboriously, the other policeman leaning his backside against the desk and running his fingers through his stylishly cropped and gelled hair. As Darren finally looked up from the screen Mick snapped his fingers at him.

'Finished now, Charles Dickens? I bet you've put loads in about you. Let me have a look in a bit: I still haven't finished mine yet.'

'Sure. No problem. What d'you say?'

'Come and look at these videos. I tell you, the sailing guy was a real nonce.'

Darren was at once excited and upset. If Mick meant that the bloke in the boat was like that it would take away a lot of the glam from his arrest, 'cos everybody said that nonces got what they deserved. But on the other hand he loved all this. He could look at really dirty stuff and it

121

made him important and excited.

Mick opened the door into where the Scene of Crime officers had dumped the bits they had finished with, and spurted a tape into the VCR player standing defenceless in the corner of the room before drawing the blinds. The TV monitor frazzled into life, spitting horizontal lines of visual rubbish before settling its picture. Darren watched. The pink bodies writhed together like an animated butcher's shop and he was transfixed and hypnotized, Mick all forgotten and unaware as the young boy in the screen served his portion of meat to the older guy, all tongue and oxtail. Darren felt his cock engorging like a black pudding, blood rushing in to meet his fat, and his loin tightening and aching until he thought he would come.

'For Christ's sake, turn it off.' His urgency was spurred on by an anxiety he could not name to himself, the thought that he might mark his trousers, the idea that Mick might notice. He felt the sweat on his back. He knew boys like that weren't really innocent. They liked it, they sold themselves for drugs, they were Pikies and other shite who got what they deserved, and good luck to the blokes who gave them a good fucking up the arse to show them where they belonged.

'Yeah, it's pretty bad, isn't it? What d'you reckon, then? Seems like a motive to me if he was screwing him.'

Darren felt his anxiety break into anger. 'Look, what we've got here is some nonce who's been killed by his low-life lover. He's dead, we've got him banged up, and as far as I'm concerned that's the way it should fucking be, OK?' Darren could not look his friend in the face in his anger and frustration. He would have to go out and hurt some woman or other tonight to reassure himself. He knew a couple of toms who owed him a favour.

Sixteen

'It's Florence Nightingale.' The joke was wearing a bit thin now but Alex regarded it as a sort of tax for drinking in the Anchor. He took the beer Les had already poured for him and drank deeply, nodding in greeting and in response to the unspoken enquiry recognisable by a slight lift in Les's eyebrows. Accordingly Les scribbled down the beginning of Alex's evening tab on the filthy pad hanging discreetly out of sight behind the bar while Alex put down his pint two-thirds full, swung himself onto a stool, and rested his elbows.

'I suppose we can all be grateful that things have moved on a bit since her day, though I am flattered. Of course it's a shame we don't get to wear the dresses. Do you think we can expect to be busy in here tonight?'

'Och Christ. We've been busy all day with people coming to gawp and reporters and that.'

'Have you heard anything? I listened to the local news on the car radio but they weren't giving much away.'

As Les filled him in on the finding of Brightly's body, Alex drank the rest of his pint slowly and divided his visual attention between the older man and his own reflection in the mirrors behind the bar. What he saw there did not altogether displease him, although he could perhaps have been allowed to get away with keeping a little more hair than his forty-five years had taken from him, and he had to squint to read the labels over the optics. The reason for his self-examination was his surprise on being recently told that he had a handsome face. The fact that the person doing so had been recovering from a psychotic episode was an even better reason for having another look. He regarded his longish, straight nose, chin and eye distribution, amount of visible stubble and height of ears with caution, as a puppy might sniff at a hedgehog. Eventually he gave it up, secure in the knowledge that he was pretty much stuck with what he had got, and knowing that as soon as he got up his primary characteristics of short legs and a pronounced beer belly would reassert themselves to drive away any delusions of beauty. Not so much Adonis, one of his girlfriends had said, but a doughnut, and she was right. He suppressed a smile at the memory, and a grin at the thought that it hadn't stopped her wanting to make love with him.

The pub was beginning to fill with the early evening regulars, shrugging off their daytime selves as Alex had put the hospital from his mind. Each had his own habitual greeting. Some did a sort of comedian's shuffle, cheerful exclamation and grin at the assembled company, others less exuberant gave what a quick nod and an 'Evening' before heading for a quiet table and the crossword. It would, thought Alex, be easy for the uncharitable mind to mistake this as being the mark of a miserable git, and but for his life-long friendships with most of the gang in the Anchor and his natural respect for the generation of Mootburgians who had known his father, he might have made that mistake. He wondered again what on earth the day trippers sitting in the picture-window bar over the river during the Summer made of, say, Roger the Syrup, or even Barges Bob when he was in his cups. He grinned again at the thought. The tobacco smoke was beginning to get comfortably fuggy now. He hoped to hell the Health Fascists didn't go ahead and ban smoking in pubs, but he was pessimistic, and drew deeply on his roll-up in compensation. In the glass behind the bar he could see the reflection of the pub doorway, and he kept half an eye on it for the arrival of members of his particular circle. This little bit of tradecraft reminded him that he always thought that he would have made rather a good spy. This was an attitude encouraged by an older friend who had done something mysterious in MI6, and whose proud boast it was, by a third of the way down a bottle of gin, that his open membership of CND had in no way affected his rise within that organisation. He and Alex had together agreed that they liked that thought and its implications, and so Alex felt less guilty about pretending he was James Bond occasionally. Hating martinis, he ordered another pint.

Andrea arrived, framed in the doorway for a moment like a rather lumpy Venus with the bright sunlight behind her and her arms above her head in loud and unselfconscious greeting, as typical as sloes in Autumn and as richly sexual as Victoria plums. Then the door shut and the moment was snuffed out and she became just Andrea again, pretty still but not as much as when she and Alex had enjoyed a thing about one another. That was at a time when Andrea was going out with a violent and abusive boyfriend, and Alex had done some handholding and nose wiping and found himself with a split lip for his pains. Anyway the whole thing had been disagreeably Platonic in the end, because Andrea was all messed up about the Abusing Bastard, and Alex wasn't going to make a come-on at her when she was in that state even though he would have liked to. Eventually it had all mellowed and fizzled out, Andrea had found herself Tom, and Alex and she, he told himself, were happy to be special friends. It annoyed him to see how, despite the initial blinding sexual impact she could make, a closer study revealed that she was now often drunk by the early evening, and on close examination you could see that she needed to wash her hair or was covering up spots on her face with her hands as she talked. He wanted to say something to her but he knew that unless she came to him first it was no place of his to offer advice where it was not wanted. Instead he kept her as close as he dared, trying to keep an eye out for her and hoping to God that Tom wasn't going to hurt her again. My God, he thought about himself, he was a patronising bugger. Actually Andrea made him laugh a lot. Best just leave it at that.

'How are you, babes?' Andrea laughed, flinging her arms around Alex and planting a wetly cidery kiss on his mouth. Alex had never been entirely comfortable with this kissing friends on the mouth thing that people seemed to go in for these days, and had been surprised when, one evening on a College reunion in London, he had seen two blokes whom he knew to be straight do it. But on the other hand it did not seem to do much harm, and he could certainly think of worse people to kiss than Andrea. He returned her kiss, keeping it just one shade shy of sexy but trying to match her tipsy warmth.

'How would you like a pint of cider, honey?' he asked, knowing that Andrea was a single mother living from hand to mouth on state benefits and some crummy cash jobs in which she was unmercifully exploited by supposed friends, and could occasionally be touchy about being seen to stand her own drinks. Personally Alex did not give a tinker's cuss if he lost out against Andrea's drinks bill permanently. 'No, darling,' said Andrea, 'let me get these.'

But Alex had already caught Les's eye.

'I have already done it, Sugar. You can buy the next one, OK, unless you're waiting for someone?' It wasn't very hard to maintain people's dignity, really.

'OK, thanks. Laura said she'd come in later. Tom's away with his mates on some works bash. And I have got loads of glorious gossip.'

'Well, come on, unload it then,' said Alex, carrying their drinks over to a corner table where the light from the ancient bottle glass windows had scored burn marks into the leather of the seats.

'Certainly not. It is far too good and you shall have to wait for Laura. I am not going through it all twice. But it's about George and all that...'

'Poor chap,' interjected Alex.

'Wait 'til you hear what I've got to say before you say that. You might change your mind.' Alex was now definitely intrigued, the promise of the evening before him reminding him of the anticipation he'd felt for the roast dinners of childhood in its rich promise of texture and variety.

'First you have to tell me what you have been up to,' Andrea continued.

'Honestly, Andrea, you are such a bloody tease. OK, I haven't been doing anything much really beyond the usual sort of stuff.'

'Busy at work?'

'When isn't it?'

As they talked Alex became aware of three elements in his excitement at the evening's entertainment. There was of course Andrea herself, always good value as long as she didn't take the excuse of Tom's absence to get absolutely rat-arsed and give anyone a reason for a go at her. Then there was the stuff about the death of George Brightly, now made the more interesting by what Andrea had said, although of course she was a terrible flirt and a drama-queen. But most of all, and with an uneasy intensity and focus, there was the imminent appearance and company of Laura Morton. He had known Laura on and off since childhood, of course, but what with her going to Cambridge and being a doctor's daughter and then a lawyer's wife, for a long time he had rather considered her a bit above his social circle. And certainly that bugger Jack, whom he had also known since he was a kid, had never greeted him with anything but the most embarrassed of nods since they were adults. But after her divorce Alex had seen how Laura and Andrea had become friends, and that made her seem nicer to him. She was a part of the regular crowd in the bar now, and her presence disturbed Alex mightily. He was still not prepared to look too closely at this phenomenon, still less to name it, in case somehow it should disappear in its delight and fragility. Still worse would be to make a fool of himself. He had done that with girls before. Oh dammit, he would have to do something about it. Or not. He didn't know even if he liked her or not. He applied himself to Andrea's voice, forcing down these thoughts as a man in financial trouble hides his heating bills.

'I don't think there's much around at the moment, babes,' Andrea was saying quietly to him. 'Me and Tom are nearly all out, all we've got left is a little bean-sized bit of mud. You could try Nigel, he usually has some but even he's been complaining recently.'

'OK, I will. I'd prefer green really. Thanks.'

'Yay, and here she is,' exclaimed Andrea as the door opened, and Alex's body responded by a sudden tightening of his stomach and suffusion of blood in his face. He rose as she approached their table and only just managed to save himself from tripping over the table leg as he moved a chair aside for her to sit down. Oh God, he was fucking this up. He could see a knowing smirk on Andrea's face and briefly wanted to strangle her. The girls kissed, but Alex hung back with a simple 'Hi. What would you like?'

Andrea finished her cider. 'Same again for me, please' and Alex briefly noted with satisfaction that he was going to get to pay for her second round despite all that dancing around earlier on. 'And you, Laura, ignoring this atrocious harpy here?' He had recovered his ground, thank God.

'Thanks, I'll have a pint of Adnams, please.'

'What's a harpy, then?' Alex could hear Andrea asking as he ordered the drinks, but not Laura's softer answer. As he waited he watched Laura, half of his mind trying to decide what precisely it was that made him feel so wobbly. Certainly she was a looker, there was no question about that. To his mind she had a fantastic face and great eyes. He didn't know much about these things but he thought there was something about her cheekbones that made her look so yummy, and she tricked herself out really well, neither too sexless not too slapperish. He supposed that would come from once having been able to afford a lot of good clothes, and inwardly groaned at the thought. He carried the drinks to the table.

'Here you go.'

'Yeah, and 'ere you can bleeding well go as well. What's all this about calling me a foul smelling old cross between a mythological wotsit and a woman?' Andrea was laughing.

'You can piss off.'

'Thank you, Alex, that's very kind,' said Laura, who was laughing too.

'Oh dear, well it seems that the least I could have done in the circumstances is to have bought the drinks. I take it back, Andrea. You are not a harpy.'

'Too bloody right I'm not.'

'They were better looking.'

Andrea picked up a beer mat and frisbeed it at Alex, who caught it, then tore a small 'V' in its side. Ducking beneath the table he placed it firmly on the bridge of his nose before popping his head up back up, the beer mat stuck to his face.

'For pity's sake, will you stop throwing beer mats?' he grinned, and Laura and Andrea laughed heartily, Laura as though it were the first time she had seen the joke. Alex felt a rush of happiness. 'Well, it's extremely nice to be here,' he said, before the idiotic words had escaped from his front teeth.

'I agree,' said Laura. 'Come on, what's all the news then?'

This was really the moment that Andrea had been waiting for. She'd been down the Queen's earlier, had a couple and heard a bit more stuff before coming on here. Andrea's succession of part time jobs as a child minder, gardener and cleaner meant that she was in an extremely privileged position as a sort of lightening-rod of gossip. An extensive network of contacts, of people who knew someone who knew someone who was useful, became in Andrea a conduit of reliable and interesting news. This was usually passed on with little malice, if just given an occasional whiz-up to keep a story going now and again. She enjoyed all of this, for it meant that she was able to hold a position of friendship and influence with people she very much enjoyed. Her miserably inadequate schooling as a dyslexic before special needs teaching had caught up with the condition gave her a horror of returning to regular employment where she would lose such status and be forced to come to terms with a disability she now found comfortable to live with.

'Well then, listen up. OK, Laura, do you remember that conversation we had some time ago about whether we reckoned George was a gay?' Alex and Laura bent forward slightly, Alex a little uncomfortable as he always was when he thought he might be in for some tricky expression of prejudice from a friend he otherwise admired. 'Well anyway,' Andrea continued, 'when I was down at John and Wendy's I met Tricia on the way home, and she said that they had arrested that Andrew, Meg Halloran's son from Lime Tree Way. Apparently he'd run off as soon as he saw the coppers, down round the back gardens, I guess to try to get to the allotments. Tricia says he was always hanging about the boatyards and sometimes George used to take him out on his lads' sailing trips. Anyway, they've got him in the police station and it looks like they think he did it, right, on the News. Then when I was in the Queen's and I tell you something else even more shocking. You know that Petronella who lives down Mariners' Chase overlooking the yard? Mad old girl who paints and has all the cats?'

'Is she mad?' asked Laura. 'How thrilling. Yes, but go on, I know who you mean.' For a moment Alex saw the bright reflection of something dangerous and hurtful revealed in Laura's flippancy and was shocked.

'Christ, mad? You should see her paintings. All bits of rubbish and stuff she's found on the beach. Objay Trewvay she calls them. Anyway, don't confuse me while I'm telling a story. So Petronella, right, my mate Sandra works for her sometimes doing a bit of cleaning, and d'you know, she's got one of them big like birdwatcher's telescopes to look out over the Quay and the boats from her top window. Anyway of course, she was watching the police doing all their stuff and she called Sandra over and

Sandra said she saw the cops take a video recorder and a pile of tapes out of the boat, and she could see they were porno tapes clear as day. She thinks they were gay ones, homosexual she called it.'

Laura felt a snaking in her mind again. Behind all the glamour and the gossip of events there was some indefinable thing she couldn't quite catch, slipping round the corners of cognition and into her memory where she couldn't quite reach it. She saw a tobacco smoke genie rising from Alex's cigarette, the back of his hand, a piece of chalk dust from the darts board lit suddenly by the window and stillness settling in her mind as she searched for what was eluding her.

'Hello? Hello? Earth calling Laura.' Laura had no idea how long her thoughts had taken her away, and for a moment was irritated that she had been torn away from them. Then she remembered where she was and laughed a little.

'I'm terribly sorry, gosh I was miles away. That's a really shocking story,' she said.

Andrea did her patient voice. 'That's just what we were saying...'

Alex broke in, 'If it's true...'

'Alex, it's all round the town,' said Andrea. 'You wait and see if I'm not right. But Laura, you worked with him or something, didn't you? I mean, you must have known him better than us two.'

'Well not exactly worked together. He was a Governor at the school where I taught. I suppose I did know him quite well. That is why I was so shocked. I mean, it is very shocking, isn't it? All of it. That poor boy. I can't bear to think about it.'

'Well, there you go, then,' said Andrea.

'I'm not going like that at any rate,' said Alex. 'Not

done in by my toy boy. At least there's still that to be said for being straight nowadays.' At least Laura could laugh a little at that. She determined to shrug off the thing in her mind until she could deal with it properly on her own, and went to the bar to order another round of drinks.

She was enjoying herself now, letting go into the alcohol and company. They had played some darts, all laughter and miss-shots, and exchanged jokes and mindless pub conversation with some of the other drinkers. For a couple of nasty minutes it looked as though Alex was going to get drawn into an interminable conversation about football with some intruder, a game about which he seemed distressingly knowledgeable. Then he had abandoned it and returned to them with a grin and uplifted eyebrows.

'Sorry about that. Just updating myself for the next unavoidable bore as quickly as politeness allows.' He really was very funny. Andrea put some money in the jukebox and they took turns choosing tunes, Alex showing a surprisingly wide taste and enthusiasm in music. The pub was comfortably full without being crowded, and when Andrea drifted away to talk to a couple of her girlfriends Alex and she found themselves alone at a vacated table. He cleared away the crisp packets and changed the ashtray at the bar, returning with more drinks, and they settled themselves opposite one another in the imagery of careful negotiation. With other friends Laura would have usually sat side by side looking into the bar. She suddenly became self-conscious, asking herself why she was positioned like that, why she suddenly found herself copying the way Alex placed his arms and the manner and timing of his cigarette smoking, and cursed herself for knowing damn well what the cheap women's magazines would have said. Embarrassed, she shifted her position slightly to one side so she could tell herself that neither Alex nor the rest of the bar would notice anything.

'Are you OK?' Alex asked, apparently in response to her moving. Laura deflected it.

'Yes, fine thanks. I was just thinking about George again. It is a nasty business.' She shivered as her white lie took hold and became reality for her.

There was a pause as Alex drew on his cigarette.

'Yes, it is,' he said at length. 'I am sorry.'

Laura reflected on this for a moment. 'Oh, it's not as though he was a real friend or anything, but, you know, I had known him for a while and there were issues, I suppose.' The alcohol, she realised, was making her inarticulate. What the hell did having 'issues' mean? She sounded like a daytime TV programme, all failed relationships and teenage pregnancies. Sloppy talking like that annoyed her. She hoped that Alex wouldn't ask her the obvious question, and his silence surprised her. They each took a drink.

'Did you enjoy teaching?' The smoke curled between them and Alex waved it away with the back of his hand as though to protect her or to see her better.

'Teaching yes, management no.' Oh God, don't let him pry, she couldn't bear it, couldn't bear to spoil the evening by going through it all. Nor could she bear the thought of him turning out to be one of those emotional voyeurs, the ones who tried to get inside your mind as a way to your knickers. She was only whisperingly aware of her disproportionate relief as he laughed.

'Oh, bloody hell, I can't tell you how many times colleagues and I have said the same sort of thing about working in the NHS.'

'Yes, I have heard it's bad in there. Tell me, do you get the same sort of thing as we get in Education, when all the best people are promoted out of the jobs they are really good at?'

'Of course. And we've got all the added buggers who come in from outside clinical experience on so-called management programmes. I don't think anybody has got a handle on what is going on, you know. It makes it very difficult to keep focussing on the patient.'

'Or in my case, the kids,' Laura put in, leaning forward unconsciously in her excitement. Here was contact, here were real issues. And he was very dishy. God, she was getting drunk, they must have had a few. What fun. She leant forward a tiny bit more, a vanishingly small abandonment to sexuality on which she fervently hoped he would pick up. Alex hunched his shoulders forwards and clasped his hands together as though he were going to impart something of great importance. He was pissed of course, or he would not be paying so much attention to her, but she was too relaxed not to enter into the fantasy of insight.

'In the end it's about values,' he said, enunciating his words carefully as the bell rang in a rather annoying way for last orders. He held a drunken index finger up and Laura wanted to hug him and laugh at the same time because he was so ridiculous and so right. 'Values,' he repeated. 'The coppers have exactly the same problem. All the good ones get promoted quickly so we're left with the very inexperienced and the terminally incompetent. We see it at work all the time.'

Andrea was a bit confused now and wondered if she were drunk enough to have missed some of the conversation. 'Do you have much to do with the police at work then?' she asked, vaguely trying to remember how many times she had seen policemen on hospital wards.

'Sure, of course. I'm a mental health nurse. Do you

want to get another one in before they kick the tourists out? I thought maybe we could go and have a Smoke on the Prom later, if you do that thing.'

'My round, and great, if you've got some,' said Laura.

Seventeen

'No no, I assure you you're wrong.' Laura felt the laughter coming from nowhere, bubbling up inside her as the spliff they were sharing took hold. 'If you can hold it in your right hand then it's waxing.' She waved vaguely in the direction of the moon as Alex took the reefer back from her and inhaled deeply, considering the proposition with care as his befuddled and relaxed mind eased itself forwards from the simple admiration which had possessed it for some moments and back into conversational mode. He looked at the water first, then at the moon, but he couldn't remember the rules although he knew he had known them perfectly well ten minutes previously. Short-term memory impairment following use of marijuana. This was an effect that he enjoyed because in the right company it made conversation appear fresh, funny and interesting. Out here at the end of the Prom you were a decent distance away from some of the bright orange cloud shed by the town's lighting, and they had been looking at what could be seen of the night sky. In this high pressure the three-quarter moon's aura was not so bright as to block out the nearer stars.

'Look, let me show you.'

Alex felt Laura take the joint and lift his hand up to make it into a crescent shape, his thumb and forefinger cupping the moon so that for a moment his concentration

137

and the shadow of his hand's cave seemed to intensify her light.

See? Now it's waxing. In a few day's time it will be a big high tide at one o'clock.'

Oh, God, she was touching him. He could feel the skin of her fingers and they were sitting close enough on the sea wall for him to smell scent and shampoo, and this was big serious business and he could feel her hip pressing into his side and for a moment he clamped his teeth together and shut his eyes with longing and his cock stirred. He was briefly at a loss, his mind caught between wanting and waiting, the caution of age balancing his desire with the horror of rejection and being hurt. Then he realised that he had to bring his hand down as though neither of them were aware of what had happened, to laugh and allow in time.

For a moment Laura felt the briefest touch of disappointment as Alex let his hand drift away from hers, but of course they couldn't sit there like that all night and somebody had to move first. The flushing in her face ebbed away and she took a big toke of cannabis that threatened to set her off coughing, but she managed to avoid it, thank God. It was neither cool nor elegant to hawk like a TB victim. She let the smoke drift from her slowly, its aromatic sweetness surrounding her in a mist of relaxed enjoyment. Briefly she thought what a hypocrite she was after organising all those drugs awareness lessons, before remembering that she had managed somehow to square that particular conscience circle by some pretty good arguments about the relative dangers of pot and alcohol a few months ago. She couldn't remember the line of reasoning now but it might be fun to talk to Alex about it one day. She wondered what he would say. He was smiling as she passed him the spliff again and as their eyes met she felt a bit embarrassed. 'I am too stoned to think about tides, but I bet I can find the Pole Star quicker than you,' he said.

'That's not fair, you've been looking already.'

'OK then, show me where it is,' Alex laughed aloud and so did she, and then their sharing turned to hilarity, both of them shaken with a nameless mirth that was like being woken to the joy which lies at the heart of the stuff of the Universe. Laura stood up and walked a few steps onto the foreshore, searching helplessly for the Plough and its path to the Pole before hearing Alex's steps on the pebbles. 'I can't find the bloody thing,' she said, and Alex took her hand and pointed it at Ursa Major and drew it upwards so that it penetrated the sky at the tiny white hole in the blackness of the night. 'One all at celestial navigation then,' he said, and this time as she dropped her hand he felt it curl round inside his palm and squeeze him so that, God Almighty, everything was all right and this was what she wanted, too. Laura felt the glow in her face and neck and knew that if they came across anyone else they would be glad of the darkness, but it was so delicious to hold Alex's hand and to hear him breathing beside her as they finished the joint and wandered back towards the park with its yellow-glare lamps. They talked of this and that, sometimes for the sake of talking, and then, she was sure, surprising each other by joyful discoveries of shared interests and opinions so that each became more convinced of their mutuality. On two subjects, nuclear weaponry and Leveller history, she felt such empathy for his passion and love of knowledge that tears pricked her eyes. Jack had never been like this. Always cynical, always decrying, his politics a posture to impose on the world as a fashion statement used to accessorize his personality, he seemed in comparison now like one of those demons in

Lewis's stories, not so much having intelligence, but using it when convenient. In the glow of the alcohol and marijuana, Alex seemed the antithesis of that past and a pattern for how she would like to see Davie grow up. God, she wished he would kiss her.

Alex was troubled. He knew well enough how what remained of the night could progress and was confident now in their unspoken conspiracy of desire. He was enjoying talking with Laura. He realised that he had more or less admitted to himself that he fancied her enormously at the start of the evening, but had then no idea of who she was. The excitement of realising that she was someone with whom he could have a proper conversation was marvellous. For four years and seven months, he supposed, he had more or less given up on the idea that he might find someone who could share with him and match him. His quiet private explorations of the world of the sciences and arts, conducted through library books and over the Internet, had been a solitary experience after Sue had decided that her continued existence would be unbearable. And now here was this unbelievably delectable woman, bubbling over with funniness and beauty, who again could match his humour blow for blow and whose morally grounded interests ranged from the life cycle of nematodes through the future of the British Labour Party and back to the writings of Erasmus. Just maybe here was someone with whom he could break a cycle of unsatisfactory relationships in which, once the sex had worn off, there was little glue to bind the participants together. He loved the touch of her palm in his, knew that if he were to kiss her that his advances would not be repulsed, and his conviction that the most erotic part of any woman is her Mind had been reinforced.

Yet that was precisely the difficulty. Dancing round one another in the intellectual rituals of human courtship each of them had managed to convey essential information to the other about their availability, past history and present values. Everybody did that in one way or another, and it was quite amusing to stand outside for a moment and to watch the ballet. As far as he could see Laura had excelled at it, dropping knowledge into inconsequence with the delicacy and come-hitherness of a geisha in a fan dance. And what was so wonderful was the openness with which she talked. Here were no boring details of how the other girls at the cash register got on, or how funny it was when people he did not know did things to other people he did not know. Instead huge issues were brought to light and exposed deliberately in a kaleidoscope of systematic self-revelation, each new pattern bold and hauntingly challenging. It seemed to Alex that Laura had seemed determined to say in all of this, this is what I am, and this is the whole of me. Each pattern had turned too quickly for him to be able to grasp its full significance, but the coloured dance was so entrancing that he was content to listen and watch, resisting the temptation to ask her to repeat herself for him. In this he was risking that in future there would be time for more thorough examination of what the geisha kaleidoscope was allowing him to glimpse. But suddenly, and crashingly obviously to him, as the patterns turned he saw one he recognised, and for a terrible moment the seductive gyrations became a *danse macabre*. He recognised it because he was trained to, because he dealt with it every day at work, and because he had been an unwittingly keen observer of Laura's behaviour for some time. Its shape had leapt out at him, as tragic as the mark of Cain, turning Laura's beauty into a symptom and breaking his heart for a moment until it surged with pity and anger so that his silence became very different from that of an admiring observer. The pattern she revealed to him in the ironic lightness of her conversation was of mood swings, of uncontrolled anger and self harming behaviour, drinking outbursts, and periods of extreme gregariousness followed by times of hellish regret, self-reproach and morbid thoughts. Now he thought about it, it chimed in with her outburst with Pete that day in the pub, much as he had admired her for it at the time. Twenty milligrams of fluoxetine a day, she had said, and nothing else for a condition that he could, he thought, diagnose so quickly. It was a horrible indictment of his own profession.

Alex turned it over in his mind as they walked together away from the Prom and onto the playing field, the grass teal green at the edge of the streetlamp's reach. He was sure Laura didn't have the unipolar depression to which she had so lightly confessed in the fan dance, the sort that had killed Sue and for which fluoxetine was prescribed under the name of Prozac. His guess was that this had been the easy, lazy diagnosis of a tired and overworked GP confirmed by a private hospital consultant whose name was a byword for idleness and incompetence. Privately Alex knew that Ronnie Lewis would not be able to recognise Manic Depression if he tripped on it on the way to his golf club. Twenty milligrams of Prozac a day, my arse: it was much more likely to have done Laura's mood states harm than good. But if Laura did have Bipolar Disorder, what was he to do? He was at a loss, he would have to think about it hard. What did all this mean for him? And what on earth should he do tonight? He neither could nor would leave her unkissed, but he did not want to do anything that might hurt her. It was pretty clear that Laura was not aware of her condition. If he were to tell her what he suspected, what would that do, and in any case, was it his responsibility? On the other hand, she seemed to have had eight years of no bugger sticking up for her and he felt that he could not simply walk away now, and nor did he want to. But now was not the time, not while he was drunk and had smoked a spliff. He would have to check it all out first, make sure that he was really sure in the cold light of the next few days. And she really was very, very pretty.

As Alex and Laura approached the end of the park's pathways and the beginning of the road, Alex realised that he was going to have to make a decision. He guessed that he would walk her back to her house, probably even should do it, although he was embarrassed at the childishness of the necessary spoken request. Damn.

'So, Miss, may I walk you home?' he asked, his comic instincts struggling to cover up his self-consciousness and anxiety. She made it easy for him, squeezing his hand and very briefly kissing his cheek.

'Thank you, kind sir. 'Tis dangerous for us girls to walk alone with no gentleman at this time o' noight.' He laughed at her mock Essex and felt a tinge of relief. Time to wind down now. 'I have had a very nice evening,' he said. No point in messing about. They weren't children. Laura found herself flushing again, her neck reddening as the warm pressure of his hand increase slightly.

'So have I.'

Laura was busy calculating now, about how far the streetlight was from her house and whether he was going to snog her under its light to the huge satisfaction of the nosey old cow who lived across the road. That would be better than no kiss at all. She felt a bit awkward about inviting him in. She badly wanted Alex to make love to her sometime, but perhaps not yet. What had happened this evening was already too big to her to risk it being spoiled by some too-quick sexual encounter in which she might be seen as being too easy. She hated that kind of behaviour in herself anyway and had been hurt by it before, quite apart from the fact that it was sinful, or rather of course, that was why it was wrong. But they had not reached the park gates, and Alex must have been thinking along similar lines because he stopped in the semidarkness between the widely spaced park lamps.

'Thank you very much,' he said, and gently pulled her towards him and kissed her on the lips. She nearly gasped in astonishment, which was stupid really because she had been thinking about it for ages, but the delight flooded her neck and breasts and as she kissed him back and their tongues sought one another she needed to draw him close to her, feeling his prick stiffen against her through his jeans. He was applying gentle pressure on her back and then searching for the cheeks of her bum, and as they kissed her cunt ached so that she damn nearly abandoned her resolve and invited him back for a fuck anyway, he was so lovely.

Alex was not prepared for the effect kissing Laura had on him. As he felt her return his embraces he was briefly embarrassed by his erection, but felt her move towards him and press herself against it in encouragement. They kissed like that for a while and then he broke away before he reached some point where his resolve would weaken irrevocably. 'That was nice,' Laura said, and giggled. He put his arm around her waist and she placed her head on his shoulder and like that they very slowly began to wander in the direction of Dogshit Alley.

'Certainly was,' said Alex, and grinned despite himself. 'I think perhaps we could fruitfully explore that particular avenue of pleasure a little more, if ever you have the time and inclination.' Laura laughed and dropped into mock Essex again, a flirtatious serving wench.

'We'll just have to wait and see about that, Sir, won't we?'

'Will you be in the pub tomorrow night?' He hoped that this was OK.

'Are you asking me out?'

'Yes.'

'Then, freak ballooning accidents permitting, I shall be there. Shall we say the same time?'

'OK, great.' Alex felt immense relief that their empathy had moved into a stage of waiting and consolidation in which they were both to be given time for consideration.

'Now you may kiss me again and walk me home,' said Laura. As their tongues met once more she heard some small animal wriggle and rustle away in the bushes and for a moment she was frightened until lust and being in love flooded her brain with their strong narcotics.

Eighteen

Inside the Cottage Laura drew threw her handbag down on the sofa and clasped her hands together, a three year old delighted at the prospect of ice cream. She kicked her shoes off and went to the kitchen to grab her half bottle of vodka, some coke, ice and a glass. There was no prospect of her sleeping yet and in any case she was for once more than content at having nothing to do except wait for tomorrow evening, a whole night and day in which she could hug her excitement to herself. She closed the curtains, shutting out an intruding world, and the privacy tempted her to bring herself off on the sofa, knowing that only the briefest of touches would stimulate her to an orgasm. But she wanted to share it with Alex, so she squeezed her thighs together, knowing that waiting would only make tomorrow's hopefully cataclysmic togetherness the more enjoyable, and that the fantasies of masturbation might interfere with the delicious anticipation of an event she so desperately wanted. She giggled at herself, wondering briefly if Alex was having the same sort of problems, and this kind of turned her on again so that as a distraction she poured herself a large slug of spirit and splashed ice and coke in the glass. Lying on the sofa with her drink conveniently to hand she asked her mind to play over the evening's events to her in as much detail as possible so that she could ponder them in all their scrumptiousness.

As the memory centres of Laura's brain obligingly came up with such of the goods as it could in its slurry circumstances, she saw herself in a succession of images and sounds which seemed to temper her aching lust with gentler promises of a home from which she had long been absent. In this state her sexuality was not destroyed but transformed, so that she took each memory of the evening and let go to see what her imagination would do with it. The effect was lovely. From Alex's conversation about the proposed replacement of the Trident missile system she drew a picture of the two of them, mud-cluttered in protest at Mildenhall or Lakenheath as the leaders of a Peace Group from Mootborough, making love in a sleeping bag as arc lights blared their anger. From the image of him picking songs on the jukebox she drew out the two of them watching the laser display at a Keane concert, Everybody Changing for the better around them. From his interest in the history of ideas she imagined them slow-wandering through the streets of Pompeii in the summer heat, fuelled by cheap Italian wine and grappa, delighting in each new discovery, laughing at the erotic frescoes in the brothels and feeling sorry for the poor now-statues left behind to smother after the evacuation failed. And from somewhere, perhaps in the way he talked, she imagined him accompanying her going to Mass and supporting her much-wanted involvement with the parish Justice and Peace group. In her desperate longing there was an echo of the hymn at Benediction in the quiet Church of her childhood, *Qui vitam sine termino, Nobis donet in patria,* as though Alex could rescue her and make everything all right. It would be fantastic, she thought with the daydreams of adolescence, to be married to Alex so that she didn't have to compromise to shag him, but who was she kidding? And why should either of them bother with all that when he wasn't even a Catholic?

Laura's glass was empty and as she glanced at the kitchen clock she refilled it generously. It was a quarter to two, and she wondered what time Alex had to be up to go into the hospital in the morning. This made her feel a bit guilty until she realised with a surge of happiness that there was no way he would have been with her if he had not wanted to be. He was old enough to make his own decisions, for heaven's sake. She had a couple more sips of vodka until she relaxed and let her mind wander again, leaning further back into the sofa and snuggling her head down against its arm. Hugo came and sat on her tummy, his purr as thick and comforting as an Irish Cream liqueur. Laura began to feel herself drifting into a doze, her hand loose against the padded sofa side, the colours behind her eyelids dancing and then giving way to the half-dream images which are the harbingers of sleep. She really would have to go to bed. And then into her mind came an image from the past, one of the hurtful images she tried to avoid thinking about but which could occasionally grab her and send her screaming for the gin bottle.

She was back in her old office at school. The sun was coming through the ridiculously warming sheet glass from which it had been constructed in the late sixties and her blouse was sticky against her back. There was something funny about her midriff, but hang on, no that was the cat here in the present. The image returned. She could see her old computer on the left from where she was sitting and felt again a spurt of irritation that she, a deputy, had only been granted an old 360 while lesser mortals such as the head of science had been upgraded to the 460s or even whizzy new Pentiums. Her desk was in front of her, in-tray overflowing with unread government consultation papers, diocesan and local authority directives that would have to be dealt with when the immediate pressures of school life had subsided in the pupils' holidays. Many of them could be simply skimmed and thrown away. Others would contain annoyingly hidden important stuff that had to be extracted from the unnecessary bullshit it was somebody's thankless task to produce. Laura felt again the sense of weariness that came with the knowledge that it was her responsibility to do all this, to filter and form plans of action, which then had to be sold to a staff made recalcitrant by what they perceived to be continual interference in their teaching.

A boy was sitting in a chair in front of her desk, his head hanging down as the tears leaked from the corners of his eyes and he occasionally wiped them away with the back of his hand. Laura watched him, partly the hard schoolmistress calculating his offence and part of her the mother whose instinct is to wrap comforting arms around a hurting child, however forbidden by law and warned against by Union advice. Before her was a blue rough book, open so that they could both see the drawings the boy had done in the back pages. 'Is there anything wrong at home, Jon?' she had asked. 'Is there something going on you should tell me about? Is anybody hurting you?' And now in her half dream she looked down at the book again and saw clearly what at the time she had dismissed as harmless doodles besides the savagely realistic biology of his penned-out and disturbing sexuality. There were pictures of a yacht, the tower of St Peter's Church clearly visible behind, and the words *Stella Maris* on her stern.

The shock of this ejected Laura from her half-sleep back into the present so that she sat upright and the cat jumped from her lap to overset the ashtray onto the coffee table. Absently she swept the spillage into her cupped hand and walked to the bathroom, where she washed the ash from her hands and decided to put her pyjamas on. She had some trouble with taking her clothes off. Her hands were shaking a bit. When she was naked she looked at herself full-length in the mirror to see if she was still the sort of thing that Alex might want, hoping in this way to chase off the whirl in her mind. It didn't work, did nothing for her, and she pulled on her nightclothes in a fury, making herself hot by tangling them up in the process. 'Christ, help me,' she said aloud, more genuine prayer than blasphemy, and returned to the sofa to try to collect her thoughts.

Things were falling into place into Laura's mind now. The vague sense of unease that had haunted her all day, the thing that had escaped down the hollows of her neurological pathways and she had been unable to retrieve had finally come to the surface. She sat and stared at the ashtray, frighteningly aware that if she were right then her narrative of the past eight years would need to be radically rewritten. It had never been Jon's father. It had been George all along, George with his smooth hands and boys' clubs, George the Governor and friend of the headmaster's who had found it enormously convenient to divert attention away from the substantive issue of Jon's disturbance and towards Laura's cracking up, George the High Tory with his ridiculous parties to celebrate the Queen's birthday, George who always took such a close interest in the boys preparing for First Communion in the Parish and who always treated them to tea. And then of course another cog turned and Laura remembered helping the Halloran boy with his tie while his Mum was in the Blessed Sacrament chapel lighting so many candles that their heat might equal the output of a small electricity sub-station. Andrew Halloran. Drew Halloran. Drew, who his Mum said had always wanted to work on the boats and had looked at her so politely and said, 'Thanks, Miss' even though of course he was too young for her to have taught him. For a horrible moment Laura imagined George's hands on Drew after catechism, seeking and probing, not as she had been with Alex earlier in the evening but with sweating pederastic lust, his eyes hypnotic to the terrified child as he presumably told him that this was love and normal adult behaviour. 'You fuck,' said Laura aloud. 'You fucking fuck,' and brought her hand down hard on the coffee table.

The pain of the impact made Laura wince and shocked her thoughts back to what she thought was some sort of reason. Her brain was working at a furious pace and she was surprised to see that it was already half past three when she looked at the clock. She didn't understand where the evening had gone, but never mind that, she had to apply herself. There were two essential questions: what was the extent and meaning of events, and what would be the likely outcome of it all, for herself and others, were the truth she had stumbled upon become known? It was impossible to think of sleep in a situation like this, she must work out as much as she could now, while the energy of discovery was fresh in her mind. It struck her that her insight was to be one of great value, and working it out presented itself to her as a moral imperative. This was something of Tremendous Importance, perhaps the most important thing she had ever done in her life, and her fingers tingled with the absolute knowledge that she held the key to all of it. She got up and paced the room, noticing again the vodka that would fuel her with its crisp white cleanliness and give her the energy to carry on the night's work. She picked up the glass and drained it, then paced across to her desk where she tumbled its assorted papers into jumbled piles and placed them on the floor.

Collecting ashtray, the vodka and coke bottles from the coffee table she placed them in convenient reach beside the flat-screen monitor. Then she opened a drawer and searched among its hugger-mugger contents for a pack of A4 and a biro, the compulsion-necessary and familiar tools for plotting and planning, the friends from all-night writing sessions at Cambridge and fundamental instruments of her success. She looked at her desk. It was the way she liked it before she began something new, bare but for the essentials to her enterprise, and she allowed herself to light a cigarette and pour another drink and stare at the white crispness of the paper before letting the racing ideas spill out of her to take its virginity in the brilliance of her arguments and the sudden connections she was making.

Laura worked through what remained of the night, her hand moving swiftly over the sheets of notes that assembled quickly on her left side. She wrote with what seemed even to her to be an astonishing clarity and confidence. Little was discarded onto the floor as a blind alley or false start. There was no trace of tiredness to spoil what she was doing. Rather her brain was alight with thought, her talents banging off like artillery in the pre-dawn silence. She drew what she thought was a list of all Jon's friends that she could remember, surprised to find that her brain quickly yielded up names and faces to the groups of boys she had so frequently reprimanded in the past. A rush of remorseful compassion for them released more energy as the voice in her head told her that the best way she could possibly help them now was to do what she was doing, and she was projected back into it again. The biro roared across the page, a sweeping arrow to connect Jon's name with Drew's in motive, and as she bullied and cajoled her memory with questions about sailing and confirmation classes some more arrows appeared but this time she needed yellow pencil to indicate possibility, so she had to find her box of crayons. A red star next to Drew indicated the murder, and she was proud of her coding and presentation. She got up, lit another cigarette and poured some vodka to celebrate, entranced with herself as she watched her mind whirl around its thoughts in disco light brilliance. Drew to Jon, Greg to Drew and back to Leo, seven names in all each radiating back to Drew in what Laura knew immediately and with religious certainty was absolute evidence of mutual knowledge and co-operation. A conspiracy, in fact. Shocked and perturbed by this new discovery, she turned the phenomenon over in her mind. There was absolutely no question of her being wrong. As she looked at it she realised that she had been uniquely placed to stumble across the truth. She knew the boys involved, and had suffered herself as a result of what George had done. Who had he betrayed, how had he got away with it, and why, should be the next step in her thinking.

Something moved at her feet, and thinking that was Hugo, Laura glanced down and saw a large snake move across the floor. It vanished as she dropped her glass. She sat down heavily, sweat clinging to her back and dripping from her forehead, and realized she was gasping out in heaving gulps her terror and there was a constriction in her throat that made it impossible to scream. As cognition overcame animal fear she suddenly knew what all this was, and that she must not panic, and slowly the room stopped spinning and she staggered to the lavatory to be sick. Grimly Laura told herself that actually this was to be expected given the importance of what she was doing this evening. She knew that what she had seen was the Snake all people have infesting the corners of their minds, the Snake from the Garden who comes up again and again in the art of the West. He had been eluding her all day but she had glimpsed him with Bob, and he had slithered away as she'd been walking home with Alex. This was the Snake whom Our Lady would crush under her feet, the Snake who was an obvious symbol of the distorted sexuality which is a regrettably common experience of evil and who had chosen to take this form for its appropriateness and to scare her off. It was extremely interesting to have seen him, but with the strength of St Michael she pulled the toilet chain and resolved that no snake apparition suggesting a prick was going to bully her no matter how much of a shock it had given her. She had thought it had just all been chance until now, but this altered things appreciably. The real truth was that her talents were being used in a battle between the Snake and goodness. It was for that reason that the discovery of a conspiracy around George's murder had come to her with the strength of a religious revelation and the snake had come in his screaming vision to scare her. For after all, how can God work except through our minds? So Laura lifted her mind to Jesus the Good Shepherd and found herself surrounded with such love and joy that she thought she would die from it all, because she had found something that He was telling her to do in sorting it all out about George, and that would be a way back for her, and tears of relief and happiness ran unchecked down her cheeks. Now she and something like an angel or even more so and yes it really was Him began to dance around the room together and she could feel Him hugging her and telling her everything would be all right and that He would give her the strength to carry on and she must tell people about what she was doing after she had finished making her notes, and Blessed were the Poor in Spirit, and Blessed was Laura, the handmaid of the Word. He hugged her one last time and they stopped dancing but Laura knew He was still there in the room as He was everywhere except this time she felt it like in front of the Blessed Sacrament although she couldn't see Him any more.

Laura looked out of the window and thought about the saints who had encountered visions similar to or as intense as the ones she had experienced. Catherine of Sienna had wrestled with demons, and Francis of Assisi had received the stigmata. Even Luther had thrown an inkpot at the devil. She thought too of David, dancing before the Lord. Up until now she had felt uncomfortable with such stories as being at the very least in need of a good deal of post-Enlightenment demythologisation. Now she was by no means so sure, for she saw in the night's events a direct encounter with evil and the power of Truth and Love which was calling her to an active sanctity, a special grace granted to her which made sense of the gifts she had been given ever since childhood. Like Jeremiah, she knew that she had been grafted into God's hand at the moment of conception precisely for this purpose, and like Our Lady in the Magnificat, she could only respond with joy and humble obedience. With astonishment Laura realised that in some profound sense she had been chosen in the same way that Catherine, Francis and the Virgin had, and that through her some great purpose was being worked out. That it should be on the stage of Mootborough should not seem too unlikely, for after all, people had despised the stable-born Christ for coming from Nazareth. She knew that in her work His was being born again, not Yeats' monster slouching towards Bethlehem but coming in the judgement of truth as He would at the end of time.

She realised that these were the birth pangs of a new Kingdom in which she was called to be a second John the Baptist and midwife to the Church. Her immediate vocation to settle this business of George's murder and to help the earthly police was probably only the first of a succession of incidents which would build up to a climax over time. She shouldn't go prying into God's future for her but concentrate on the task in hand, secure in faith. Again a joy and love surrounded her, the lights in her mind flashed and she spun around on the computer chair for happiness' sake.

It was half past six now and people were passing her window on their way to work. For once the sight of them did not make Laura feel inadequate or unhappy because there was something for her to do now, a definite purpose which had given her life direction. She did not feel tired at all, and of course that was because she was filled with the Holy Spirit. But she knew that her body needed fuel, so she ate some natural yoghurt from its tub. The vodka bottle was getting dangerously near empty but she noticed that if she couldn't hang on until the shops were allowed to serve more there was a bottle of rosé left three-quarters full in the fridge door, and that would do. Accordingly she poured half of the remains of the spirit into her glass and filled it up with coke that had long since become warm and flat. The ice had disappeared and the oily vodka made it taste of petrol. Oh, and while she was about it she would need some more cigarettes, so she went to the cupboard under the stairs and took out another packet of duty-free Silk Cut from the cartons kindly smuggled to her from a one day van trip to Belgium by Tom and Andrea.

Laura sat at her desk again and quickly rearranged the piles of notes she had made about the Boys. Taking up her biro again, she marked a new page 'George' and underlined it heavily. She waited for a moment and then her mind began to race once more as she knew it would, tapping into inspiration that seemed to be immediately available and could therefore only be rationally explained by divine intervention. Beginning by what she knew of George's various posts and interests in the community, she worked outwards again, the hours speeding by unnoticed as her brain worked in exterior silence and inner shouting fever speed. The notes grew again beside her, and in an hour and a half she had a new diagram interfacing George with the original one, showing a detailed spiders' web of times, points of shared activities and places. This she illustrated after the manner of a mediaeval manuscript, which had been a special hobby of hers at University when she could get the time. In one corner she drew and coloured in the Blessed Virgin, her hands wide and pointing downwards towards the planet Earth beneath her feet. In the other *Stella Maris* appeared in full sail and close hauled to the wind, flying from her stern not the red ensign, but a wine-dark flag emblazoned with a snake, all poisonously green body, eyes and teeth. She did this because she knew that when things came to be researched and remembered, as they inevitably would be, this would be a key document. As an historian she knew the importance of posterity. Finally she made some notes for further essays about the theological understanding of visionary imagery, the connection between Freud's theories of sexual disruption in childhood and the Augustinian view of Original Sin, and how George's story could possibly be used to illustrate her underlying thesis that post-enlightenment language often finds its correlation in mythological and imaginative terms, the essential truths remaining the same. By the time all this was finished it was well past her usual lunchtime, so she sat on the sofa and finished the rest of the yoghurt and wine.

Laura's nightclothes felt sticky against her now as she drained her glass, the collar grazing against the back of her neck where perspiration had made the skin sore. Her hands were dirty and her eyes stung, while her mouth was tired and sour from cigarettes. The room had acquired a haphazard look. There were papers on the floor and the wicker basket that should have contained them was lying on its side like a broached oil tanker, disgorging its contents on the shore of the carpet. She yawned and stretched. Sleep caught her by surprise to still the squalls in her perception as she stretched herself out and let her exhausted consciousness drift away on the swell that she noticed was making her surroundings pulsate and swing. Her final thoughts drifted to the exciting luxury of seeing Alex in a few hours' time. She would not be late.

Nineteen

Alex was beginning to think that maybe it wasn't such a
good idea to have arranged to see Laura in the Anchor.
Last night he had been too tentative, he told himself, and
what he should really have done was to invite her out to
dinner or something. Looking round the bar he could see
Andrea talking to Pete's brother Mark. She hadn't noticed
him yet, but was quite capable of imposing a good-
natured monopoly on Laura when she arrived. Either that
or she would twig what was going on and draw the right
conclusions before he was really secure about them
himself, and become archly embarrassing. He didn't know
which would be worse, and could do without either. He
should have given this more thought and he hoped that
Laura wouldn't think him a complete fool. The prospect
was vaguely upsetting and he sighed unconsciously as he
raised the pint to his lips. Andrea had seen him now and
waved, but she didn't seem anxious to leave her
conversation yet. He didn't hold out much hope for the
rest of the evening. God, he mustn't get too drunk. He
had made the decision today that he liked and admired
Laura very much, and that the events of yesterday evening
were to be welcomed and pursued. Her condition was
one he knew to be manageable, and his professional
conscience was clear. She was not, after all, his patient.
He was rather pleased when on reflection he had

discovered that much of his confusion yesterday evening had been caused by questions of ethical practice. He'd been vaguely surprised to realise he cared deeply about them. The reason for his final decision had happened somewhere around mid-afternoon when he'd been struck with the contrast between the relationship he had with the patient he'd been talking to and what he felt about Laura. And in fact, he suddenly thought as he stood in the bar and lit his roll-up, as a supplementary argument you could say that if he didn't carry on with this thing with Laura that was a kind of discrimination. It was like saying that you are not allowed to fall in love with the mentally ill, and they are not allowed to experience love themselves, however enchanting and intelligent they were. That was like the old lunatic asylums where patients had been separated, men from women, in case they had sex. He grinned at himself, wondering if this was not a neat but fallacious argument for him to do what he wanted to do anyway. Oh, to hell with it. He'd already thought about nothing else when given the leisure today, and had made his decision as best he could. He would have to face the consequences, one of which he fervently hoped would be getting the opportunity to fuck Laura. He hoped to hell she hadn't gone off the idea.

Alex continued to sit on the barstool, his favourite one in the corner where you could lean against the wall. He had arrived about an hour before his date mainly because that was his time for arriving at the pub anyway. But he also wanted to appear casual, as though nothing were out of the ordinary. In a word, cool. He had finished his pint even though he had forced himself to drink it really slowly, exchanging idle conversation with Les. He glanced at the Guinness toucan clock on the wall, an object of some justifiable local pride. Blast it, there was still another half hour to go. He would have another slow one.

'Same again please, Les,' he said, and noticed with affectionate irritation the magical appearance of Andrea beside him, finished with her conversation and empty cider glass in hand. 'And a cider, if you would,' he added. Les met his eye briefly, the stern Scottish face looking a lecture in people buying their rounds and not being taken for a mug. Alex met the other's gaze with equanimity. Les was a nice bloke but he hadn't quite got hold of the human relationships thing. Although he would of course have his parting shot.

'As ye wish,' Les said, and as Alex grinned, walked abruptly off to pour the drinks. Alex returned to thinking again what an idiot he was not to have foreseen the likelihood of interference this evening. Never mind, he mustn't take it out on Andrea, and waiting with her would both pass the time and increase the insouciant thing. He handed her the pint.

'There you go.' He looked at the clock again.

'Thanks, darling. Waiting for someone?'

A kind of strangulated feeling came to Alex's throat. He felt hot and rubbed the back of his neck. Damn and blast it all, he needed to recover from this quickly.

'Only for you, my sugar lump.' He watched Andrea to see if it had worked. She smiled briefly and let him off the hook.

'Oh, you are so sweet.' Thank God for the power of compliments. But as they continued to talk he found it hard to keep his eyes from wandering to the toucan and his mind on the inconsequential trivia that seemed to constitute Andrea's conversation more than usually this evening. An hour came and went. Andrea made a minor show of buying her round, which he let her do because of Les and the dignity thing. Now he was matching her drinking and at last beginning to relax, conscious that his earlier feelings had been the product of first-night nerves and insufficient alcohol. He promised himself that he wouldn't begin to worry that he had been stood up until another hour had passed. Laura was cool, and so was he. Still, he wished he had got her mobile number or something. He knew Andrea would have it, but it was impossible to ask her and for a moment he felt ridiculously jealous. He smiled at himself. That really was too absurdly adolescent for words. He took a great gulp of beer and felt it buoy him up as the habituated pleasure responses kicked in, little synapses sparking off and going 'Yummy, give me more.' Briefly he wondered if knowing about how this worked reduced or enhanced the pleasure itself, and he decided that it probably enhanced it. Less chance of going over the top badly, too. Or at least too often. Well, in theory anyway. Where the hell was Laura? He gazed at the sweep of the dart player's arm over Andrea's shoulder, noticing the dull sheen on some guy's tattered jacket as he chalked the score on a blackboard also in need of a better coat.

Alex had bought another round and he and Andrea were halfway down their pints when, Oh my God, here she was, and he could hardly bear look at her, and when he did he felt a rush of something that felt very like what he imagined old-fashioned joy was all about. He waited as Laura kissed and said some kind of greeting to Andrea, and this time she embraced him too, which felt like some kind of token of a promise and he wondered if that was what she meant, or if a beer-bumbled brain was playing its tricks, although surely he hadn't drunk that much. His head felt as though he were a child about to cry from excitement and he did not dare look her in the face, but he had the dazed impression of some skilfully applied and tastefully understated makeup, a hint of citrussy scent, stylish top-and-skirt, and jolly bead necklace. A warning sign flashed up in his head to tell him that he was in danger of guzzling her up, so he broke away to order her a drink.

'What would you like, Laura?' he said, and she looked him in the eyes and held his gaze and grinned, and for a moment the bar slipped away and she laughed, and he was laughing too.

'A drink would be nice for now,' she replied, and they laughed again as somewhere a mobile rang. 'A pint of Adnams, please.' She came and stood next to him at the bar. He looked in manful resolution at Les, but was aware of her turning her head towards him and that, fractionally, she was leaning her weight against his as lovers do. As he handed her the glass he felt her fingers deliberately touch and rest on his. Relief swarmed over him as they made their way to a table, leaving Andrea on her phone to join them or with any luck, not. As they sat down Alex could hear the end of the conversation, 'Yeah. OK, see you in half and hour then.' He touched Laura's hand very briefly, a sign-back of complicity, and felt her quickly entwine the index finger of her hand with his.

Here it was again, Laura realised, as Andrea came to sit with them, a friend betraying her. She was eating crisps and scrunching the packet, which sounded like a reptile's skin, as of course it would. Fuck off, bitch. Which reminded her that Alex didn't know what he was getting caught up in yet, but she really needed him and knew that she would make it up to him with fantastic sex, and they would live together and that would be all right with God, and maybe they could get her marriage to Jack annulled, and Alex would ask her to marry her and they could do it properly. In the meantime Andrea was always around him and just because they had once had some sort of a thing together she thought she bloody well owned him. What in fact she did was leech on his good nature and cadge free drinks and just, always just, keep him on the edge of a promise of sex. Laura had been sitting next to Alex and instinctively she moved closer to him, knowing that he had unwittingly been given the power of prophecy and that Andrea for the moment had in some sense been turned into a harpy.

'What are you laughing at?' the harpy asked her, and Laura realised that a whole thought-train had passed through her head and she had no idea how long it had taken. She decided it was time to go into well brought up mode and stopped in snorts.

'I'm most frightfully sorry, I seem to have lapsed into a trance,' she said. God, how she hated them. She was righteously glad that she it was so easy to make this one feel small with a bit of Oxbridge English and snottiness.

'Take more water with it,' came the retort, so the thrust hadn't been deep enough, and while she participated in the compulsory laughter Laura realised that what she really needed to do was to make an obvious sign in front of Andrea. This would be a powerful thing against the enemy, because he hated love and sometimes when she wasn't a harpy Andrea wasn't all bad so after a clear sign the enemy might relinquish her, leaving her to bugger off with Tom. And of course that was what the phone call had been about. How brilliant of Laura to realise it.

Whether it worked or not, it would be great to hold Alex's hand anyway. She reached over to do it but couldn't help herself when she touched his fingers, and she had to cuddle him around his neck and kiss his cheek, although really she wanted to snog him there and then. When she had finished she found herself laughing in bliss, but knowing that for appearances' sake she needed an excuse, even if it wasn't a very convincing one.

'Thanks for the beer,' she said, and saw at first hesitation and then realisation cross Andrea's face, which made her want to laugh again because the harpy had disappeared from behind her friend's eyes and that was proof of the power of sign and sacrament which was flowing through her since her visions today and in her love for Alex. She could chat normally now.

At least the occasional uncertainty that he had suffered from during the day could now be dismissed, thought Alex as Laura kissed him for a second time. He felt himself colour up. As she released him, he was aware of Bob the Bargeman's amused observation of their behaviour from his habitual table. The old bugger actually dared raise his pint to him behind Laura's back. Alex didn't care, he wanted to grin back. He and Laura were in some strange bubble of their own, where, he realised, his earlier anxieties were ridiculous. He was enjoying the feeling very much.

'Andrea and I were just saying what a fantastic day it's been,' he said, now released from Laura's arms and playing games, fending her off with small talk and keeping Andrea in the loop, serving to her a ping-pong ball of conversation to watch in admiration how she might bat it back. Somewhere he was aware his sense of social propriety was reproaching him, but it was from a very, very long way away.

'Gosh, was it? I mean, it has been a lovely day, hasn't it?' said Laura. 'I had a super walk down here, I do love doing that and seeing what everybody has in their gardens. I hate gnomes though. Alex, do you know much about Original Sin? I've been working all day and most of last night actually on some ideas and I would be really interested to know what you think about them, from a psychological point of view I mean.' Laura looked for a moment in astonishment at Alex and Andrea as they burst out laughing before her brain presented the image back to herself. She joined in, mirth flooding her mind and loading her up with pleasure as they watched one another's laughter, each new wave breaking on top of the last until lack of breath forced tears from their eyes and the joy-storm subsided.

'Original sins? I reckon I've done some of them,' said Andrea.

'Not with gnomes though,' Alex replied. 'For that you need medical advice.'

Laura and Andrea laughed. 'Oh, I am sorry,' said Laura. 'I wasn't thinking what I was saying.'

'Totally mad,' said Andrea playfully, and Alex watched her bite her lip and turn her head away to bury it in her cider glass. So Laura must have told her why she had been laid off work. Andrea was a silly cow for making such a slip, but Alex knew her well enough to be certain that this was all it was. Anyway, it seemed that he didn't need to protect Laura anyway at the moment. She was carrying on quite well enough on her own. Maybe she had some kind of filter system switched on.

'No, but seriously, Alex, I mean, I would like to talk to you about it, I mean, Augustine and all of that. I have actually been wondering how much the *Confessions* may have actually influenced Freud.'

That was a bit of a wowsa, Alex thought. Nobody else he knew would have chucked him a line like that in a provincial pub, paying him the compliment of no-nonsense intellectual equality, being hungry for his professional knowledge and making assumptions about the width of his reading. And in itself her thesis was an interesting one, although to be truthful he'd only skimmed the *Confessions* and read occasional references to them. He was a bit hazy on that score but she could talk about that and he could talk about the history of psychology. There was no doubt about it, Laura was really exciting him.

'OK, that sounds really brilliant. I should like to knock that idea around with you,' he said.

'I didn't know Clement Freud was a Catholic,' said Andrea, and Alex was impressed when Laura didn't make to catch his eye.

'Actually that's his grandson,' she said. 'I meant the other one – he was a psychologist I think, like Alex, but with a beard. I think they were Jewish.'

'Isn't there some painter called Freud? I really like his stuff,' said Andrea. 'Tom and I saw this exhibition place full of it up in London.' While he was recovering from the shock of hearing himself cast alongside the great Beardy Weirdy Alex got another kick as he realised that he could be a terrible intellectual snob absurdly surprised to hear that Andrea had ever looked at a proper painting. He listened as Andrea and Laura sorted out the Freud family and discussed what they liked about paintings and the way Lucien showed the colours of skin. It seemed to him that Laura was brilliant at this, providing information when it was needed but doing so with such a lightness of touch that she brought out Andrea's enthusiasm and allowed her to take the lead in the conversation. And then of course he remembered that she had been a teacher, and his delight at watching her was increased by professional detachment and observation. She really was very good, and he wondered what it must have been like for the kids in her classes when she was on good form.

'OK,' he heard Andrea say, 'now tell me who this Augustine bloke was.'

'Oh, he was a bishop ages ago,' said Laura, 'and he wrote this thing about how he was converted to Christianity.'

Andrea's nod seemed to indicate her satisfaction with this answer, a lack of desire for further information, and she reached for her pint. A hiatus in the conversation was looming, and Alex needed to say something.

'Was this before or after he did the stuff in Canterbury?' he ventured.

'What?' said Laura, immediately the outraged dominatrix of fantasy school stories. 'Sit on the Naughty Chair immediately and wait to be spanked. Such lamentable ignorance of chronology shall not go unpunished, nor shall your wilful lack of catechesis. I shall attend to you later.'

Oh, bugger, thought Alex, but he laughed at the way Laura kept command and turned his ignorance, so gently dealt with in Andrea, to a vicious humour that was in itself flattering. He loved this, loved the way she could run rings around him and transform the beer-aged bar to brilliance.

'Ah,' he said. 'I take it that I have made a fundamental error.'

'Quite so,' said Laura, now the patient special needs teacher. 'Listen very carefully. There are two Saint Augustines. One was Bishop of Hippo…'

'Did you say hippo?' said Andrea, and snorted with laughter.

'Indeed so. An amusingly named Roman colony in North Africa. He was the one who wrote the *Confessions* and he lived right at the time of the Fall of Rome in 410.'

'So when was the other around then?' asked Alex, as Andrea continued to say 'Hippo' and giggle.

'Late sixth century. Do not mess with a medieval

historian.' Laura replied. 'There will be questions later this evening.' She winked at him, if he was reading things right, salaciously.

'How excellent,' he said, 'I'm looking forward to it,' and he had never heard anybody get so much sex into a few words as when she replied softly, 'I hope so.' There was a pause between them and she touched his hand, and somewhere in the protection of their bubble Alex was concerned that they might be making themselves obvious.

'For goodness sake you two, book a room,' said Andrea, and they all three could release the tension by laughing, and everything was OK again. Laura gave Alex a twenty-pound note to go to the bar for more drinks, and the feel of its smooth newness for some reason made him think of thighs.

Away from the protection of the tables the pub had become more crowded. Alex waited behind a sea of familiar backs, nodding greetings as each turned towards him with their orders while he made steady progress towards Les's recognition. Pints were passed with dancing dexterity and carried three to two in clasping hands beneath the whirr of the Ventaxia. Someone had lit a pipe and the vanilla sweetness of Dutch tobacco made Alex think of sea-shanties and sailors' hats as the light bounced from anciently-stained lampshades and onto the unnecessary jauntiness of so many brass fittings. He was at the bar itself now, scoring the tipsy weekend victory against a world which seemed too often to be conspiring to deprive him of beer. He was happy in this and in the contemplation of promised sex.

'You want to watch that one, you know, mate.' Cigarette smoke was wisping away from the speaker's deeply orange-stained fingers as he nodded towards where the women were sitting. Alex was surprised in his thoughts and turned to look at his former classmate's contemptuous face while keeping part of his attention on the progress of the drinks being served in his peripheral vision. Despite himself he was becoming hot as a response to the other man's apparent aggression, and he felt his heartbeat accelerate. He tried to think his way out. 'Do we run from the bear because we are afraid,' he remembered, 'or do we fear the bear because we run?' He reminded himself that he had never liked Mark much at school, where his idleness and flippancy during their shared classes had driven Alex into furies at the weaker teachers' lack of control and Mark into a miserable list of failed qualifications. His conversations with him since the Sixth Form had usually consisted of the pub-confined football blag and lazy chumminess of indifference.

'Oh, Andrea's all right,' he said, more self-assured now, taking command of the conversation with a deliberate show of misunderstanding. He turned his attention back to the passing of the glasses as though the topic had been dismissed.

'Not her. You know who I mean. That Laura who's been hanging round your neck all evening. I tell you, mate, she's bad news. I mean, I know Pete can be a wanker sometimes...'

'Yes, I know,' broke in Alex. 'I was there.' He was beginning to be angry now. It was time for Mark to drop it.

'Yeah,' said Mark, apparently nonplussed. 'He doesn't do himself many favours, but he is my brother, and the way she went off at him was like, well out of order. And she's always at it, making a fool of herself. I tell you, mate, she's a well known head case. Course she says she's got fucking Stress or whatever they call it this week.' He spat the word out like venom. 'Bloody mental health

170

problems be buggered. She hasn't done a stroke of work since her old man kicked her out way back, and gets well paid for it on fucking Incapacity. Of course we all know what her real problem is.' He took a great draught of lager. 'Bit too much of the old sauce. She's a bloody nightmare. I know what I'd do with that lot, take their bloody benefits away and force the fuckers back to work.' Les had reached Alex and he ordered the two pints of Adnams and one of cider. Now that he had nearly achieved his objective he decided that he couldn't be bothered any more with this self-righteous public-bar ignorance and knowing malice. They were, he thought, the hallmarks of a deep stupidity whose main characteristic was the inability to empathise. Mark had fallen out of the great DNA cocktail shaker with some inordinately unpleasant attributes, and he was briefly interested to note how one could see some of the same coding expressing itself in his brother. That was tough on both of them, of course, but they did after all have to make some sort of an effort to live in society. It would be noisy, absurd, ridiculous and therefore wrong to beat Mark's head to a bloody pulp with the conveniently placed and heavy bar bell, so instead he said, 'Yes. And of course it's a shame we've all got to pay tax for hospital consultants when you're so much better qualified to do the job.' As he picked up the glasses he was pleased to note the puzzled expression on Mark's face. That fucked you, he thought triumphantly.

'I think it's brill,' Alex heard Andrea say as he rejoined them. She was leaning forward on crossed arms in conspiratorial smiles while Laura had one elbow rested on the scratched brown veneer. 'Thanks, love, cheers. I must go and talk to him in a minute, then we'll be over, OK?' She was nodding towards the other bar, and as Alex followed her gaze he could see that her Tom had been drawn into conversation there and was looking around him, apparently searching for her. Andrea looked excited as if full of some Great News, and he and Laura watched as she swayed, beamed and dodged her way through the cigarette-smoked crowd. Laura attacked her new pint with enthusiasm, and for a moment as he sat down Alex watched her in erotic fascination as she took the glass to her lips.

'Cheers,' he said in response to her smile and raised glass, and then they both spoke together, 'With any luck…' 'Maybe she'll…' and for Alex the moment was sparky with that extraordinary synchronicity which he had occasionally experienced in his previous relationships, and especially with Sue. Every time it happened he was almost thrown off balance by the comic romance of its reality, and had often compared it to the reality of experiencing déjà vu, although that was definitely more unpleasant. And of course he and Laura were laughing together, because the telepathy-thought had created an unexpected tension, and laughter was the way you got rid of it. The brain represented the overload to itself as humour.

'Oh dear, we are naughty,' said Laura. Alex told himself that he must stop analysing everything as though he were at work. It was just because he was nervous.

'We are,' he said. 'I'm sorry I got Augustine all muddled up. But he, the early one, so he was the one who invented the idea of Original Sin, was he? Sounds like trouble to me.'

'You and a few million western Catholics. He's not a saint of the Eastern Church so they get off lightly.' Laura felt a slight pang of conscience about this implied certainty in Theology and unfairness to the old guy, especially after everything that had happened today, but she was enjoying being dramatic.

'I shall move to Greece then, when I get religion,' replied Alex. 'In fact I think I shall move there anyway.' He affected a ridiculous accent and waved his hand in a controlled but theatrical gesture to indicate the bar. 'Let me take you away from all this to my olive grove in the sunshine and we shall drink wine and eat smelly cheese among goats.' This was better. He felt ridiculously happy.

'Ooooh yes,' said Laura, 'and when I get old I shall have a black dress and ride down into the village every day on a donkey, and you can be all strong and brown and full of peasant wisdom like Yves Montant.' She loved the idea of a future together, it was right that he was talking about it, this was how things were meant to go.

'That was Provence.'

'Don't argue with me when I am fantasising,' retorted Laura.

There were hanging baskets on the wall of the pub, and Alex gazed at them as he waited for Laura to come back with more drinks. The colours were jostled together in sweet-jar gaudiness and swung together very slightly in the evening's easterly breeze. In places the low mellow sunshine hit the plants in such a way as to shine through leaves and blossoms and reveal their inner structures. Alex noted the green-veined intricacy of a leaf, the subtleties of pink and white in some trumpet-shaped flower. He had been rather remiss about his botanical education, and Sue used to laugh at him for it. He should make an effort about it sometime, it was a gap. A flash of electric blue from across the road attracted his attention, the magpie's back suddenly resolving to black again as it landed at the foot of a yellow bush. Alex regarded it warily and nodded it a mental greeting. It seemed unfair that such a beautiful bird should be saddled with so bad a reputation, he thought, but its place in folklore was too heavily entrenched for him to overturn in his mind, and it did have disgusting habits. It flew off chatter-nagging and monochrome again towards the park, seeming satisfied. Strange how powerful these traditions can be, thought Alex, even for a Modern Renaissance Man With a Firm Grasp on the Enlightenment, and he smiled as he realised that he liked to think of himself like this. The sun was striking him on the face and warming him through the glass and he felt at ease. The L word was hanging between him and Laura, he reflected. He was content to leave it unspoken while dancing with her in its hypomania. He was thankful for the monoamines that he knew were doing their magic stuff in his brain because of her presence, happy to swing along with her in their shared high spirits, too glad to want to press or question her thoughts this evening after all.

Twenty

The walls were grey. People had scratched dirty words on them, especially above this thing you lay down on. Drew didn't know what to call it, it was much harder and narrower than a bed and there was no duvet or anything, just an old fashioned blanket like Nan had got. It was like a single berth, but he knew you only got them on boats. There was a toilet and a basin. He hated the toilet. He hadn't wanted to use it because there was no curtain or anything, but after the pasty and chips they had given him he had had to have a dump and somebody had lifted the flap thing in the door and laughed at him while he was wiping himself, and he'd felt embarrassed. He thought it was the big policeman who had caught him running away. He was the one who always stared at him in the other room with the table and the chairs. They asked him questions there, but most of the time that one had just given him the evils like they used to in school when he was younger. George used to help him with stuff like that, told him he would protect him and not to take notice of bullies. He'd even promised to talk to the headmaster about it if Drew wanted, but Drew hadn't. George had made him feel special. Mum had liked him, you could tell, what with the way he spoke and everything. He couldn't really remember when he'd started hating George. When he was young the other stuff had happened when they were on their own and didn't really seem to count, because then you thought that anything grown-ups did was bound to be OK. Then gradually it wasn't like that any more. When Drew had got older George began taking him out on his boat with the others and was always giving them whiskey and putting dirty films on when they had moored up for the evening and eaten tea. Once or twice it had happened in George's house at what he called one of his Special Parties, and then they would all be there, but usually it was just Drew and one of the others on the boat. Often it was Jon. The films had women in them to start with and Drew would watch them while George used to get drinks and chocolates and that. Drew had enjoyed that, it made him fascinated and excited to watch the girls undressing and playing with themselves and doing it. It was sort of like a Playstation Game only more, the way it made you go on and on watching. Then George would ask them if they were enjoying themselves and said that it was OK with him if they wanted to play with one another, and he would change the films to ones with men and boys in them. Then the stroking and sucking would begin again and the probing until they got to what George called the Ultimate or some word like that, which was too rude to think about and hurt especially when he did it with his fist, but afterwards George always said that it was simply an overflowing of love and nobody should feel ashamed. Afterwards Drew had felt dirty and miserable. Once he had even burned the clothes he'd been wearing, and it was awful when anything came on the telly about gays because Mum hated anything like that. Drew shut his eyes and wanted to cry out to keep the pictures in his head away, but he knew the policemen were about outside and it escaped through his teeth in a moan as he pressed himself against the wall.

He'd wanted to ask for cigarettes while they were asking him questions but he hadn't dared. He was scared they would tell Mum he smoked. She had come to see him earlier on, but she just kept crying and saying, 'Oh Drew, they're asking me all sorts of terrible things, terrible,' and he didn't know what to say to her, so eventually she had just gone away and his tummy had felt all empty inside. But really he had done it for her as well, because George had said that if he ever said anything about the sex he would see to it that her life was made a misery and she would never get another job again. And he had meant it, too. Drew could tell. He had told him how powerful he was on the Council and all of that stuff, how many high-up people he knew in Mootborough and even in the Government and police and that. Drew didn't understand all of it but it frightened him to think that he would be to blame for hurting his Mum. George said she was a wonderful woman and if he did anything to hurt her he would be even more of a worthless little turd than the boys at school said. But apart from all of that Mum would be terribly shocked about what had been going on if she ever found out, and she would start blaming herself like she always did when he knew it would be his own fault, because George had said so. He hadn't wanted to hurt his Mum, she was worth so much more than him because he was dirty like George said, so for a long time things had gone on like before and Drew and the others had gone on the boat and all of the usual stuff happened, and he hated George more and more as well as loving him.

One day ashore when George was doing something in the chandlery Jon had told him that George had said the same sorts of stuff about Jon's dad, threatening Jon and that. He'd told Drew that at school once he had been really upset after an evening with George. He'd seen him at school the next day on a Governor's visit, and he'd smashed up some PE stuff and he'd got really near telling Mrs Morton everything, her from Church, because she was deputy head then and he'd got sent to her. But there had been what he called a fuck up, he was always using bad words. Mrs Morton had lost it and had a nervous breakdown or something, so after that he couldn't do anything.

Drew couldn't really remember how long after that they had got together, five of them meeting in the drizzle on the bandstand with their hoodies drawn up and wandering around the farthest of the Park's fields as they talked. Jon had talked a lot. He was really clever when he wasn't all angry or drunk. The thin wind had whipped wavelets in the river as they walked and was bending the long grass down beneath their weight of water. But Drew hadn't minded the weather, he had felt all excited being in a group. The drizzle had turned to rain and hid the trees on the far shore at Saltbridge, and they talked about what they could do with George. Jon had said there was no way they could go to the Police, his Dad said they were useless and no way did he want everybody to know what had been going on. He said he would like to tie George up instead and torture him until he died to see how he fucking liked it, and that would stop him doing it to any other kids. He said how he would do it with a pair of pliers and a blowtorch, and as he talked like that Drew had felt like he did when he watched the women films, all sweaty and with his thing hard. The others said they all felt like that too, and then Drew'd had his big idea that made them listen to him and he'd felt proud and important. It would be easy to kill George out at sea and to drop him over the side.

They paddled the idea around, imagining together the sharp swift blow from behind and then how they wanted to cut his cock off and show it to him and shove it in his mouth while he was still alive. Then they'd weight him down with rocks and stuff they'd carry in their sailing bags and push him under the guardrail to bleed and drown to death. The eels and lobsters and that would do the rest, Jon had said. As long as they were careful to do it somewhere deep no one would ever know. All of them were good enough to get the sails down and the boat back to Mootborough under motor, where they could say he had slipped and they didn't know how to use the radio. Even better, they could even break a wire in it and say they had tried to use it, but George had said it needed fixing. They'd have to throw George's mobile away and make sure they didn't bring their own, get rid of the porno films and clean up, but they could do all of that on the way back if they were careful and used the autohelm.

The wind had started coming in gusts then, sending the gulls spiralling inland, and they'd had to turn their backs on it and wander back towards the Town so that they could hear one another.

Drew had imagined George's voice saying, 'It wasn't *cold*, dear boy, but it was *persistent*,' and he'd wanted to spit in his face and do everything that Jon had said, and he was really glad, he felt like the other boys had given him permission to think like that.

As they walked towards home it seemed like they'd all made a decision already, so that when Jon said, 'I reckon the first time we get the chance we should do it,' they'd all agreed. Drew had been really excited, it was like being in Robin Hood or something because you knew it was the right thing to do even though it was against the law. Like Jon said, it was the only way, and although usually you

179

weren't allowed to kill people sometimes you had to, like in wars, and this way nobody would get hurt except George. Drew had carried his exhilaration through the rain, hugging anticipation to himself for days afterwards and half imagining that he might be able to do it all by himself and get to be a hero with the others, especially Jon.

It had been George's fault it had gone wrong. He'd been drunk when Drew went on board that evening and he'd been all over him, giggling and kissing and taking off his trousers and that even while Drew was trying to put his bag down. Drew had tried to push him off, he hated him when he was like that, but George had just laughed. Then like a light going on in his head Drew had realised that all of this made him feel sick, the slobbery grown man's mouth with its beard ends and huge aggressive tongue, the perfumed cheeks and chipolata hands, his stupid Thing standing out between his legs, and as George had turned to struggle with the last bit of his trousers over his sailing shoes he'd realised he had a chance now, and he'd taken the bolt croppers and hit him hard over the side of the head, and George had just fallen down with a thump and he'd gone on hitting and hitting and hitting and hitting and then cutting and cutting and cutting and cutting. He'd cried as he did it, he didn't know why, it was like all of the bad stuff George had done tumbling out of him all at once and he was cutting away the past. Then he'd washed himself as best he could and sat in the cabin as the light went down, trying not to look at George's body. Afterwards he went out to cast off and motor out for the night so that he could get rid of him in the deep water off the Beacon, he thought he could manage that even though it was several hours away, but when he got outside he realised that he had forgotten about the tide and it was gone, so he'd had to find the keys and lock up, which he knew was dead risky, but he couldn't think what else to do. Then he'd changed his clothes in the dark cockpit, and stuffed the bloody ones in his sailing bag.

He was early when he got back, of course, so he'd told his Mum some story about George having cancelled the sailing outing. As soon as he'd dared he'd phoned Jon and told him that he must, absolutely must, meet him for the evening tide, but Jon said he couldn't until the day after. So it had been a really horrible day. The weather had changed and it got really hot, and he kept imagining George all smashed up in the cabin, and when Mum was out working he had washed and washed his clothes and sailing bag in the bath because he didn't know how to use the washing machine, and then the bath was all bloody so he had to do that, too. When she came back Mum had asked questions about the clothes on the line and he said that he had fallen in the mud around the moorings and hadn't wanted to give her an extra job, and she had said that he was a very thoughtful boy, and that made him feel really nervous. It was hard to eat any of his tea and he had thought about stuff on and off all the way through the evening and the night, hearing the chink-chink of poorly stowed halyards against the masts in the boatyard and counting off the chimes of St Peter's clock, and it had been hot, really hot, and he couldn't get the picture of George's smashed up face out of his mind.

Drew had realised he hadn't got much of a chance left when the policemen came. He'd seen the car stop outside and he'd felt kind of sick, he'd known they were going to come to his house. His first idea was just to try to get away to find some place to hide until the evening, and that was when he'd tried to run away. He hadn't realised until much later that they'd already found George. Maybe if he

181

hadn't run he might even have got away with it, he didn't know. They'd hurt him when they caught him and used bad words, and now everything had gone so wrong he knew other people would use them about him too. He looked at the scratched wall again. That was what he was, that is what Jon and the others would think of him because he'd tried to do it on his own. Whatever happened now he would have to shut up about the others or it would make everything worse.

Twenty-one

Dom McGahan rested his head on his hand and rubbed at his forehead as he continued to make the preliminary draft of his report. The sequence of events was pretty clear now, and Andrew Halloran's guilt established with easy sufficiency. Fingerprints matching those taken from him at arrest had been found all over the bolt croppers recovered at the scene, whose shape matched that of the injuries to the body of George Brightly. Mr Brightly's blood had been found in large amounts in seams and tucked-away places on recently washed clothes identified as Andrew Halloran's by his mother. The magistrates and CPS would nod it through; it was simply a matter of adding the additional evidence as it came in and feeding it to where it was needed. A quick result made easy by the youth and stupidity of the perpetrator. And a load of stuff that Dom knew he would have to face sooner or later but didn't quite want to yet.

Reading through his work from where it began with Mr Armstrong, Dom remembered talking to him earlier in the day. The sharp, fox-like little face had relived its moments of puzzlement and then revulsion, and he seemed to be half enjoying and half nervous of his own importance. Dom mimicked the man to himself silently. Mr Armstrong, call me Ted that's what most people do, see, well he'd been walking on the far side of the moorings, see, you know not many people go there but he does because he likes to be on his own and have a bit of a think. And see, there'd been a bit of a smell, and he'd thought see, one of them old seals has died again and got caught up on the staging. So he walks down there and has a look around and he followed the smell, see, and told the Police when he realised it were coming from this boat all tied up, see, at the far end and he'd had a look through the cabin windows and there was this bloke all smashed up, it gave him a fair old turn, he could tell you. Dom had rather liked Mr Armstrong. It was he too who had suggested that they talk to Meg Stubbens, who did a lot of cleaning nearby and sometimes worked in the chandler's. Dom had asked him if he knew who used to go out on the boat, and he had said that Meg knew everyone around the boatyards. So Dom had sent a couple of DCs off and after a bit they had trotted back with a list of names and some addresses.

It wasn't a matter of rocket science to send Uniform off to knock on doors, and as luck would have it Darren Wright and Mick Earl had arrested the Halloran boy. He had obviously panicked when they arrived to question him, Dom reflected, which was a good job because even somebody as obviously dim as Halloran might have been able to confuse those two if he'd kept control. But he drummed his fingers on the table in irritation that it had not been a couple of the dimmer drafted Amblehurst coppers. Wright and Earl were a dreadfully bad influence in the Station, and were now crowing around the place, full of renewed vigour and self-confidence. That was all he needed. He'd been pretty certain that one or other of them had been behind all that stupid nonsense about BNP stickers on the Civilian Assistants' locker last month.

Their equal insolence when he had questioned them at the time had spoken volumes, but without proof he hadn't been able do much more than produce platitudes and empty threats. Not much good for Ayisha Patel or the other black CAs who had to use the locker room, although he'd tried as best he could to reassure them. Dom sighed, finished reading, and swung around the Executive-Style-Look-at-me-I'm-a-Chief-Copper chair he hated in order to get up and go to the window.

The normal scenes of Mootborough life were going on below him, watched over by the Town Sign. This had been erected in 1973, and a curious inscription described it as being the gift of the Town Council to the people of Mootborough. Dom had never quite understood how something given to taxpayers by the tax receiving authority could be called as a gift. Even in Mootborough, where an interest in local politics often seemed to be a necessary precursor to madness or social disgrace, the weirdness of the logic defeated and amused him, and he smiled briefly. Much else about the High Street had changed since his childhood. Grocers, greengrocers and fishmongers had given way to estate agents and mobile phone shops, and as the drift towards out-of-town supermarkets had continued, charity shops had moved into the gaps once occupied by now-unsuccessful small businesses. From where he was standing Dom could only see one shop recognisable from his youth, where Joe Rampton was carving a late evening ham for an elderly lady, clinging onto trade by the quality of his produce, his family's considerable shared charm, and the snob appeal of offering butcher's accounts.

Lamb chops now. Dom watched the cleaver drawn back and raised, the sudden descent and miraculous cleaving of the meat. Or he would have done if he hadn't looked away at the last moment because the sudden image of Andrew Halloran and George Brightly came into his mind. For a moment he was horribly aware of the reality of what had gone on in that boat once you stripped it all away from talk about evidence and the CPS, results and prosecutions. It took a good deal of hatred to kill someone like that, some unimaginable depravity or unimaginable hurt. Of course in a sense it didn't really matter. There was more than enough evidence to secure a conviction and he wasn't for him to do the Defence's job for them. He had absolutely no doubt that Wright and Earl would consider questions of motive, let alone Andrew Halloran's welfare and future, quite irrelevant in the face of a Result. That was another reason to regard them as ill equipped for duty, now he came to think about it.

Halloran hadn't looked depraved to Dom, but then of course, it was difficult to tell so far. The boy was clearly extremely distressed, too terrified to answer questions coherently or to think straight at the moment. It was all right to let that go on for a while. Even Darren Wright's presence in the interview room had its uses there, although Dom had some nagging reservations about what could be interpreted as psychological pressure and had taken the precaution of getting the boy checked every half hour. What he really wanted was a confession, not in the sense of a simple police statement, but for the boy to open up and yield his painful knowledge. After Dom had seen the pornographic tapes he had a fairly clear idea of what might have happened, and if that were the case the lad could only help himself, and those who had to guard him and look after him, by letting go. In any event Dom reckoned that the key would be to find out the things which frightened the boy and then, kindly, to try and put his mind at rest as much as possible. Dom had a number of strategies and a lot of experience for that, and in a little while he would get rid of Wright in favour of a motherly woman constable so as to talk to him.

Twenty-two

Alex lay with his head snuggled on Laura's breast, her arm around his shoulders so that for both of them to be comfortable he had to be a bit lower down in the bed than she was. She was stroking his back with her fingertips, running little figures of eight over his still-hypersensitive skin to produce ripples of sleepy pleasure. He touched her sex lightly with his fingers, feeling his own wetness mingled with hers in its smoked-salmon silkiness. Laura mused contentedly on how the lubricated openness into which she had invited him with tender eagerness, and his gentle phallic urgency, had shouted their restlessness each for the other. To be filled by him had been like being made as complete as you could hope for in this life, and she was certainly up for a good deal more, only not now because she'd come three times and him twice. She looked at his face, at what seemed to her to be the kind perfection of his nose and half-closed eyes, and here and now it all seemed so right to her, the absolute mutual self-giving in which they had seemed to reach out together and touch the place outside the Universe where God was. This had been no lustful porn-fed coupling, all right as they were in their limited way, but as near as she thought she had experienced to the platonic Idea of lovemaking, unless of course she had forgotten what it felt like. The reality of it all struck her with the force of a blow, and she realised that this had been an existential, a life-transforming experience, just as when she had seen the Snake and danced with Christ. It was no coincidence that things were coming together as they were. This was further proof of her special mission and of how the God who she had touched again in sex with Alex was working his purposes out through her and now, how joyfully, through them both. She stroked his cheek. 'You know,' she said, risking everything and nothing, 'I am in serious danger of being very much in love with you.'

Alex opened his eyes and shifted up the bed to look at her. She was crying, he noticed, small tears leaking unhindered from the corners of her eyes as she returned his gaze. Then she sat up and laughed, and wiped her cheeks and sniffed a little like a child. 'Sorry,' she said, 'how stupid. Just happy tears.' But Alex knew it wasn't stupid at all and he sat up too and hugged her to him and his breath bounced out in a trembling whoof as her hair enveloped his face and he tried to get her as close as possible.

Some minutes afterwards as they sat still hugging on the bed, Alex reflected that while this was all very nice his shoulder was beginning to hurt like hell, his back was shouting for relief from the job of having to support most of Laura's weight as well as his own, and politeness demanded that he should make some sort of a verbal response to what she had said. Who was it, he wondered, who had said that humankind cannot bear very much reality? He had a feeling that it was that old fraud Eliot. At any rate, transcendent sexual experiences were certainly at the mercy of the corporeal nature of existence.

'Laura,' he said softly, and eased her back down onto the pillows, lying down beside her and pulling the duvet comfortably over them both so that now she lay with her head on his chest. 'That was very nice.' He felt her dig her fingernails into his side.

'Watch it, buster. "Very nice" does not get you many brownie points.' They laughed.

'I didn't mean just that,' said Alex. 'I meant the whole thing, the whole evening.' Oh God, how was he going to do this without making a complete arse of himself, what possible metaphor could he use in front of this terrifyingly brilliant woman? 'As to the love thing,' he began, and there was a pause now and he could feel her tensing on his chest, her breathing suspense-shallow in the warmth of their closeness and her hands minutely contracting on his skin. He decided to go for it for her sake as much as his. 'Well, I have to tell you that I am noticing symptoms of the heightened states of awareness and obsessive behaviours in myself which, when combined with raised libidinous thoughts and tendencies, and centred on a single human object, I think we may objectively diagnose as the syndrome that is commonly referred to as being in love.' He felt her hands relax, and she kissed his chest.

'You're a bastard,' she said, and laughed.

'Quite so. In fairness to you, I have also to say that in simple terms, I am extremely, crashingly happy.'

'Great,' said Laura, and kissed him again. 'So am I. So you want to carry on?'

Alex felt a moment of unease, his years calling to him from his testicles, before realising that Laura might be talking in the longer term.

'Of course,' he said. 'That's what being in love is all about, isn't it?'

'So do I. I want to be with you always,' said Laura, and the clever ambiguity that was meant not to scare him wasn't lost on Alex, who took her hand and raised it to his lips.

'Sounds a great plan to try out to me,' he said. 'Laura, making love to you, I mean the sex, well you know, it was, I mean I haven't…'

'Nor me.'

They slept like spoons in the bed, Alex surprised and delighted by the warm curve of her backside as it pressed against him. In the small hours of the morning he woke up with an urgent erection and Laura stirred and pushed herself against him lasciviously so they made love and Alex came with quick surprise. Before she drifted back to sleep he heard her murmur, 'There's going to be an awful lot of work to do, darling.'

Alex smiled into the darkness. Nobody had called him Darling like that since Sue. He asked himself how he felt about all that now, and whether Laura being on the scene would help. He remembered the cold churchyard where he had stood slightly to one side of the family, the sympathetic country clergyman with his talk of God's absolute love and forgiveness, his own feelings of yawning blankness and, somewhere, fury. Since then he had always known that if he were to develop an illness himself, that period in his life and these thoughts would be his trigger for acute episodes. The empty futility of Sue's suicide would wreak its havoc again, and the evil it contained despite Sue herself would be released to whip through history like a Shakespearian curse, starting with his own life and who knew ending where. He shuddered very slightly under the duvet, making Laura stir but not wake. There were very good reasons for keeping a sharp watch on these thought patterns of course, but loving Laura might finally be a way of saying goodbye to Sue. Alex felt comforted by the idea, and was able to dismiss the issue from his mind, save only for a resolution that he would talk to Terry about it next time he was up for the compulsory counselling that went with his job. As to what Laura had meant about there being a lot of work to do, he hoped she might be thinking aloud about all the business of how they might see as much of one another as possible, considering the needs of the children and so on, and even maybe living together, although he knew it was really ridiculously early for that last one, and he should play it very cool. Despite all that he went to sleep with images of Laura and himself opening boxes and arranging possessions in his mind.

Laura was still asleep when Alex woke, her small snores filling the room with contentment as the early morning sun filtered through the pale cotton curtaining. This had been designed to fit some other house, and from where its edges now did not quite meet the window frame, brightness splashed in pools onto the laminate flooring and the bed. It had been this that had woken him, some edge of brilliance finding his eyes and forcing them into wakefulness. Leaning over the side of the bed he retrieved his wristwatch from his tumbled clothes, and as he registered 07:45 Laura turned over towards him and half woke.

'Hello, lover,' she said sleepily.

'Hi there. I'm going to make some tea, OK? Don't get up, I need a pee anyway.'

'Lovely. No sugar. It's all in the kitchen.'

Alex gazed out of the tiny window as he waited for the unfamiliar kettle to boil. Christ, her garden was even worse than his. Bindweed was threatening to engulf the far end, crawling up some young tree he couldn't name and spreading over the remains of a trellis which he could see also supported one of those climbing plants, wisteria or clematis perhaps. Nearer the house an attempt had been made to cut the small lawn fairly recently, but the push-along mower had been abandoned in the middle of the task, leaving the unmown half more than ankle deep and sporting a fine crop of daisies and dandelions. In the flowerbeds, plants he tentatively identified as hollyhocks and lupins fought with knee-high grasses, while dried out and weedy pots containing the carcasses of God knew what adorned the decking area he could just glimpse abutting the wall. Above everything a washing line was stretched on a pole, and the sun was doing its best to steam the dew off a pair of jeans, some knickers and a bra abandoned there since they were washed. Well, perhaps he could help with the garden sometime if she would let him, it might be fun to do it together. He sloshed the boiling water onto the teabags and wished that he hadn't got to go into the hospital today. Perhaps he could put it off, he mused, but dismissed the idea almost immediately. Unless he caught up with his paperwork his clinical time was going to be badly threatened, and he couldn't bear the self-reproach that would bring. Besides which, he'd been stupid enough to tell people he would be in, and if he didn't turn up it would look odd and embarrassing. At least on a Saturday he could more or less choose when he appeared, but he felt a moment of hopeless anger that they were all in a trade in which to get the job done properly you had to eat into your own time. The bottomless pit of NHS spending had a sharp end, and they were on it. Damn, blast and buggery bollocks to it all, he wanted to be with Laura, and it wasn't fair. He extracted the tea bags and poured the milk.

Actually that was pretty childish, Alex thought. He was meant to be a grown man and he would be able to see Laura this evening. Which reminded him that they still hadn't given one another their mobile telephone numbers.

That was important, he didn't like the thought of them not being able to get in touch, he'd had enough of that yesterday when he'd been waiting for her in the pub. Now there would be no embarrassment about asking her. He'd traversed the small distance to the foot of the precipitous stairs and was preparing himself for the ginger ascent with scalding liquid when the sound of a small snore reached him, and he smiled. Tea could obviously wait for a bit, and in the meantime he could write down his number. Placing the mugs on the coffee table he searched in the pocket of his jeans for his tobacco, producing at length a crinkled and dangerously near empty packet of Golden Virginia into which he had also stuffed his papers. He rolled himself a satisfactory cigarette from the drying strands and dust with the dexterity taught by perpetual and largely self-inflicted shortage of money, and took his tea over to Laura's desk. On the left hand side of this was a pile of papers, the top one a blank sheet of lined A4, and in front of the computer monitor there was a biro. He took the paper, lit his cigarette, wrote "ME," his mobile and landline numbers, and as an afterthought added the first line of his address just in case she wasn't sure.

For a moment Alex hesitated as to where to put the note he had created, in front of the monitor or back on top of Laura's papers, before deciding that she might miss it if he jumbled it up with the other stuff. Accordingly he placed it on its own in neatly isolated prominence and weighed it down with the pen. That would do, he thought, and he leaned back in the chair and took a sip of tea, idly letting his eye wander over the whole desk as he smoked in quiet enjoyment. He looked at the pile of papers again. There was a picture on the top sheet now which he thought at first might be a gaudily coloured piece of the children's homework. Davie and Lizzie they were called. He'd seen them in the pub sometimes and he thought they were nice kids, although recently according to Laura, Lizzie had been showing signs of all the grumpiness of adolescence. But surely no child could have done these drawings. He looked closer, taking the page from the pile. The image of the Virgin was excellent. He'd no idea that Laura could do this stuff as well as everything else, although of course he'd heard her discussing Lucien Freud with Andrea. For a moment he felt mildly threatened by what seemed to be the inexhaustible variety of her talents, until he remembered the state of her garden again and grinned. He didn't like people too perfect.

Alex's mood changed as he read the rest of the paper and looked at the final illustration. Too perfect maybe not, but now he was getting seriously concerned again. He'd almost forgotten about his worries in the warmth of their lovemaking. But he had seen material like this before, the constant repetition of words, the apparently meaningless diagrams that were the expression of an interior logic that only the patient could see, but he or she with absolute clarity. An empty, clinical feeling crept over him as he read the recurring words 'Brightly' and 'Murder' with their splashes and lines carrying whorls of colour across the page. This can only have been done within the last couple of days, and with growing desperation he tried to shut out the memories of endless Art Therapy Groups with patients in full-blown mania. He looked at the page again, at the whirling words and the boat in full sail. Surely there must be something he'd missed, maybe Laura was simply too clever for him and he hadn't seen some other obvious pattern, but he couldn't make sense of anything. And it wasn't as though she were using mathematical formulae, for instance. He'd known one chap, a brilliant former professor of Mathematics, confound his own diagnosis simply because nobody could tell if he were mad or a genius or both. But Laura wasn't like that. She was using things he could understand like words and drawings.

Alex's need to reassure himself was stronger than his misgivings about Laura's privacy, and he pulled the rest of her notes towards him and began to flick through them. None of the pages offered him any comfort. Each was as frankly barmy-looking to him as the last, names and places conjoined without any apparent sense or order in an Underground map of coloured pencil, rambling notes interrupted by outbursts of Anglo-Saxon against, of all people, the man Brightly. On the very last page were some extremely recondite-looking references to *Civ. Dei.* and *Conf* followed by 'Speak to A. about Aug. and Freud' in heavy double underlining. He could at least understand that bit, it was what she had been talking about last night in the pub, and so probably these notes were the day and night's work she had spoken about then. He groaned inwardly and his mind began to grind towards a hypothesis, doing its own thing despite his reluctance and fear.

For a horrible moment before she'd noticed Alex's T-shirt, shoes and socks on the floor and the smell of tobacco drifting up from downstairs, Laura had panicked after she woke up. Now smiling with desire and relief she tiptoed to the top of the stairs to surprise and mock-reproach him for the lack of tea, and he was all lovely with his top off and his back half turned towards her at the computer chair. He was reading her work from yesterday, and she was again instantly filled with the certainty of the rightness of connections and coincidences which were not coincidences at all but the magical way in which things were working out, and she wanted to laugh aloud for happiness, except that would spoil the surprise, so instead she offered a silent prayer of thanksgiving.

Then she said to Alex to tease him, 'Hello again, gorgeous, have you forgotten me already?' It had just the right effect. He jumped and turned around hastily, doing his best to wave her notes around casually before placing them with a shamed face on an approximation to their correct position. He looked like a schoolboy suddenly caught at the wrong end of the playground, his ridiculousness causing her to bubble up inside with suppressed giggles. 'Make some more tea,' she ordered to play with him. 'I'll be down in a minute.'

Damn, she'd caught him, thought Alex as he did as he was told. He shouldn't have pried like that, he would be cross if someone had done it to him. His folly and arrogant failure to stick to proper practice concerning permissions and privacy could make life difficult now, and he was a bloody fool for not thinking of the reasons why they were there in the first place. On top of that, the thought of displeasing Laura filled him with the kind of dread that somehow always made him feel hungry for comfort food, banana custard or porridge or something. A promising looking tin yielded up some digestive biscuits and he took a pile to munch in the sitting room, turning over in his head what he should say and wondering whether he had snookered himself. He heard her foot on the stairs and then Laura was standing in the room and picking up her mug of tea, dressing gown clad and in brushed-hair delightfulness despite him.

'Glad to see you've made yourself at home,' she said, and took one of his biscuits. Oh God, she really was cross, Alex thought, and as usual she had been too quick for him and got in first, before he'd had time to get his brain in gear. He took a deep breath.

'Look, Laura, I'm really terribly sorry, I shouldn't have been reading your stuff, it's really very rude of me, but I was looking for a piece of paper to write my phone number on, and I sort of got intrigued.' He watched as Laura crossed over to the desk and took up the single sheet in his handwriting. He was confused as she turned to smile broadly at him.

'What on earth are you talking about? I meant the biscuits,' she said. 'Don't be so silly. Thanks for the numbers: I'll ring you and then you can put mine in.' She went to sit next to him on the sofa, placing the tea and telephone numbers on the coffee table and turning his face to kiss him on the lips, sliding her tongue into his mouth and stroking him through his jeans. Thoughts of banana custard were driven from Alex's mind as he kissed her back in surprise and relief.

'Anyway,' she said, 'I wanted to talk to you about all that stuff. I already told you about some of it. I'm glad you read it, it's all part of something much bigger.' This was good, Alex thought, although he registered enough to wonder what was bigger apart from the obvious, and the nagging thought still reproached him that what he had done without her permission was an intrusion and only Laura's elevated state of mind had let him off the hook.

'That's nice of you,' he said, 'but it was still cheeky of me.'

'Oh, balls, darling. That's what it's all about, love and communication in community.' She was baffling him now.

'I don't understand,' he said, but his clinical experience rose to the surface as he realised that here was a possible opportunity to engage Laura in some meaningful exchange and to probe her awareness. But Laura just laughed and hugged him, and whispered into his ear.

'You will, I promise you.'

'Laura, darling, what do you mean…' but it was no good, she had undone his jeans and simply said, 'Later, honey bunny,' and was taking him in her mouth. This felt extremely pleasurable and for some time he gave in, but it was ridiculous to carry on in front of an open window giving straight onto the street at a time of day when people were going to work. She moaned in pleasure and he could feel himself tightening up.

'Laura,' he said, 'Stop it, there are people outside.' He wriggled away from her just as he saw a man in a pork pie hat passing on the far side pavement. Laura laughed.

'Let's give them something to watch then,' she said, and stood up, threw her dressing gown to the far side of the room with a dramatic gesture and strode naked to the low window.

'We're fucking because we're in love,' she proclaimed loudly and triumphantly, raising her arms above her head and then bringing them down to cup her hands around her breasts, which she proceeded to wobble at the glass, making 'Obble-obble' noises and laughing.

Precipitated by panic, Alex stuffed his still-tumescent member painfully quickly into his jeans and sprinted round the side of the coffee table to take Laura in his arms and get between her and the window. Glancing hurriedly up the road he noted pork pie hat's apparently unconcerned progress towards the Town with some relief. But who the hell else had seen was anybody's guess. Laura was still laughing and waving over his shoulder, shouting, 'Coo-eee, this is my lover' at anybody who might care to hear. Suddenly the absurdity of the situation was too much for him, and as despite himself he started laughing too as a pleasurable plan of possible rescue formed in his mind.

'Upstairs, you naughty girl,' he said, and slapped her on the rump. Laura yelped, giggled and ran towards the bedroom with Alex in slightly out of breath but enormously thankful pursuit.

Twenty-three

It was bacon roll for breakfast. He'd enjoyed that. He was always glad when they brought him food, because he was sometimes scared they would forget but they never did. He'd eaten it carefully, rotating it round and round as he took nibbly bites and watching the pattern in the bread getting smaller and smaller until he'd just been left with one round bit he could put in his mouth all at once. Then he'd drunk the rest of his tea, which was sweet and nice. It made him think of the kitchen table at home with its plastic top and Mum and him talking. Mum was always drinking tea, she said it was much better than what his dad used to drink all the time. Sometimes Drew felt like she was telling him off for what his dad had been, which wasn't fair because he'd upped and offed back to Ireland when Drew was still a baby. He'd never had a real Dad. George was the nearest thing he'd ever got.

Thinking like this wasn't helping, it made him want to cry again. He lay on the bed-thing and tried to concentrate on the patterns in the ceiling. If you looked carefully you could join the cracks in the plaster together and see a man's face, and a cloud, and something that might be a rope except that if you forgot about the man's face and let your eyes go out of focus his nose became a head and then the rope turned into a scary snake. He'd used to buy them in the corner shop when he was little, rubber ones to tease his Mum with, and she'd always pretended to be frightened and he would laugh. He couldn't see any of the patterns any more, his eyes were swimming and he wiped the tears angrily from his cheeks. He closed his eyes and tried to sleep away everything horrible.

'OK, Janey, you go and get him and sit in, OK? Lots of tenderness like we said. Got some fags?' The policewoman nodded at Dom, her black hair bobbing prettily against the lovely Afro-Caribbean face. 'Good. I bet he smokes. Tissue box to hand?' Another bob.

'Certainly have, Guv.' She smiled. God, she was something, Dom thought, and for a second his mind was full of Motown Music and the Three Degrees squirming in sequinned dresses before he realised with a comically heavy heart that to such a girl this was ancient history. He smiled back at her, thinking fondly of his wife as he had taught himself to do in such moments. In fact Janey's good-humoured intelligence and sensible sexiness reminded him a great deal of Deborah, and that was why he probably had such a soft spot for her. He hoped he didn't let it show too much.

'Right. The social worker's Karen Hunter-Waddington. I think you already know her?'

'Yes, I've worked with her before. Nice woman.'

'Yes, she is. Very efficient, bang on with the law and absolutely on the side of getting the job done in everybody's best interests. I rate her enormously. OK then, let's go.'

Dom followed Jane Roberts down the corridor, vaguely trying to practice the Guardianship of the Eyes taught to him in his youth by not looking at her bottom.

'Hello, Andrew.' A lady police officer had come into his

cell and she was smiling at him. She was black. Drew hadn't had much to do with black people before, there had only been one or two at school, and when they came on the telly sometimes Mum would say that they should go back to their own country. Except for Stevie Wonder and Lenny Henry, he noticed she liked them. Once he had fallen off the slide at the Prom and hurt his leg, and when they had gone to A and E the doctor had been black and Mum had been rude about him afterwards. But Drew hadn't minded, the doctor had nice hands and was kind to him and he'd got to ride in an ambulance, which was great because he was only seven. So he didn't know what to think really. Once he'd asked George about it and George had said that everybody was made in God's image, dear boy, and colour and sex had nothing to do with it. That sounded nice to Drew but since talking to Jon he'd realised that you couldn't trust anything George had said. So he just looked at the woman with her black face in her black uniform and said, 'Hello' back and wondered what was going to happen now.

'Did you enjoy your breakfast?' she said, still smiling.

'Yes, thank you,' he said.

'Good. Now listen, we're going to ask you a few more questions, OK? Mrs Hunter-Waddington will be there again to make sure you're OK, and me. I'm called Janey. And Inspector McGahan. Have you seen him before?'

Drew thought so, he remembered a fat thoughtful-looking man who didn't say much but seemed to be in charge because everybody called him 'Guv' like in *The Bill*. He nodded.

'I think so.'

'OK, then. You've got the boss today, so you're quite the celebrity. Come on, let's go.'

Drew did as he was told and went with the black

woman called Janey down the corridor. He knew what she was trying to do, he wasn't that thick, being nice to him and all that. But nobody had smiled at him for so long that he couldn't help feeling better because of her.

By the time Janey knocked on a door Drew's mind was already responding in its conditioned way to the easy seductions of kindness.

Insp. Patrick McGahan
P.C. Jane Roberts
Social Worker: Mrs Karen Hunter-Waddington.
Andrew Halloran

Insp. McGahan: So, Andrew, what we want to do this morning is for you to help us to understand a little bit more about Mr Brightly. Do you think you can do that?

Halloran: I didn't do nothing, I said before.

Insp. McGahan: OK then. Maybe there's been a mix-up. Sometimes things like that happen. Sometimes the police get it wrong and then it's up to people like me to find out what really happened and put it right. Perhaps you can help me with that, what do you think?

Halloran: I don't know.

Insp. McGahan: You did know Mr Brightly, didn't you, Andrew?

Halloran: Yes. Doesn't mean I done anything though.

Insp. McGahan: Andrew, I want you to try and put that stuff on one side for a moment. Nobody here is trying to catch you out. This isn't like school. Teachers were always trying to catch me out, pinning the blame on me for things, yes? What we want to do is just to try to understand what Mr Brightly was like for a while, OK?

Halloran: OK.

Insp. McGahan: You used to go out sailing with him, didn't you? Did he teach you to sail?

Halloran: Yes. Me and a lot of the other boys from School. We used to go out weekends and that. Still doesn't mean I done anything.

Insp. McGahan: Did you enjoy it?

Halloran: Sometimes. I liked the sailing.

Insp. McGahan: OK, that's really interesting. So there was a sort of club, was there? A kind of weekend sailing club that George ran?

Halloran: It wasn't like a club, I mean there weren't any rules and that and we didn't have a name or anything. George would just like, get us together and we'd go out.

Insp. McGahan: So there weren't any subscriptions or stuff like that. George paid for everything?

Halloran: I think so.

Insp. McGahan: That seems very kind. Was he a very generous man then, do you think? I mean, he never asked you to do anything in return?

Halloran: Mum liked him. She always said he was nice.

Insp. McGahan: OK then Drew, it seems like George was very good to you. When did you start being friends with him?

Halloran: When I was doing my First Communion classes at church. George like helped teach my class, and he use to walk me back home to my Mum, and he got to know her and started taking me out for treats and that.

Insp. McGahan: So you would have been what, about ten, eleven then?

PC Roberts: For the benefit of the tape, Andrew is nodding.

Insp. McGahan: You said your Mum liked him? Did you like him?

Halloran: Yes.

Insp. McGahan: OK. Drew, were there ever any bits of your friendship with George that you didn't want your Mum to know about?

Halloran: *Pause 35 secs. (inaudible)*

PC Roberts: Here, Andrew, have a tissue. When you feel a bit better can you speak up a bit? Take your time, love. OK now?

Insp. McGahan: Those videotapes we found on George's boat. You know the ones I mean. Was that the sort of thing you didn't want Mum to know about?

Halloran: *(inaudible, then)* Yes.

Insp. McGahan: Did you just watch the tapes with him, or did he make you do other stuff?

Halloran: Other stuff as well. I really hated it at the end but it was like I couldn't stop him. I'm sorry.

Insp. McGahan: With the other boys or was it just you?

Halloran: *Pause 15 secs, (inaudible, then)* Just me.

Insp. McGahan: Did you feel angry about it?

Halloran: I didn't, like, when it started because I was just a kid, but I did when I got older.

Insp. McGahan: Well done, Drew, you're doing really well. I wish we had talked to you sooner. Drew, I've got to tell you something. We've found your fingerprints all over the bolt croppers we found in the boat. We know they were used to kill George because of the shape of the wounds you made in him. Plus we've got his blood from your clothes, although I know you washed them.

PC Roberts: Are you OK, Andrew? Do you want another tissue?

Halloran: What will happen to me?

Insp. McGahan: Drew, you killed George Brightly because of the sex things he did with you, didn't you?

Halloran: Yes.

Insp. McGahan: Before you did it, did you ever think of

talking to anyone about what was going on?

Halloran: I couldn't, like, say anything to nobody.

Mrs Hunter-Waddington: I think that may be enough for this morning, what do you think Inspector? Andrew has done very well.

End

'This is awful.' Karen Hunter-Waddington looked in Dom's eyes as though hoping for some sort of reassurance. It wasn't something he felt he could give her. This confrontation with real horror filled him with an emotional nausea. And he'd winged it. He'd never had any real evidence about why Halloran had killed Brightly, just a list of material that had combined what he knew to be his prejudices to form a pattern in his mind. And if Halloran had clammed up, if he hadn't just then been at some critical emotional stage in which the added pressure of questioning had been too much for him to hold the pain back any longer, things might really have gone wrong and made matters worse for him. Certainly Karen would be behaving very differently. She would never have let him get away with it, and would have been right not to.

'Yes, it is,' he said. And he was pretty awful too. He was overcome with self hatred for what he saw as a wicked irresponsibility in his over-reliance on a supposed ability to see patterns that might not be there. It was as though some foul thing left over from what they had discovered was seeking to destroy his lack of confidence and self-esteem.

A police officer passed them in the strip-lit corridor. Here a miscellany of posters and notices were presided over by Sergeant Hibbert, whose frequent and increasingly furious series of reminders about keeping boards tidy had become an amusing diversion from the tedium of station life. Dom shook himself slightly, feeling with surprise his tight, dry mouth as the thought of Ted Hibbert's frenzied rages lifted his spirits slightly. Word would have got round the station by now, and he framed in his mind what he was going to say. Only please don't let them clap, but that was too much too ask of the idiot section. As they approached the door to the briefing room he became aware of Karen again, who had stopped just in front of him and appeared to want to say something. Of course, this was where they were to leave one another, the quick bond of intensity of experience being broken by the intrusions of life.

'OK,' she said, searching in a pretty but, Dom guessed, practical large bag in some sort of Indian pattern. He bet it was a fair trade one, and liked her for it. 'I'm going to the office to report back, and then I am with his mother. I want to come back and see him in the late half of the afternoon, all right?'

'Of course it is. I want you to have access all the time, any time you want. If you have any problems, get directly in touch with me.' He handed her his card, all blue and red and resplendent. 'I'm sorry it's so pompous-looking but I suppose it saves time, not to speak of my memory.'

'Thanks. Here's mine.' She looked at him carefully. She didn't feel that great herself, it was quite a hammering she'd got and she badly needed a cup of tea and to talk to someone about it in the office. Vaguely she wondered if she looked as grimly upset and inappropriately tired as he did, and the thing that had made her a social worker started pushing at her mind again.

'Are you OK?' she asked, and Dom laughed grimly.

'Do I look that bad? Well, I suppose I could say that I've had better days. Like you I suspect.'

'Yes,' Karen said, 'you could say that.' For a moment there was a silence between them as each were lost in contemplation. Dom broke it.

'No, I shall be OK. But thanks,' he said. 'Listen, it'll be over to the Prison Service and the courts soon. I think it's important we keep in close touch. You'll be all right?'

'Sure. Fine. I'll talk to one of the girls at work. We're agreeing to keep one another in the loop, then?' and despite his professional liking for Karen he could not stop from wincing internally, and he rebuked himself as they said their goodbyes. By the time he had his hand on the briefing room door he knew that during his conversation with her his mind had already framed what he was going to say there by some mysterious process of its own.

'Right, ladies and gents, Andrew Halloran has confessed.' They had been sitting or lounging around comfortably, and he had noticed the sudden quickening of tension as he came in, the backsides removed from desks and the keyboards clattering to a stop with his first words. Now as he looked at them he saw the equal and opposite reaction working, the smiles breaking out, Darren Wright rolling his fist into a ball and jerking it back with his elbow as if in some triumphant moment in a football match, and the predictable ripple of applause. He held his hand up.

'All right, that's enough. Well done everybody.'

Wright and Earl were preening themselves, probably in expectation of being singled out for praise.

'Good team work all round, from the arresting officers to the result.' That was enough. It was all they were going to get, anyway. He looked around the rest of the room.

'There's something else I want to say. While we're all no doubt pleased by the speed and success of this investigation, the major reason it's been so easy is because of Halloran himself. He was a pretty incompetent murderer. He left enough forensic lying around to convict him five times over. What we've learned from his confession, and from some of the other evidence as well, is that Andrew Halloran was systematically sexually abused by Brightly, a pillar of the community, from when he was aged ten.' Dom felt the anger rising in him now and he cleared his throat in an attempt to keep his voice steady.

'Andrew Halloran killed George Brightly because he felt he couldn't tell anybody about what was going on and there was nobody who could help him. I think we all of us need to reflect on the fact that Brightly was a criminal menace nobody picked up on. Not the social services, not the schools and churches he associated with, not the sailing fraternity, and certainly not us. As a result he's dead, and God knows how much other information has died with him. You can probably all imagine what Halloran's life is going to be like from now on. I want us all to think about that in terms of what we have been saying about the importance of getting out into the community and forging those relationships of trust where kids like Andrew can feel they can come to us. In the meantime, while he's still with us, Mrs Hunter-Waddington is to have absolute free access to him. Those of you who have to see Halloran are to treat him with kindness and kid gloves. This is a boy whom society has profoundly failed, and the beginning of repairing such damage as we can is going to start here, in co-operation with our colleagues in Social Services. That's all.'

Inspector McGahan half-turned to speak to Ted Hibbert and the room was relaxing again. Papers were being picked up, brisk movements were being made between desks, and heads were turning back to computer screens. Darren Wright was confused and angry, he'd expected more than this, it was bloody typical. He spat his resentment quietly at Mick from the side of his mouth.

'Bloody wanker, he makes it sound like it was our fault.'

Mick shrugged minutely. 'That's them for you, though, isn't it? They haven't got a clue.' Dom saw the interchange and felt his jaw tighten with anger.

'Ted,' he said, 'I don't want Wright or Earl anywhere near the Halloran boy from now on, understand?' He was making a mental list, and it was getting longer.

Twenty-four

Alex spun the wheel of his ancient and battered Fiesta so that its tyres scrunched the new gravel of the Maple Centre car park together a little more. It was rather a satisfying noise, like biting into a chocolate wafer, and the car's slight sliding to its stop reminded him of childhood and go-carts made from odd bits of wood and pram wheels bouncing in the alley behind his house. He liked the small pleasures that accompanied his daily arrival at work. They made a marker between the two halves of his life, easing the transition from Mootborough to hospital and clearing his mind for the day ahead. Today he had a little more time to enjoy them and in any case he wanted to be alone to think about Laura. In front of him were the hospital fields, land owned by the Trust but not yet built on, new cut by the gang mower beneath chestnuts to make the delightful play place of squirrels, rabbits and even, it was rumoured, the occasional badger. There were several wooden benches dotted about. He walked towards one, vaguely hoping but unconvinced that his toes kicking against the tops of cut and discarded grass bundles were releasing more of the summer smell of cricket fields, childhood picnics and first kisses.

Sitting down, Alex contemplated the image of sharp, modern efficiency projected by the Maple Centre. It was very different from the blankly frightening aspect of the former Victorian workhouse in Amblehurst where he had done his training and first job. There each aggressively angular gable, the dim, tunnel-like corridors and the cheap dark bricks seemed to him to have been deliberately designed to oppress the spirit. He guessed that the nineteenth-century architect had taken it for granted that his job was to remind the uniformed and de-sexed inmates that they were the refuse of society, migrants and failures for whom an industrial time had no place and who, in the vicious self-righteousness of the golden age of the Queen Empress, were to be held responsible for the poverty and degradation into which famine and the Market had placed them. Alex had hated the place both ideologically and aesthetically. Remembering the old building he rolled a cigarette in angry solidarity with the Proletariat and the mental patients who had succeeded them. No tailor-mades for him. Even patients he had known had been pushed out of sight, an embarrassment to be ignored or spoken of in hushed tones, successors of the workshop inmates in more ways than the architecture that symbolised for him their alienation. The grey, sweet smoke surrounded him as he exhaled, and he thought of Doris Carter's hair nodding frantically up and down at him from above her ancient face. An inpatient at Amblehurst, she had talked incessantly of the baby that had been taken from her when she was sixteen after whose conception she had been forcibly consigned to a psychiatric hospital as a moral imbecile in the late Twenties. By the Eighties it had been frankly admitted that there had never been anything wrong with her or the others like her except the damage done by decades of institutionalisation. A handful of people had gone to Doris's funeral, all of them patients or staff, and Alex had been one of them. So on the whole he was pleased by the low-rise, large windowed Maple Centre with its neat notice board and inside, its bright murals and jolly plastic-covered fittings. Budgetary overspends, the uncaring cost-cutting exercises of successive governments and the shortage of acute beds notwithstanding, Alex had long ago decided that he was permanently committed to the Care in the Community of which the Centre was the local hub while still supplying secure and acute accommodation. He and Sue had spoken of it as the active expression of compassion in a society that was at last learning to turn its back on the canting hypocrisy of a Christianity that had long forgotten that even on its own terms, its God had gone out to the outcasts, the lepers, tarts and possessed.

Once, Alex remembered, he and Sue had been at a party and there had been this very posh elderly woman, all tweed skirt, cashmere jumper, teeth and pearls beside the fire. When she'd been told that Alex was a mental health nurse she had begun to complain loudly that, My goodness, everybody these days seemed to be talking about depression and Post Traumatic Stress Disorder, and what a Lot of Nonsense it was and in Her Day you just had to Get on With It, you Never Heard any of that Sort of Thing. Alex had been furious, he'd wanted to tell her that was because you lot just locked the poor bastards up, or about the patient of his round her age who didn't dare sleep with the light off or look at a graveyard and who sometimes ate his own shit ever since he had been a bulldozer driver at the liberation of Belsen. Instead he had merely said, 'You're right, we are wasting our time,' and walked away to refresh his glass, leaving Sue to make her excuses and raise a concerned eyebrow at him over the drinks table. Speaking later about it at home she had told him that according to the rumours, Mrs Carter was a tremendous busybody at church. They had a nice bitchy time then, discussing how for some it appeared that their certainty of being made just by their faith seemed to obviate the necessity for imagination, empathy, or any desire to inform themselves.

Alex didn't think Laura was like that. The marginally difficult fact that she was a Catholic and that he felt slightly out of his depth there slightly disturbed him, but so far it seemed to have had no impact on their relationship. Certainly not, he reflected with cynical amusement, on the sex. Laura had said it was a sacrament, and he guessed that this was maybe how she used the highest language she could find to express their shared joy and perhaps stop herself feeling guilty. Although he wasn't absolutely sure what a sacrament was that was certainly fine with him, and for a moment he felt himself stir with pride and lust as he remembered the absolute open nakedness with which she had presented him. As far as her faith was concerned, he was well used to coming across that sort of stuff in his work and would offer her what the textbooks said, 'supportive and non-critical acceptance of the patient's cultural beliefs'. And damn, now that P-word really meant he had to follow where his mind had been leading him this morning, and for once permit the two halves of his life to integrate with one another, so contrary to his usual inclinations and practice. Though transmitting their images still to his optic nerves the trees and buildings receded from his attention as reluctantly he turned it towards this new and painful act of love.

Evidence, hypothesis, test and conclusion. Alex forced himself to think of Laura in these terms, the tools of a social science taken to her personality as one might in an absurd moment take a pair of pinking shears to a Van

Gogh. For a few seconds the sense of disloyalty he had felt on reading the pile of notes on her desk returned and he nearly abandoned his train of thought before telling himself that was too easy and the anxieties that had been knocking at the doors of his intellect would merely return. If they were well founded then there were significant issues about Laura's health that he could not in all conscience ignore if he were serious about loving her. He had to be careful about casting himself in the role of Saviour, though. It could well be that his concerns about her were really to do with his desire to have saved Sue, an egotistical projection from his past with him as hero. There were good reasons why mental health workers were discouraged from counselling their partners, and Love was not always a good diagnostician. He sighed. The mental gymnastics of all of this were beginning to weary him and he was aware that he was in danger of getting into a paralysing circle of indecision of the kind that could sometimes lead to a dangerous inactivity. He had to get on with it, it would not leave him alone and he had done his best to think about the possible pitfalls.

The tattered, ancient briefcase Alex loved and which he had bought at a Peace Fair in Cambridge had a gently abrasive texture where the polished surface of the leather had been worn by who knows how many years of handling. It rubbed against his hand agreeably as he ground out his dog-end with his deck shoes and walked towards the Centre. He had intended to do as many as possible of the Care Plans it contained and which were making its sides bulge today, but now he had decided that he wouldn't start them until he'd tried to get this Laura thing more worked out.

Twenty-five

'So, what we gonna do?' Leo's face was half lit by the sunshine as he looked at Jon, the shadows on his features mimicking his anxiety. The others were there too, gathered by phone calls and Internet messages to the Prom. Jon felt a weight of responsibility overcome him together with its excitement. As soon as he'd watched the News he'd realised why when Drew had rung him he'd sounded so weird and uptight. At first he'd nearly panicked, he'd had to have a smoke, and then he'd wandered over to the Mootborough Arms to sit with a Guinness and a whiskey. It had been dark in the pub, the high-sided pews like confessionals against the nicotine stained glass and the magpie priest colours of the Guinness working in his mind to make a careful self-examination. Had they really meant what they'd said about killing George? What Drew had done had made the situation urgent and dangerous, and the question required them all to have the same answer. As he'd contemplated his pint he knew that as the oldest the others would be looking to him for leadership, that he was going to have to pay now for his easy dominance by protecting them and himself and making sure they were all agreed on a line. He'd finished his drinks and within an hour set up a meeting.

Now the river breeze was chilling the sun-and-anxiety

sweat on Jon's face and under his T-shirt, as he leant against the field's fence. The chain link hammocked under the weight of his back as he used the rolling of a cigarette to make the others wait for his answer to Leo's question, drawing out the tension until he could sense their nervous concentration. The brass Zippo lighter he'd bought in a head shop in London felt smooth and cold under his fingers, its leaf design finely tracing itself on his palm as he flicked the top back, closed and thrust it into the pocket of the thin jeans that emphasised the uncompromising skinniness of his frame.

'OK, I guess we're all a bit tense. I've been doing a lot of thinking and I reckon I've got the situation sorted. But first, has anybody spoken to the police, or had the coppers talk to them, anything like that?'

Around him Jon could sense the circle relax, and that was good, that was what he had wanted the reaction to be because it meant that they would be willing to do exactly as he told them, as long as they remembered it of course. Christ, one of them was only fourteen. They were all shaking their heads.

'Good. They haven't talked to me neither. What I think is this, OK? Drew's obviously killed George. He's managed to balls it up and get himself arrested. And we're all nervous because of the shock and that conversation we had last time we were here. If Drew tells the police about that, if he tries to grass us up we could end up in deep shit. Am I right?' There were nods and murmurs of assent.

'OK, listen. This is what we do. First, I don't think we should assume that Drew is going to tell the coppers anything about us. We've all been keeping one another's secrets for years and I don't see why Drew should suddenly change. We're his mates after all, and although

221

he's thick in lots of ways I reckon that he'll know that when all of this is over in one way or another he's going to have to face us. It's in his interest to keep shtoom.'

'Yeah, but wha' if they get it out of him somehow? We don't know what the coppers are like, do we?' Greg's freckled and ginger-topped face was screwed up and there were tears in his eyes. He looked as though he was going to lose it, and Jon made a quick mental note.

'Right. I was coming to that. OK, let's suppose that Drew does tell them everything. What do we do then? The way I see it is the coppers will come looking to talk to each of us. What we've got to decide is what we are going to say and each stick to it. Otherwise we'll be contradicting one another and we'll all be fucked. Understand?' Again the nods of agreement. He had them so far, this was going well.

'The most dangerous thing we can do is to say that we never had that conversation about getting rid of George. The police are bound to think that's bollocks.'

'Why?' Greg again, now leaning forward with what seemed to be interested hope, definitely Jon's yardstick for how all this was going down.

'Well, wouldn't you? I would. I mean, the police will see that it's pretty unlikely Drew would be able to make up a whole story about our conversation and stick to it. Apart from anything else he wouldn't be able to remember the details. And it's dangerous as well because on that day we met there were people walking their dogs and that, and somebody is bound to have seen us together. It would only take one of them to say something and we would have to explain what we were doing against what Drew had said. See?' They saw.

'OK. Now this is what we do. We admit to everything about the conversation, how we discussed bumping off

George and that, but we each say that we didn't take it seriously. As far as each and every one of us is concerned we were just fantasising, pipe dreaming and that.'

'But why should we want to do that?' Leo asked. 'They're going to want to know why, and I don't...' His voice trailed off and he stared out across to the green and red buoys which marked the deep channel at high tide, but were now aground on the slickness of the ebb's mud. Jon looked at Leo. He had anticipated this danger and had felt it himself. It was all about the fear of humiliating exposure, the agony of parents and of facing them, the dread of a help which was even more terrifying than the fear of punishment, the cruelty of sideways looks and silence and the distaste of friends.

'OK,' he said again, 'This is the clever bit. We fantasised about killing George because we had heard rumours that he was a nonce, and we said that was what he deserved if he was one. None of us really took it seriously and it was only after Drew did what he did that we realised that George must have been noncing Drew. And, if anybody sees us here today and we get asked about it, that is what we have been talking about. We have been going on about how shocked we all are, and even whether we should go to the Police ourselves, but we hadn't decided yet because we were a bit scared. None of you have been nonced, you are not sure about anyone else except you realise about Drew now. Unless of course you want to say you have been nonced up and go down that path. But don't involve anyone else.'

Leo looked at him sharply. 'OK, it's a personal thing. I'm like you for now. But some of us might want that kind of help.'

They went over it again and again, even explaining to Tim what a nonce was and telling him that it would be a brilliant idea for him to say to the police that he had actually first learned that word in the fantasy conversation about George's killing. They walked round and round the field, Jon badgering each of them in turn to check they had remembered what they were going to say. Eventually Jon stopped pacing and they came to a halt.

'We're all agreed then?' he asked, a final grasp at them to shake them into confidence and purpose, a coach in the dressing room in the seconds before play, a teacher in the classroom doing absolute final revision before exams. Greg blew his cheeks out and, Jon noticed with relief and pleasure, looked relieved and even happy.

'It's good, Jon. Really good. I mean, thanks.'

'Yeah.'

'Yeah, thanks Jon.'

Jon felt pleased with himself after they had each left. His reconstruction of events and the way he had sold it he knew had been brilliant, and he felt proud and powerful to have helped the others. Actually it had been so good that he nearly believed it himself, and he pushed away the thought that he knew it wasn't true, and so did God. Fortunately it would take somebody with the insight of the angels or the knowledge of the demons to know the truth, and he very much doubted the police had those sorts of resources. He'd enjoyed RE at school. He'd had a brilliant teacher and some great textbooks, and done his GCSE on St Mark. So today's talk hadn't left too bad a feeling. Little Tim had actually been crying with relief and couldn't speak as he left, but just gave Jon a kind of embarrassed hug, who'd tousled his hair and for a fraction of a moment had wanted him.

Twenty-six

Laura hugged her happiness to herself as she sang, the sparkles of water from the showerhead falling on her shoulders as the soap's smell of rosemary replaced the musk of lovemaking. Rosemary for remembrance, she thought, not that she needed any help to remember because she was alive with the suddenness of a joy in which it seemed for her now that the whole of life had become a sacrament. In this state of grace, she told herself, she was experiencing the world in its wonder for the first time, and she was finding the most acute pleasure in every sensation and object. The design of the shower gel bottle made her marvel at the ingenuity and functional artistry of mankind, the soft enveloping of the bath towel she was now gathering round herself of the lamb's wool clothes of the blessed in Paradise. She felt no need for invocatory prayer when the things around her were smiling out to her the wonders of creation as they must have smiled to Eve before the Fall. Rather to say an *Our Father*, as she had done for Alex after he had left, was to concentrate and interpret an immediate and apparently permanent sense of the presence of God, who was heaving out his love and walking in the garden of her mind. She towelled her legs vigorously. The Roman soldiers had worn their sandal straps round those muscles there, and look, there was the place where they had driven in the nails the day He paid the Snake for what Eve had done.

She pulled on her jeans, they were her best new ones, she really liked them. They had a funky understated Indian pattern near the hem and that was good because it reminded us all of the richness of cultural diversity, like that day when they'd had an African Mass at school. That had been cool, the kids had really woken up to the idea that Liturgy could be fun. She knew Alex would like the jeans. It was interesting this Alex thing because it was proof of how God can work in really unexpected ways. She would never have dreamt that he could all be part of his plan too, she was half thinking that what with the divorce and the sex and everything God might be cross, but it wasn't like that at all. When they'd made love she'd known that it was all right, God had been lurking there sacramentally behind the veil of orgasm. It had been the ultimate three-in-a-bed-experience.

Laura giggled at the idea and helped God to wriggle her into a T-shirt. It was golden yellow, the colour of the Resurrection morning and of Easter hope. Her own Easter was going to be found with Alex, he'd made love to her and she'd known that they were together and that if she was going to get to the bottom of this Brightly business he was going to have to be with her. But it was more than that really, it wasn't just like God was using Alex to prop her up so that she could do what had to be done. More like Alex had always been part of the Plan, part of her life all along which she had only needed to be revealed to her, and the extraordinary thing was how now she could see everything falling into place around her and it made her want to laugh aloud for joy.

Instinctively Laura chose muesli for breakfast, its sweet graininess reminding her to buy more healthy, organic food, although she wondered whether the issue was really about Fair Trade, organic production, or both. As she finished her cereal she decided that she had enjoyed it, which was good because often she didn't feel like eating and knew that she would most likely skip lunch. Also Fair Trade was best, and organic farming to be encouraged where possible. She consulted God about this briefly, and found him in agreement, which made her happy. She was eating with Alex tonight, he was coming round after work at six o'clock and she was going to do a Thai Chicken Curry, which was dead easy but impressive. She'd be able to talk about it all to him then, she'd known he'd wanted to this morning but she had been too excited and there hadn't been enough time and besides, you didn't tell somebody they were part of a divine plan every day. There were some supermarket chicken breasts in the freezer.

As she placed the breakfast things in the dishwasher Laura told herself that before Alex arrived there was no time to be lost in applying herself to what needed to be done about Andrew Halloran. She had already realised after her work of the other night that she had to go to the police soon to tell them what she knew. She had to admit that she was rather enjoying all of it. It would be fun to tell Alex about her day this evening. She knew it was going to be all right because look how everything had worked out so far and it was fun to feel so full of life and energy. What she needed to do was to get in touch with that police inspector, McGahan she thought he was called, and arrange to see him. She hadn't ever done that, she supposed you just rang the police station. But if it were possible she would like to see Drew as well, and she certainly didn't know how to go about arranging that. She wanted to see him because she felt so very sorry for him and she wanted to tell him that it wasn't all his fault and that people loved him and were praying for him. She wanted to take God with her into his cell, or wherever it was, she supposed it was a cell, how terrible even though of course he had done a very terrible thing, and she knew with a certainty that she had been specially chosen to do just that.

Jack. Of course, that was the obvious answer, Jack would help her. She knew they hadn't been getting on too well recently but with things as they were it would be OK, and even Jack would be caught up in this purpose and mission and their relationship would be made better by it. She smiled as she thought how that would surprise him. Anyway he would know all the answers, about whether it would be possible for her to see Drew and how she ought to go about it and about where they might send him after magistrate's court and all of that. That was an inspired idea, she thought, and smiled again as she realised the literal truth of the words and sent out a prayer in thanks. The telephone felt small and heavy in her hands as she punched in Jack's number and pressed the little green button. There was the dial tone and then the sound of the exchange, the ringing tone and finally, Jack's voice, and she realised that she had been holding her breath and sighed with relief that it wasn't Poppy.

'Hello,' he said.

'It's me.'

'Yes, I can see your number. What do you want?' Laura passed over this as deadpan humour.

'Look, Jack, I need your help. I need to see you.'

'When?'

'Well, now would be a good time, to be honest.'

'I'm extremely busy, Laura, it really isn't very convenient.'

'Oh come on, it's a Saturday.'

'Surprisingly enough you may remember that there are those of us who actually have to bring work home over the weekend. Is it about the children?'

'No…'

'Well, I honestly don't see why it can't wait for a bit. I suppose I can see you on Monday at about five o'clock.'

'Jack, it's really very important…'

'Laura, I wish you would get it into your head that unless you are in direct danger or there is something wrong with the children, there's no reason I have to do anything for you whatsoever. Last time you rang up it was nearly the middle of the night and you really upset Poppy, and I do think that she and I should be allowed to spend our weekends alone together. Now if you don't mind, we're planning a dinner party tonight, and I have to go.'

'Jack…' But Laura heard the click of the disconnecting line with astonishment.

Jack rubbed the back of his neck in frustration as he replaced the handset on its charging cradle and walked the length of the wide and high-ceilinged Georgian hall to the breakfast room and his interrupted perusal of *The Independent*. He had bought the house a couple of years ago and felt comfortable in it after the dismally designed four-bedroomed Lego-land semi he had been reduced to following his divorce. His immediate neighbours had compounded his misery there, an estate agent and his wife, for God's sake. They had treated him with an egregious social climber's bonhomie to which he had been too weak to respond with what he knew would have been his mother's marvellously crushing put-downs. He could imagine what she would have said, of how she had warned him all along about Laura and how she would plunge him into the company of the unsuitable. And of course that was exactly what had happened.

Jack very much disliked Laura and tried to think of her as little as possible these days. This was partly to protect himself. To receive a telephone call from her was to be filled with anger at her for having reduced him to those years of living well beneath the lifestyle of his friends and partners. Poppy and he could actually hear the estate agent and his wife through the walls. He hadn't lived in a house like that before except when he had shared some pretty vile digs at Cambridge. And of course it hardly helped that Laura was frequently drunk when she telephoned and would often go off in one of those blind rages, which were so bad that Poppy was frightened of even answering a call. The children, of course, realised what was going on despite his best efforts to keep his own voice level and reasonable, and naturally he was aware of the difficulties this brought them. Lizzie was an extremely sensible girl, though. From what she talked about and her choice of company it was clear that she had little time for her mother's histrionics and found them embarrassing and irritating. Often he and Lizzie had laughed about Laura when they were alone together, and he had felt proud at the way she was growing up so levelheaded, independent and amusingly cynical. Davie was another matter. He was soft and sentimental to a fault, and Jack knew his mother would have said that he got that from Laura's family and would have made some reference to dog breeding and bitches. He knew too that while Lizzie would more or less shrug off Laura's bad behaviour merely as evidence of Mum being tiresome, after a quarrel Davie would look downcast and troubled. He and Poppy had done their best to cheer the boy up when this happened, offering to take him to the cinema and such if they had the time, but he was pretty recalcitrant material to work on. Maybe it was just adolescence, but Jack didn't think so. Davie would usually say, 'No thanks, Dad,' and go off and talk on MSN on his laptop, or tell them he was going out with some of his school friends.

Of course Laura was officially meant to be ill. Jack had been having a couple of pints with Russell in the D'Aubery Hotel last week and that had come up, and he had felt as embarrassed as always in the difficulty of acknowledging that Laura was off the rails. The senior partner's huge fingers had curved around his beer mug and created the impression that he was only holding a half, but this was miraculously transformed into a pint as he laid it on the bar. Jack had nearly made a joke then about lawyer's bills, but he didn't think Russell would appreciate it and had checked himself in time. And to be honest he was getting a little sick of lawyer jokes himself, partly because Laura had enjoyed them so much, but more because since he'd been with Poppy he'd realised that they had constituted a way Laura had developed of putting him down. But people like her who made jokes like that were quick enough to come running for his time when they were in trouble. That was time which, as Poppy said, was going to be expensive because look at all the hard work he'd had to do to get where he was. Expertise like his only came free in the Health Service, and there wasn't a National Legal Service yet, thank God. It irritated him to think that probably Laura would have been able to get away with pulling Russell's leg, and that she could have carried it off with her usual show of sexy brilliance which always threatened to tip over into downright naughtiness.

Somewhere in the attic there was a picture of all four of them at Christmas, Frank's arms around Russell's shoulders and his own around Laura's waist, each of them tipsy in paper hats and hilarity. For a moment Jack felt a tweak of nostalgia as he remembered Laura's gales of laughter when Frank had pursued him round the table with a bunch of mistletoe, and his tiny ideological jealousy at the easy way in which she had accepted Frank and Russell's boisterously gay commitment to one another. It was a shame that Russell didn't seem to care for Poppy so much. The invitations had been reduced to men's drinks after work, and he knew that she was angry and jealous about that, so he took good care not to mention them.

'Presumably you still see Laura from time to time?' Russell had asked. 'How is she these days?'

'The same as she has been for a while, I think. As far as I know she's still on antidepressants. She's drinking a lot.'

'Well, don't we all?'

'Yes, but…'

'Oh, don't be such a fart, Jack. Come on, how are things really?'

So he'd risked it. Russell was an old friend, but also his boss, and he'd been conscious of how opening up to him could be useful if he played it right, cementing a kind of mentor and protégé relationship between them. So he'd talked to him about how Laura behaved, about the phone calls and the fury, about the sheer unreasonableness of the whole business, of how he had tried to do his best despite everything, about Poppy's fear and the anger he felt at his own inability to make Laura see sense. Russell had bought crisps and another couple of pints. The snacks were on the bottom shelf, and the beauty of the barmaid bending over was a delight Jack thought he was enjoying alone.

'Oh, my dear,' Russell had said, 'I didn't know it was so bad. Poor Laura.' And Jack realised with unease that Russell had outwitted him, had stood outside and picked through what he had been saying to reconstruct a story more acceptable to himself. There was a rebuke in Russell's words which was best dealt with rueful manliness.

'Oh, piss off,' he'd said, laughing.

'No, come on, seriously,' Russell had said, and Jack began to feel himself sliding into desperation. 'It sounds really horrid for her.'

'Well, it's not been a bundle of laughs for me and Poppy either.'

'Well, you've made that pretty clear anyway. Do you know, I think I am becoming tired, dear boy. I shall stagger onwards, the knowledge of your moral rectitude in the face of so many difficulties fortifying me as I go.'

'You really are a bullshitter, Russ.' Jack was near to anger, he could feel it banging against the back of his eyes.

'I know, dear heart, I know. But isn't that the joy of our profession? We, after all, are surely in some sense licensed bullshitters, and you more than most.'

'I would have thought that applied more to barristers.'

'Barristers? Dear God, you're right, they really are the Punch and Judy of the law, sweet and old-fashioned self serious thespians and ancient queens in wigs. I love them but I cannot take them seriously. So I take your point. And now I must leave. You know, I don't at all mean to be intrusive and these things are very difficult, but I don't know if I've told you that I have a niece who suffers very badly from depression and has been in hospital because of it a few times, so I do understand a bit about what Laura and you all must be going through, particularly with the children and everything. Sally has got two, and when she's ill she misses them very much.'

Russell hefted his massive bulk from the barstool. Gosh, thought Jack, even with Laura and everything it was a bit of a shock to hear him talk about family madness in such an open way in the pub, considering his position in the town and seniority in the profession. But of course maybe being an out gay you get to empathize with all sorts, and maybe Russell was senior and respected enough for it not to matter so much. Jack didn't really know what to make of it all. As he walked home and turned the conversation over in his head he was caught between Poppy's absolute, common sense diagnosis of Laura as an irredeemable alcoholic and pot-head and that other idea lingering idea in the back of his mind and now made the more urgent by what Russell had said. Laura might, just possibly, after all be really ill, even more ill than wicked, and he should have done more to help her when they were together. He didn't like thinking about all this. At the time of the divorce he'd said that he should have custody of the children. His argument had depended on the idea that Laura was not capable of looking after them, but if he was honest with himself he knew really that it had been driven by his unremitting hatred of how she had embarrassed him by losing her job, not eating, drinking their money and behaving so badly. And whenever Laura crashed into his life now she managed to humiliate him, even in her so-called illness. If she had got cancer he would have kind of known what to do, but what she had was just unfair shite for him. After all, his only contact with that sort of stuff was when you tried to make a case for diminished responsibility, and there was no way he could be responsible for Laura.

Oh my God, now came the even worse thought that people might get the idea that he had not done enough for Laura. Maybe they might think that he'd been too quick to assume that she was just being difficult and resisting treatment when the Prozac and psychotherapy didn't work. Is this was what Russell really believed? It would explain why he wouldn't invite Poppy to anything, if he suspected that she had distracted Jack from the real issue. And of course he and Laura had promised one another that it was for sickness and as well as health and all that jazz. Ironically it would have been Laura who would have pointed out that when those rules were made you were guaranteed that one or other of you would snuff it quickly, most often the woman in childbirth, and that the average length of a marriage was considerably shorter then than it was now. It was part of her argument for a liberalisation of the Catholic procedure for annulment, but Jack had never really thought very hard about those things before except as amusing mind-games.

'Who was that on the phone?' Poppy was in the kitchen doing some frightful things to a pair of ducks, the air blue from singed feathers and sweet with the smell of honey and orange.

'Guess,' said Jack, coming up behind her and wrapping his arms around her to touch the top of her legs for a reassurance he needed in its mother-sweet neediness.

'Oh, Christ, the Bitch Woman.'

'You have it in one, my dear.' He moved his hand over to her crotch and stroked her through her jeans.

'Get off, peanut brain, I've got work to do. What did she want?' Jack laughed despite himself and released his hand to search for a glass instead.

'Christ knows. She said she wanted to see me, absolutely sodding now. I'm afraid I gave her the bum's rush.'

Poppy looked up at the kitchen clock, a rather splendid number that she and Jack had picked up in Pisa last year that registered ten to twelve.

'Bloody hell,' she said, 'it's a bit early even for her surely?'

'Well of course there is that. But come on, Popsicle, I'm having a drink. Do you want one?'

'Oh, go on then, but don't make it too strong. And don't you have too much either.'

'Thank you very much my dear, but I think that I can probably handle myself.' As soon as he had said it Jack knew that it would set her off, she was laughing like some bloody magpie and saying that she was busy so maybe he would have to. Once all this had seemed charming, but now that the novelty had worn off his patience sometimes wore pretty thin. Similarly he'd never thought that *Coronation Street* would be something to which he had to accommodate his life, or that his children would learn to say 'pardon' and 'pleased to meet you'. In a weak moment he had talked to Laura about that when they were going through one of their good communicating times. But she had just laughed at him and said she didn't give two stuffs about language as a social shibboleth, and he needed to realise that he had made his choice and that the kids would survive whether they said 'pardon' or not. Then it had seemed to Jack that sometimes Laura didn't care enough, that she was too willing to leave things to Poppy when he really needed her to back him up, and this made him even more cross with her and made him want to ignore her more.

They were having syllabub after the ducks, and Poppy directed Jack in lemon squeezing and sugar weighing so that his fingers became sticky and delicious. He sucked them and wiped his hands on a tea towel in order to take up his gin and tonic, the tiny bubbles woken into action again by the movement of the glass. Surreptitiously he topped up his gin level while Poppy's back was turned, and after some excellent club sandwiches they did enjoyable things for the evening meal with vegetables, smoked salmon and table decorations for an hour or two. In this way the disturbance of the morning gave way to afternoon in the sweet idleness of the weekend. Davie was off with his friends somewhere, and Lizzie, who had briefly raided the kitchen for her share of lunch, was ensconced in her room with homework, TV and her computer.

Jack was wondering if he might try again for some surreptitious sex when there was a series of loud knocks on the front door. There were two means of gaining attention there. One was an old but still-functional electric push recessed into the wall that gave out a heart-stopping ring from the ancient black-cupped bell in the hall. Jack and Poppy liked to think this dated from the time when people still had maids, because you could hear it all over the house. Poppy in particular seemed rather pleased with this idea, and to Jack's embarrassment would mention it to guests. The other was a splendid brass knocker in the shape of a stylised greyhound. This had been used now, with the rat-a-tat-tat of urgency.

'What the hell...' Poppy began to say, and fumbled to retain the bowl in which she had been whipping the cream and other ingredients.

'Calm down, darling, it's only the door,' Jack said, although truthfully the volume of the repeated bangs had awoken his curiosity too and only his pleasure at seeing Poppy disconcerted had prevented him from an involuntary exclamation as well. 'Probably one of Davie's mates.'

'He's meant to be out,' Poppy snapped. Jack was so sluggish sometimes, except of course about one thing, he was quick off the mark enough for that, and it was so out

237

of place. She had a sudden memory of his hands on her while she was working earlier. He didn't seem to realise how distracting it could be when she was trying to do her best for him. Cooking was the one thing where she felt she could be in control and compete with him on her own professional terms, and it made her angry when he did that thing of disrespecting her. And kids didn't knock like that, anyway, they beat out cheeky rhythms announcing their intention to play console games or kick balls around. The staccato thing she had heard had intruded into her mind and coalesced with the anxiety that had remained there since the morning's telephone call. She was already prepared to be really angry and began, 'If that's Laura...' but Jack was already half way down the hall and had waved dismissively at her from over his shoulder, so that she banged down the bowl on the work surface and began to spoon the mixture into ramekins, wishing that the sloppy whiteness were his emulsified brains.

Jack cursed inwardly as he recognised Laura's familiar shape distorted through the dimpled glass of the lights in the front door. These were not entirely in keeping with the period of the house but he tolerated them as a concession to illumination and because he could not persuade Poppy of his keen appreciation of architectural integrity. It was an irony that his liberation from Laura had now landed him in a situation in which he was less able to discuss stuff like that, or much else either, for that matter, including sex, which Laura had always been open about. Occasionally it had occurred to him to think that Poppy used sex as a kind of reward or as a means of getting what she wanted, but he couldn't bear to think that he had really made that kind of a mistake. Nonetheless he felt his irritation rise at both women, fuelled by the knowledge that there was going to be the most almighty row with Poppy unless he could rid the territory she had gained of Laura. But he wasn't really puzzled that Laura had appeared. In fact, although he would never have admitted it to Poppy, he had half suspected and half dreaded that it had been her knocking, although it was unusual for her to go so far as to come to the house. She must have done that thing that Poppy called 'going off on one.' He braced himself and opened the door.

Standing on the doorstep Laura looked unnaturally well and bright-eyed, and to Jack's astonishment and irritation she was laughing, brimming with some secret excitement of the sort he had occasionally seen in her before. For a moment he was uncannily reminded of the time he had come home from work to find her dancing round the sitting room to Madness's *It Must Be Love*, clutching the positive pregnancy testing kit which was their confirmation of Lizzie's presence in the world. On that occasion she had taken him in her arms and they had laughed out their joy together and ended up in bed. Now of course there could be no such mutuality of communication. Instead her words were tumbling and gabbling out ideas that changed with the dizzying rapidity of the machine gun fire Davie directed at him on the rare occasions Jack could rouse himself to play one of those stupid games with his son on the console. In the rapidity of her sentences Jack could barely listen to the meaning of what Laura was saying before it was replaced by something else. There was something about being sorry, honey, for phoning earlier and not wanting to make life difficult for him, and that she had stumbled across something terribly important, and how she knew she was the only one who could solve it all, and how she had suffered but that she knew they both still believed in God and she knew He wanted Jack to help her, and how terribly important it was for kids she knew and on, and on, wheeling words clashing and colliding and frighteningly torn from language's logical framework.

Despite the onslaught of words Jack's mind suddenly clicked into gear as it caught up with something Laura had said. All this God stuff was embarrassing and more deranged than usual even by her standards. He'd deliberately kept her standing on the doorstep in the admittedly rather vain hope that Poppy would be unable to hear much of what was going on, but now in his anxiety he took a step forward and pulled the door half-closed behind him. Leaning slightly towards Laura he caught a whiff of lunchtime beer, the sour alcohol-and-cigarette smell of that dreadful Anchor place she went to. He wondered what else had gone into the mixture, she seemed as high as a kite. He couldn't smell cannabis so the word *coke* occurred to him. He'd never known her take it before, but couldn't think of any other explanation for her irrational behaviour, and once or twice he had seen colleagues use it at parties. He'd even tried it himself sometimes. So now red alert signals were flashing on in his lawyer's mind, all sorts of potential embarrassment for him making it imperative that he got rid of her. At the same time he vaguely wondered where she might have got the money for the drug, and it occurred to him with irritation that if she were doing Charlie then her limited income would certainly mean that the children were being sold short. She was still gabbling, her voice streaming out sentences as though they were part of the *Minute Waltz* as she leant towards him and took hold of both his arms with her hands unexpectedly and began to rock him back and forth, her eyes fixed on his and her whole body seeming to tremble unnervingly.

'Laura, get off,' he said, and felt her grip tighten as she

pleaded with him to listen. Behind them, Poppy flung the door open.

'What the hell is going on?'

'Poppy, please, I'm dealing with it,' Jack said, although in truth he was beginning to panic that the situation was getting out of hand now, and Laura was still refusing to let go of his arms. Poppy ignored him and, stepping as near as she could to Laura, pushed her hard in the shoulders so that she relaxed her grip on Jack's arm and he was able to step backwards towards the house. She leant her face near to Laura's, her cheeks red with anger.

'Go away,' she hissed, 'Go away and stay away. We've already told you we don't want to see you. Go away to live your own miserable little life and leave us alone.' She turned to Jack. 'Get inside,' she told him.

'Jack...' Laura said, and for a moment she sounded to him as though she were in despair and he had to steel himself against a shiver of lovingkindness. But it was too late, Poppy had somehow propelled him into the hall and was closing the door. When it was half closed he heard Laura say something he didn't quite catch, and Poppy wrench the opening wide again.

'Fuck off and stop causing trouble,' she said loudly, and slammed it shut.

It wasn't meant to be like this. Laura stood astonished at the smooth paintwork in front of her, still feeling in her hands the memory of Jack's shirt beneath her fingers, the familiarity and oddness of being so physically close to him tingling in her mind and on her skin. She turned away from the house and walked down its short path to the street, and was surprised that she was feeling nauseous and slightly unsteady on her feet, dazed and somehow unconnected to the world around her, a bit as though she had the 'flu. Only a little while ago in the pub after her 'phone call to Jack it had all seemed so obviously easy. She'd understood among the beer glasses and ashtrays that despite Jack's initial reluctance, the purpose and guidance she had been experiencing over the past few days would stay with her, that she only had to talk to him face to face. She'd known with the certainty of absolute knowledge that she had to walk to Jack's to see him and in this way she would be enabled to reach the next stage of her purpose, which was to find a way of seeing Drew. Then it had seemed that the interconnectedness of events in which the hand of Providence was so clearly discernible was still then making itself apparent and could be trusted to continue, and her actions had been the living out of an Act of Faith. But now for some reason she could not fathom yet it all seemed to have been thwarted. She walked towards the Post Office, its pillar-box an unexpected splash of blood against the brickwork.

There was a low wall in front of one of the houses at Post Office corner and Laura sat on this, barely seeing the passing traffic or the lime and laburnum trees lit by the sun which was warming her as she struggled to make sense of what had happened. She'd practically begged Jack to listen to her and it was all wrong that he hadn't, and instead Poppy's hissing loathing had spat humiliation in her face, not that any of that meant anything because all that mattered was doing what God wanted and having something to show to Alex at the end of the day, not her own reputation or anything daft like that, and she prayed desperately for help in her helplessness.

A car mechanic's van drew up opposite her, grubby white with oil and usefulness, the reflection of the sun splashing from one of its windows onto Laura's face and forcing her to look up as its boiler-suited driver closed his door and disappeared towards the Market Square. Estuary

Repairs. Brakes and Exhausts. MOT Testing. The last word stood out for her and burnt itself into her cognition as though the world had stopped, it was like St. Francis at Mass in the Portiuncula, hearing the words of the Gospel and the apostolic call to Holy Poverty for the first time. Then she gasped aloud as the cosmos clicked over again for her, and she felt the excitement and adrenalin flooding over her once more. Of course there would be Tests, it was ridiculous to think there wouldn't be and anybody with half a knowledge of history would have realised it. She laughed at herself out loud, and thanked God that He had pulled her to her senses with a little miracle, which she decided that from now on she would call the Little Miracle of the Van, and in her laughter and joy she tried to think of what that might work out as in Italian. And of course it was ridiculous to think that the Snake would just bugger off and hide, that he wasn't all the time trying to trip her up and work against the Plan, which explained why Jack hadn't listened and Poppy had hissed. Poppy was being used, was keeping Jack from hearing. Laura just hadn't seen it because there was so much history between the three of them, but of course when you thought about it she had been on the other side all along, whispering in the garden of their marriage and trying to take the children away like a snake stealing eggs and making Jack not see what was happening all around him. God had given her Alex now, but still Laura saw that for Jack's sake as much as for all the rest of it, she had to get him away from Poppy and try again. Full of what she believed to be the Holy Spirit, energised, and fearlessly angry for righteousness, Laura began to retrace her steps towards the house.

'I thought you were a bit harsh with her, you know,'

Jack said once he and Poppy had regained the kitchen. It was true, of course. Anybody could have overheard what was going on. Some passing neighbour, a postman, even one of their close friends by bad chance. Of course it hadn't turned out like that. It was like when he had nearly crashed his MG on the Cambridge road, driving too fast and with insufficient attention up a slip road he had somehow mistaken for a main carriageway. Before he'd known what was happening he'd discovered the roundabout at the top and only just managed to wrestle the car round at high speed. Afterwards he'd stopped with the noise of howling tyres still in his head and filled with the thought of what could have happened. It had made him feel sick. Of course Poppy's lack of discretion wasn't absolutely life threatening but it really was terribly important to keep things as smooth as possible when they lived so near to the practice. Maybe it had been a mistake to buy a house in the town and one of the outlying villages would have been better. There would have been trouble with Laura, of course. She would have moaned that it was making it difficult for the kids to come and see her, although Lizzie didn't seem that much interested nowadays and Davie would soon grow up too. Then it would all be OK, he told himself. But for now it seemed to Jack that the world was blowing a particularly ill wind against him, and in response he blew out through his own teeth in vexation. He watched Poppy as she placed the syllabubs in the already-overcrowded fridge and begun to wipe the work surfaces vigorously, clearing things into the dishwasher and drawers with angry efficiency. She was refusing to answer him now, for God's sake, and Oh, screw all of this. He headed for his study-sitting room where he poured himself three fingers of scotch and switched on the twenty-four hour news. Not that he was really interested, but Poppy certainly wasn't and the noise would have the agreeable effect of irritating her. He knew he wouldn't get any tonight now, so sod it all.

After the first two or three gulps of whisky Jack began to feel better and was even wondering if he might not try to go and work things out with Poppy when he heard the door of the study open and shut behind him swiftly. He was surprised that she should make the first move like that, usually she managed to make a sulk last a while longer. Maybe he was having a good effect on her. He looked round and the grin he had been preparing was swirled off his face, disappearing down panic's plughole to be replaced by the cold water of very considerable trickiness.

Laura had got in through the French windows, rather cleverly she thought. She'd been able to remember the way quite clearly from the party for Davie last year, the last time they had all tried to do something together, but she knew it was more than just that, just as she knew that as she checked the windows for Poppy's presence she wouldn't be there. Looking at Jack's face now she nearly burst out laughing. He looked really scared and she had to reassure him.

'It's all right, love,' she said, 'I've not come to kill you or anything…'

Jack was suddenly angry. 'Don't call me that,' he spat, his jaw thrust forward in an unconscious but characteristic attitude that Laura for a split second recognised, but her mind was unable to process because of the howling sense of purpose in her head. 'You can't just burst into places, you know. People have homes, for Christ's sake.'

'No, no, no, Jack,' she said, 'I know all that.' She knew she was talking very fast, tripping herself up on her words. 'I know you're a very clever lawyer and I've had to bend

245

the rules a bit to come and see you, but that's why I have to see you, do you see, that's why, because you are clever and I must, you don't understand, it's really important, it might be the most important thing I've ever done in my life and please listen, Jack, only please listen and you'll understand, and I'm sorry I called you love but of course we still do love one another in a way, we both know that, please listen to me, it's really important, it's what God wants for us both, I know it, please listen.' She took a step towards him but he was already out of his chair. He was really angry now, his head felt as if it were full of blood and he was trembling as he strode past her to fling the door open to the hall.

'Get out,' he shouted at her. 'Get the fuck out of my house.' Poppy was coming down the stairs as he marched into the hallway to point towards the front door. As Laura saw the other woman her face seemed to go all wrinkled up and she screamed and covered her face with her hands and ran towards Jack to bury it in his shoulder and whisper urgently at him.

'It's her, don't you see? It's her that's making you like this. She's making you not listen and trapping you into doing evil things. Just listen to me. Look at her eyes and the way she hisses when she's angry. She's like a snake, Jack, it's the bloody Snake, don't you understand?'

Poppy was heading with quick, purposeful steps into the kitchen. She'd had enough of this, it was time to put a stop to it once and for all. If Jack was too spineless to do anything then she certainly wasn't. As she dialled the brief number she heard Laura's voice, shouting now, 'For God's sake, Jack, don't let her make you more stupid than you are. You're being an idiot.'

Jack was furious. Laura had always put him down no matter how much money he earned, no matter what he did or whatever position he'd had in the town. He'd put up and put up with her weirdness for ages, and now the last vestiges of restraint seemed to snap inside him.

'And you're a fucking alcoholic nutter,' he screamed at her, relieved that he could say it at last, to tell her the real truth without the necessity for compassion because she had done all of this and he wanted to be rid of her for ever. He pushed her away from him and she banged her back against the wall, but came at him with claws and fists. 'You bastard, you bloody fucking bastard, I hate you, I hate you, why can't you see what's right, why can't you just talk to me,' and she tried to scratch at his face and pummel him on the chest and bit him hard on his right arm so that he turned away from her in the shock of the assault, and then she jumped on his back so that he fell heavily on the stairs, and she was trying to hit him in the balls but he kept his legs together so that it didn't work, but she was raining blows down on his back and he felt blood erupt from his nose as it banged against the carpet, and she hit him again and again and there was more blood seeping through the back of his shirt, maybe from a spot, and he didn't know what to do because you don't hit women and in any case part of him thought that in some obscure way he deserved it.

Glancing upwards Laura saw Lizzie standing at the turn in the stairs, her daughter's honey blond and Alice-banded hair framing a mask of tears, and her love and compulsion shouted out 'It's all right, my darling, it's all right,' and she scrambled over Jack up to the landing to join her. She went to reach out her arms to encircle her, to comfort, help and protect her from Poppy, but she stood with her arms rigid, her body quivering with compulsive shakes before suddenly she held both hands up in front of her, fingers spread wide as though in defence of her face or to push her mother away.

'No,' she said, her hands reiterating the word. 'No. Just go.'

Something happened behind Laura's eyes then, a kind of cold feeling that made her mouth droop and shifted the focus of her mind with painful suddenness, that made her stare at Lizzie for she couldn't tell how long as the terrifying realisation of the girl's frightened alienation crept over her. She stepped forward to reach out for her again, but Lizzie stepped back and shook her head, dropping her hands to reveal the nakedness of her weeping and lips uncontrollably trembling so that she stammered as she said, 'Please, Mum, just go,' and something in the Universe seemed to break.

Laura hardly saw the stairs or the hall, though as she closed the door behind her and walked briskly, half-ran away from the house she realised that she hadn't had to climb over Jack on her way out, so he must have moved. There was something wrong now, there was definitely something wrong, and she increased her pace.

The roads were hot. The freshness of the morning had given way to a sticky sweetness, the air seeming a suspension of Laura's confusion and that terrible sense of knowing that something really awful has happened but not really being able to apprehend its meaning, a bit like when Dad died. Her eyes and her head hurt terribly from crying as she'd walked into the yawning despair that was beginning to open up inside her during the hanky-sodden trip from Jack's house.

At the top of her street there were men at the side of the road repairing something or other. Laura knew one of them by sight. The smell of hot tar, she thought, was like some awful linctus being offered to her but she was nauseated and could not breathe in. Oh Christ, don't let it all be her fault, not again, please not again. The image of Lizzie on the stairs kept coming back to her, and when it did she wanted to fall to her knees and weep on the tarmac and cry in the arms of the Mother whose Heart was pierced with a Sword, but she was so afraid that would never happen again because of what she had done, ruining everything so terribly and she was so bad and there wasn't a way back. The temptation to run came over her and she felt her heart quickening and beating inside her as though it would kill her with her own life, but she had to get away, get away fast or the pain in her eyes would get worse and she would just disintegrate onto the pavement and there would be nothing left except a big pool of salty water and trace elements because it didn't seem that anything was holding her together any more. She staggered as she half trotted around the final corner, and this did something to her ankle that forced her to go more slowly again, although there were still furious rainbows in her head.

Darren reckoned that was her coming down the road now. He'd left that black cow Jane Roberts back at the Mortons' house to get on with the rest of the stuff and taken the car straight round to where he'd said his ex missus lived. He liked all this sort of stuff, trying to nick them quickly and that. This copper he knew, one of the good old boys who'd been a proper front line professional all his working life, he'd told him that if you could get them while they were still upset you had a much better chance of getting a fast confession while they were still confused, like. And if you had a confession the lame arse victims were much more likely to press charges because they wouldn't have to appear in court. Loads of brownie points there, and he was fucking certain he wasn't going to share them with any blackie.

Christ, she looked pissed though, staggering about like a Saturday night slapper after sixteen Bacardi Breezers. Morton had said she was an alkie, well 'had a drink problem' anyway, but Darren knew damn well what that meant whatever snob language you used. He grinned. This was going to be a piece of piss.

"Scuse me, Laura Morton is it?' he said. But she hadn't even noticed him as he'd got out of the car, either too pissed or too stuck up to care about a policeman looking directly at her. That annoyed him, he was proud of the way he filled out his uniform, it made him look like someone you didn't mess around with. Then he felt his anger joined by another feeling as the first trickles of excitement seeped into the back of his neck and groin, the hope she'd give him some lip, some excuse to have a go, really get at one of her sort. He'd not had many chances of that, most of his time was spent dealing with low life scrubbers. But one of his mates, Andy, had told him how he'd once dated this ballerina, real top class bird she was, and he'd always told him how great it was to see her on her knees swallowing dick and dribbling like some dirty slut. Darren thought about this and felt his knob stir as he saw the Morton woman come up and walk right past him as though he hadn't spoken. He watched her arse cheeks tightening the fabric of her jeans on either side alternately as she walked unsteadily and raised his voice at her just before she reached her door.

'Oi, I'm talking to you.'

There was somebody shouting now, and dimly Laura realised that she'd actually already been spoken to. She'd been too distracted to listen because some vague idea of reaching the sofa in her sitting room had formed itself in her mind. She'd known pet cats wander away to die, half slinking and half wobbling from the world to some secret place of safety whose privacy had spoken to her of their silent dignity. Bobby in her six year old arms, his stripes cold against her touch under the yellow tree in the garden, the death colours of his ginger fur present to her memory and contrasting oddly with the blue-black brutalism of the policeman's uniform as she turned to look at him. He was big, this policeman. You could see the anger beneath his shirt and in the hard, young face. And she knew that she'd seen anger like that before, in sixth formers following hopeless vocational courses that made them laughed at and looked down on by their peers, in Pete's nasal racist rants against the immigrants for whom he could blame his own inadequacies, in the hatred people had shown her and the others at church when they had tried to get a few toys and things organised for some asylum seekers' children living in town with their mothers while their dads languished uncharged in prison. Then her historian's mind heaved into action unbidden, and as she looked at Darren she saw the police defending the black-shirted men of Cable Street, knew even that the disaffected and embittered of his sort, in another country and not so long ago, had flocked to wear brown shirts instead of black ones. She continued to stare at him, trying for a moment to work out what so malign a presence was doing so close to her, what the pattern might be to all of this, but there was a kind of light-headed feeling and a buzzing in her brain now, and she realised she was badly frightened.

Darren walked up to the woman. He was standing close to her now, just outside the limits of her special privacy, and instinctively Laura stepped back, but he raised his hand in a peculiar half-point towards her and his voice another step up in harshness so that is was now only a shade beneath a threat.

'Don't you walk away when I'm talking to you. You Laura Morton?' Laura thought she recognised him, he was one of the police who had been outside the Anchor talking to Inspector McGahan after the boys had killed George. For a moment she felt a surge of relief, the idea occurring to her that perhaps nothing bad was going to happen here, that somehow a message had got through and that McGahan wanted to see her and things were going to be all right.

'Yes, I'm Laura Morton.' The men at the top of the road had started to drill at a different place, the febrile banging of the air adding to the oppressive, slick warmth and making it difficult to think. The policeman sniffed conspicuously.

'So how much have you had to drink today?'

Oh God, of course it wasn't going to be all right at all, Laura could tell that, she could see this guy was out to get her, and she realised what was happening as her mind clicked over and out of the corner of its eye she saw Poppy, coming out of the kitchen at Jack's place with the telephone receiver in her hand and placing it on the hall table. Rage was heaving itself up inside her now as though from some vile internal organ, so that she dug her fingernails into her hands and wanted to claw at her own face in misery and misdirected fury. That bloody bitch, that bloody bitch, how dare she send this monstrous, barely educated thug-in-uniform after her to humiliate her and compromise both Jack and the children? And more despairingly, how had she managed to get herself in such a stupid situation? Fleetingly she thought of her mother. Christ, she was going to have to try to out-think this blue-shirted bastard, stop Poppy's plot now or at least delay it until she could get time, only her head was raging and she felt unsteady on her feet. She tried to smile.

'Yes, I had a few pints at lunchtime, actually. I hope it's not a crime yet.' The policeman didn't smile.

'Bein' drunk and incapable is. You were staggerin' all over the place up there.'

'Yes, I know, a bit too much sun on top of the beer I expect. I'll go and sleep it off – my place is just down there. Thanks very much for being concerned.' Laura turned to go, but as she did so heard a kind of snorting laugh behind her.

'I don't think so, love, do you?' Love. He liked that, that was clever of him, that would get right up her snooty fucking nose, it was what you called shop girls and old bags on buses. He saw her freeze minutely as he laughed and said the words, sly knowingness Mick called it. It never failed to rile them. For a moment he thought she was going to really wind him up by walking on again, but she turned back, and he was disappointed.

'I'm sorry?' Laura asked. She'd definitely taken the bait, but for a moment Darren was disconcerted by the direct arrogance of her question. Taken aback, his mind went blank. Laura's, on the other hand, was racing. She was going to hit back now and hard, with a clever argument delivered in language chosen for its locker-room effectiveness. It was too bad she didn't know much about Law, of course what with Jack and everything there was an irony there, but surely to God she could make some mincemeat out of this idiot. Even if he were determined to do something really stupid it would only confirm what she thought of them. 'What exactly are you implying?' she continued, warming to her theme. 'I'm going home, and I'm going to fucking sleep. Neither of these is so far as I am aware a crime, and nor is having two or three bloody pints, as you doubtless know from even your limited experience of the world. So if you'll excuse me, I shall continue on my way rejoicing. If you want to talk to me about something you can make an appointment so that I can have a legal representative present. Unless of course you want to arrest me. If you don't, I suggest you piss off and leave me alone.'

Darren swallowed hard. He wasn't going to have this, there was no way he was gong to have some snotty bitch talk to him like that, that was well out of order, and fuck me, she must be either mad or pissed anyway to talk to a copper in that way. He'd wanted to talk to her and get a confession from her of course, but after this and with a bit of luck he could do that down the nick in a few minutes. He knew what he was going to do. He was going to wind her up a bit more. As she turned her back on him and made for her front door he fell in step close beside her and leant his face near to hers, which was staring rigidly ahead, though sweat was revealing her agitation and he liked that.

'I'm warning you, if you swear at me once more I'm going to arrest you for being drunk and disorderly.'

'Oh go screw yourself,' said Laura.

Twenty-seven

Jack pinched his nose delicately into the tissue, staunching what he hoped would be a final trickle of blood while trying to maintain some sort of authority and as dignified an aspect as was possible under the circumstances. He knew the young police officer sitting opposite him slightly. Already he had been impressed and reassured by the way she had been handling things. She had been able to cut through Poppy's angry near-hysteria and take control of the situation with calm and patience, and from this he thought that she would be reasonable in the conversation he was steeling himself to have with her, if only Poppy would stay shut up. The big chap who had come with the woman PC had left after whispering something in her ear. Jack could guess what that meant, and now that his own pain and anger had subsided he was becoming uncomfortably aware of the need to wrest the immediate situation away from Poppy and into his own control. It was more than irritating that Poppy could not see the potential damage all this could cause, even to her own well-being, for God's sake. Not for the first time he had the uneasy feeling that she was really rather dim as well as being tiresomely vindictive, and he was sufficiently self-aware to recognise that his present discomfiture contained a good deal of ironic regret. In an equivalent situation and before she started going off the rails at least

Laura would have shut up and left things to him, he was the legal expert for Christ's sake. Surely now the stupid woman he had lumbered himself with could imagine what might happen if all this got into the local newspapers? He thought of Russell perusing the Mootborough Standard, and a drop of nervous perspiration began to tickle the nape of his neck. Desperately he again sought to catch his wife's eye before she did more damage, but she wouldn't be drawn. He would have to go in feet first.

'Look, Jane, I think things are getting a bit overblown here.' He kept his head down as he said it, unwilling and too scared to watch Poppy's reaction. 'My ex-wife has been under a lot of stress recently and it's true, as Poppy says, that she came round here and made a bit of a fool of herself. There was a bit of a to-do between her and me and I stupidly tripped and banged myself running after her on the way out. Poppy just got scared and angry and rang you, that's all. I'm not surprised really. A lot of raised voices and so on, and then me having a nosebleed like this. But she couldn't really see what was going on from the kitchen.' He attempted a laugh. 'I am so sorry that you have been troubled, but there really is nothing to worry about.'

Jane turned herself in the seat to look at him, at the expensively comfortable jeans and chequered country-style shirt now smeared here and there with blood.

'Really? Are you sure, sir? Only from what Mrs Morton has been telling me it seems that your ex-wife was being very aggressive.' Jane's last job in the leafy suburbs of Amblehurst had taught her to recognise the noise of the upper middle classes whining their way out of embarrassing situations involving the criminal justice system. She was thus disinclined to believe a word of what Morton was saying, although it was true that most of the Poppy woman's stuff had simply amounted to a long tirade against the awfulness of the former Mrs Morton. She watched as Morton exchanged the briefest of glances with his wife, and had to suppress a smile at Poppy's numbed and furious expression. She certainly hadn't been expecting her husband to take control like that. The new Mrs Morton had better learn to catch up with the game quickly, Jane guessed.

'Mrs Morton?' she asked, but it was already a formality, she knew that without the victim's co-operation there would be a zero result. Morton would stick to his line and his wife would follow him. And after all, no real harm had been done whatever way you looked at it. She watched the couple stare at one another for a rather longer moment, the woman blushing and, Jane guessed, torn between humiliation and loyalty. That idiot Darren Wright had already hared off to find Laura Morton. The thought made Jane impatient to go. Just get on with it, she thought as she waited for Poppy's answer.

'I suppose so,' the woman said at last. 'I suppose it happened like that if Jack says so. After all, I was in the kitchen for a lot of the time. I'm sorry.'

Jane closed her notebook. There was no point in telling them off, and it would pointless anyway. Put it down as community policing.

'Don't be,' she said. 'It just looks like a bit of a misunderstanding, and we'd much rather you were safe than sorry. I think that unless you remember anything else we won't be taking things any further.' She got up from the chair and took Poppy's hand. 'Goodbye, Mrs Morton. Thank you.' Morton was ushering her out in a kind of creepy all-colleagues-together way, as though they were at some posh Lawyer's Ball or something, and he stopped her in the hall.

'You won't be talking to Laura, will you?' Now he sounded like a doctor or priest, inviting her to share some quasi-confidential information with him. Jane felt herself become annoyed at so naked an attempt at manipulation and briefly she was tempted to think that if he started pushing things she might decide to change her mind and start making things awkward for both of them. 'It's only that, well, she hasn't been very well recently and Poppy does rather get over-upset about things. I'd really hate to think of things being made any worse for Laura. She's a poor thing really, and one does have the children to think about, after all.'

'Mr Morton…' but he held up his hand.

'Jack, please.' As though they were in the pub. They'd only ever exchanged the briefest of conversations in the Mootborough Arms, for heaven's sake.

'OK, Jack. As I say, I don't expect that at this stage we'll be taking things further, and I promise that if any further evidence arises we will take account of what you say about your ex-wife's health, OK?' She looked him full in the face, and saw his muscles relax and his shoulders slump minutely before he saw her to the door with meticulous good manners. Once out onto the street she moved her hand up to her personal radio, guiltily delighted that Darren Wright was about to make a fool of himself.

Twenty-eight

'Hiya.' Alex spoke into his rather ancient mobile phone, delighted to see Laura's name on the scratched plastic screen. He'd half hoped she might give him a call some time during the day, which had already been a good one, much more successful than he'd thought. He'd sat at his desk with the windows open and looking out onto the field and made much better progress on his case notes than he'd anticipated. There had even been a cuckoo calling from somewhere in the trees. Most of all, he felt a good deal more confident about the Laura business. He'd been jotting down some notes about her symptoms as he had promised himself, and then Terry had come in and he'd been able to speak to him confidentially and thrash the thing out between the two of them. Terry was a damn good counsellor, there was no two ways about it, and patients who were assigned to him usually counted themselves very lucky to have him as their Community Psychiatric Nurse. By sharing the situation with him Alex had almost been asking him to make sure that what he felt professionally about her wasn't in some way distorted by the racing brain chemicals produced by love. So they'd worked on it together for a while, with all the due provisos that Terry hadn't actually had a chance to assess Laura, and they'd come up with a few ideas. Alex had written them down. It always helped him to do that:

- There is no objection to a relationship between Laura and A, as L is not A's patient.
- There are good grounds for suspecting that Laura may be suffering from bipolar disorder. She appears to have had manic as well as acutely depressed episodes.
- Laura has been treated for unipolar depression and believes herself to be a unipolar depressive.
- Alex has a moral duty to care about Laura's mental health, and should consider gently introducing her to the idea that her previous diagnosis may need revisiting.
- Should Laura's condition deteriorate dramatically, she and A should involve the local Mental Health Team.

So on the whole Alex thought he had a pretty well conceived plan of action. He just had a few more case notes to do and then he'd be on his way, speeding as fast as Ford's rather less than finest would allow towards the pub and the girlfriend at the other end of these electromagnetic pulses or however the hell mobiles worked.

'Alex, I'm terribly sorry, but I've been arrested. I'm at the police station.'

'Oh Christ.'

Within less than five minutes the trees were hard speeding past the car's windows, then Alex's crunch-gravel urgency gave way to tarmac and then to the seemingly slowest wait in traffic's history before the swing right onto the bypass. Foot down, squirting fuel fed by anxiety, he had to keep an eye on the speed limit, there was no way they were going help him if they caught him. It wasn't as though he would be recognised as a nurse in a hurry. The road surface rolled away, swinging underneath his car and below a lorry, and there was the left turn to take him through that ancient but now hateful village, its inhabitants maintaining a fantasy of tradition though its men drove their gas-guzzlers to London, or took the train and read the least demanding of the broadsheet newspapers. There was impatience here. The carriageways were narrowed and speeds slowed by the exigencies of economics and geography. Alex tapped out his frustration onto the plastic of the steering wheel and only glancingly noted the ducks on the pond as he passed. He normally delighted in them but now the absurd noises they made seemed merely ridiculous to him, and he was annoyed that he could hear them above the noise of the Fiesta's near-idling engine. At last he was on the Mootborough road, the fields to either side rolling away and down towards the Estuary and distant power station. As he pressed petrol into the engine the various idiosyncrasies of the clapped out car asserted themselves. The gear lever started up a noisy shaking in its housing, and from somewhere that he had never quite been able to figure out the driver's door had developed a mysterious and worrying intermittent metallic rattle. He passed the church where Sue was buried. He had his customary but now fleeting mind-view of her grave beneath the squat East Anglian spire with its white weather boarding, the new polished stone which perhaps might cause the odd rambler to pause and wonder what had caused so young a woman to die so late in history. He gulped in grief and brief self pity, and as though in determination never to allow such a thing to happen again, allowed the gentle downward slope beyond him to overcome his caution. The speedometer crept over seventy-five. He slowed only as he reached the outer limits of the town where harassed-faced parents could be seen struggling with recalcitrant shopping trolleys and fractious children outside the supermarket.

Mootborough police station was an imposing nineteenth century brick building, set just off the Market Square and shouting late Victorian civic pride in its three storeys of red stocks. One of Alex's visiting college friends had described it to him as giving off a reassuring Dixon of Dock Green atmosphere, and certainly its cast iron and blue glass lamp gave it that appearance. Alex had felt regretful as he'd pointed out the ugly little rectangular metal box attached to the side of its main entrance. For years the station had shut at five o'clock, and this now served to connect the town's citizens to the County Police Headquarters in Amblehurst after hours. Nor had the station's design anticipated the impact of the internal combustion engine, and as a result during the day its tiny yard became crammed with police cars and vans which spilled their gaudy stripes and Crimebusters messages out onto the adjoining streets, an inconvenience accepted for the most part with shrug-shouldered good humour by a populace who generally liked the old building.

Usually Alex would have taken his time to find a parking space, trawling round several little known places where it was sometimes possible to shove a car down for free and without restrictions even so close to the centre of town. Today there wasn't enough time to go messing about like that, he would have to make an exception to his habitual practice, for once paying the ruinous charges imposed on high street shoppers in the District Council car park. As he manoeuvred the car and began to hunt for a space he once more wondered whose palm had been greased so that the out of town supermarkets got their car parks free of council tax while the High Street traders were struggling. A yellow hatchback drove the thought from his head as it reversed out and he swung the Fiesta into its vacated space, quick-leaping from his seat as he cut the ignition and, once outside, fumbling in his pockets for pound coins.

'I've already got that Morton woman. She's out the front now on a D. and D. We was just waiting for you here.' God, thought Janey, six foot two of testosterone and gristle. She wondered briefly if he and Earl shared a brain cell, passing it between them like the Graeae with their single eye. She had been reading about them in her OU course.

'What for?' she asked, pushing past Wright and so forcing him to follow her down the corridor. 'There isn't anything. The Mortons say it was an accident. There was a bit of an argument, Mr. Morton tripped and banged his nose, and the new Mrs. Morton got frightened. All very regrettable, no hard feelings, *et cetera*.' Jane had delivered this over her shoulder and now a kind of snorting exhalation came from behind her.

'That's a load of bollocks and you know it.' Now Jane felt that he had justified her giving in to the constant temptation to needle him.

'Do I? Seemed like a reasonable explanation to me, but of course I was on my own at the time. No doubt had you been there, with your well known skills of detection and knowledge of the Law, you could have run rings around a solicitor and his wife. As things stand we may have missed the opportunity of a result, of course. I am in the unenviable position of having to rely only on what I've seen and heard. In any case the Mortons won't shift from their story now.'

'So what you're sayin' is, you've fucked it up.'

'I prefer to think of it as a small domestic dispute amicably settled in the best traditions of community policing.' A twinge of guilt here as Jane wondered whether she would have shown the same leniency to a less comfortably off and well educated couple, and she resolved to try harder not to pre-judge. But she certainly wasn't going to share this with Wright. Instead she stopped, crossed her arms to face him and asked, 'Why did you arrest Laura Morton?'

'She was pissed.'

'How do you know?'

'She was all over the place. And she said she'd been drinking.'

'Perhaps she was upset. You know she's not very well?' He looked surly now, his fists clenched as he too crossed his arms and his uniform strained against his arms.

'She looked all right to me.'

'Doctor now, are we? Did you cuff her?'

'She told me to go screw myself.'

Jane sighed. Wright was an idiot but the D. and D. thing would have to stick now. Not even she was willing to allow that kind of stuff, but having observed Wright in practice she could well imagine the circumstances which had brought the offence about.

'Yeah, well, OK, but I've no doubt you deserved it.' She was bored now and in any case needed a wee. She moved off towards the ladies.

'What d'you mean, you bloody...?'

'That, Darren. Just that. You're a bully. And dare I say it, occasionally something of a moron. Think about it.' She let the door close behind her, shook her head as though trying to free it from some malign influence, and resolved to talk to Ted Hibbert.

Alex took the last few paces of his short walk from the car park at a trot. The unaccustomed exercise was heaving in his chest and prickling his skin as though he were wearing too many heavy, tight clothes, or maybe his epidermis had swelled up and was acting like the cover of a hot water tank. His flabby belly certainly made him look like one of those sometimes, anyway. A momentary concern flickered across the back of his mind. Maybe he ought to think about giving up smoking, but as he slowed and recovered his breath his habitual excuses reasserted themselves. He and Sue had always said that there was no vice worth giving up in order to spend a few extra years sitting round the walls of a ruinously expensive old people's home. The memory reassured him and almost made him smile briefly as he passed beneath the gaudy blobs of what he thought might be lobelia and busy lizzie slurping their tongues over the hanging baskets round the town sign.

The police station reception area was sparse, stark in its plastic-chaired and lino functionality. Posters hung to the walls in various stages of blu-tacked decrepitude, part of the cutting edge of various government initiatives. Think Don't Drink and Drive and Lock it or Lose it curled their UV-cracked corners by the windows. Drugs Ruin People's Lives and Having Sex under Sixteen is Illegal were imprisoned under scratched plastic and were faring somewhat better. Alex knew several patients for whom the sex one's depiction of pretty girls in their school uniforms would have provided masturbation fantasies for a year, and wondered how many more were wandering about undiagnosed to be similarly fed.

Laura was sitting forward on one of the chairs, head down and hands clasped tightly round a handkerchief that was obviously now far too wet to be of any real use. Alex watched her try to smear the tears away, but no sooner had she done so than more succeeded down her cheeks, the bouncing light shining back off surface tension and accentuating her signals of distress. He sat on the chair beside hers and pressed his reasonably clean bandanna into her hands. He'd used bandannas for years and was rather pleased with his collection of spots and paisley patterns, and seeing Laura look up and feel her press his hand he felt better, less tense and in a territory with which he was familiar and in which he thought he could take a degree of control.

'Thanks,' she said, and gave a wan half-smile.

'No problem. You OK?'

Laura looked away. She wanted to be able to say that she was fine, to deal with it as she imagined Andrea might have done with a self-protecting mixture of humour and self-righteousness. But she couldn't. Her interior dialogue was too one-sided, shouting at her that she was a loathsome fool, filling her mind with self hatred and despair so that all she wanted to do was curl up and never have to think or do anything ever again. And it was wrong of her to have involved Alex, wrong to have dragged him into her stupid sodding shit life although of course she was grateful he was there because she was frightened. She knew that without him if that horrible policeman upset her again she would make a terrible fool of herself and certainly make things worse than she had managed to make them already. Unbidden and unexpected, a memory came into her mind, one of the sort that made her want to put her hands over her face in sudden humiliation and fear of herself. She did that now, taken back to years ago and the scene of her sister and herself systematically smashing her father's greenhouse panes in the sunlit garden, urging one another on in their seven-and-eight year old emotional sadism. She bit her lip and her fingers trembled on her forehead as the pictures dissolved themselves and their place was taken by a succession of others, bleeding their evidence of her failure and wickedness into her mind and forcing her to say, look at this, this is who you are, this is what you have done, until she arrived at the final horror of today.

Alex continued to watch her as he noted that a good two minutes of silence had passed since he had asked her if she was all right. She'd only moved once, to place her head in her hands. He knew about this of course, knew from experience and textbooks and talking to patients that silence and stillness can indicate an internal storm which made communication difficult and voluntary movement an unwelcome distraction as the mind fought back to maintain a balance. It was like watching a man intently reading books and making notes in a quiet library. It was so peaceful a scene on the outside, but when you'd actually done that stuff yourself you realized that on the inside it was quite different. What looked like doing nothing very much was actually an interior roar, a racing wrestling match with ideas. But even so it was important not to jump to conclusions. He could see that she was pretty bad just at the moment, and felt rotten for her. He desperately needed to get her away from here so that he could take some sort of a history, get clear in his own mind what had been going on before leaping in with some possibly inappropriate course of action. After all, getting arrested would be a bit of a shock for anybody, even if she had been showing some other rather worrying behaviours recently and it all rather begged the question of exactly how she had managed to end up here.

The copper looked angry now. He'd banged through the door into the reception area and slapped down some paperwork on the counter with the air of a stroppy thirteen year old. He seemed to be studiously ignoring the pair of them and Alex didn't recognize him, but he felt

Laura tense and wriggle under his arm, so guessed this must be it. He took his arm away and Laura looked up briefly before stuffing the handkerchief away into her pocket and wiping her face on the back of her hand. For a moment she looked like a little girl sitting terrified and in trouble outside the headteacher's office. The policeman was taking an inordinate amount of time filling in some form or other, leaning over the counter and holding a biro awkwardly with the base of his thumb as he wrote, leaving the rest of his hand free to form a fist against the paper. At length he turned around, clipboard in hand, his body language screaming what seemed to Alex a seen-it-all-before aggression disguised as the indifference of efficiency. From somewhere in the recesses of the station an older man with receding hair and sergeant's stripes on his uniform had appeared to stand behind the counter. He seemed to be pretending to do something with envelope files, shuffling them over in his hands, but Alex had already caught the look he had given the younger man and the way he was now discreetly observing him. Eventually, and without looking up, the younger policeman gabbled off that he'd arrested Laura for being drunk and disorderly and, after due warning, she had told him to screw himself. Despite himself Alex was mildly amused at this new information as the young copper turned his attention fully to Laura.

'Right, you've been arrested for drunk and disorderly. This is how it works. You can admit it and pay up now or you can plead not guilty and go to court. Up to you.'

Laura didn't know what to do. Her mind blanked out and that frightened her almost as much as when he'd grabbed her and put on the handcuffs and hurt her. He'd pushed her roughly into the police car. He'd got really close to her then, she could see him enjoying her fear and she'd felt him touch her between her legs through her jeans. Her skin could remember the warmth of his hand there and she heard again his grunting and saw his grinning, bestial face as he covered up his sweaty pleasure by telling her to get in, as if she'd been were resisting arrest or something when she hadn't been, she'd just been so shocked by the ridiculous suddenness with which the situation had seemed to escalate. His erection had tented his trousers as he'd got into the front of the car. But of course that couldn't really have happened, policemen didn't really behave like that except in books and in the newspapers. She trembled and reached for Alex's hands.

'We'll pay up now,' Alex said. 'Let's just get it over with.' The policeman seemed to notice him for the first time.

'Who are you?' he asked. 'I don't remember you.' From the corner of his eye Alex could see the sergeant put his files down on the counter and stand cross-armed to watch.

'I'm Laura's friend,' he said.

'Boyfriend, are you?' Wright almost spat the word. 'Maybe you ought to keep a better eye on her then. You just keep your mouth shut until you're spoken to.' He didn't care any more, they were all scum anyway. That old bastard Hibbert looking at him could do what he liked, after today he'd half decided he'd had enough of the way the Force was going anyway. He turned on the Morton woman, stupid weeping cow, as though tears made any bloody difference to anything.

'Well, go on then, ignore lover boy here, what are you gonna do?'

It was easier now all she had to do was repeat what Alex had said and also because she could feel him trembling with anger beside her which was comforting and dangerous all at once. And she knew he would want her to include him and get her own back at the policeman's being rude, so she said, 'Alex is right, I'll pay now.'

'Right, shame you can't make your decisions on your own though.' Slam went the clipboard back onto the counter as he turned his back on her and hesitantly marked a green form with two crosses. 'Sign here and here. The fine's forty pounds, and you can count yourself lucky I'm not making it eighty.'

Laura got up. The plastic low-backed chairs seemed to have made her unsteady and Alex was quick to help her, taking her elbow with discreet old-fashioned courtesy. As she reached the counter and looked at the green paper with its words that she could read but somehow couldn't force to make sense, she felt him press the paper money into her hands. The policeman hissed through his teeth and then his finger suddenly appeared in front of her, jabbing at where he'd marked the form. She noticed, absurdly, that he had carefully manicured fingernails.

'Look, there and there. Christ, not too difficult for you, is it?'

Alex felt his neck warm and his back teeth clench. He watched Laura sign her name and his necessarily impotent anger derived some vicious satisfaction from the way her dramatically flowing signature contrasted with the childish looping scrawl Wright had driven into the paper. The copper watched as Laura held the money up tentatively and saw it taken with a wordless, contemptuous snatch, and clipped it to the board which he passed to the sergeant. As the older man took the papers he looked up and for a moment his eyes met Alex's. Alex was sure it was deliberate, and suddenly he realized that he knew him slightly, he'd forgotten where from, probably from one of the pubs. Strange how uniform and context made people look different. He'd forgotten the guy was a copper. Emboldened, Alex allowed his eyes to shift to indicate the younger policeman and was rewarded with the briefest of nods.

'Right, you can go,' the PC was saying. 'But before you do I'm giving you strong advice to stay away from your ex-husband's house. You know what I'm talking about so don't stand there looking all innocent. People like you are a bloody liability. Go on, get out.'

For a moment Alex opened his mouth to speak, but saw the sergeant's shake of the head just in time. He took Laura's hand and walked with her towards the door.

'That's right, you comfort her, mate,' Wright called after him. 'Maybe you'll get your leg over.' It was only after the door had closed behind them and Ted Hibbert had counted to ten that he turned to Wright and said:

'I think we'd better have a talk, son.'

Twenty-nine

Laura had felt numb when Alex had driven her home. She'd sat in the car and looked at the dirt patterns on the windscreen and couldn't feel anything at all. Once on their journey she had heard something like a child moaning and was surprised when Alex put his hand on her knee to comfort her. Only then she'd realized she was making the noise. When they reached the cottage he'd made tea and he'd put a lot of sugar in hers, and she'd drunk it although she never took it that sweet, although of course she knew why he'd done it and it was nice of him, and actually it was sort of comforting. He'd eaten some biscuits and a bit of cheese, but she hadn't had any appetite at all and they'd sat smoking one cigarette after another until she had to stop because her head started spinning and her tongue tasted awful. Then they'd sat on the sofa together and she put her head on his chest and he placed his arms round her. The infrequency of words passing between them somehow made a space for her, and she'd begun the first of the crying fits which had come over her for ages now. Alex had watched her as she'd forced her hand into her mouth and bite on it to stop the shameful tears that terrified her with their evidence of madness. Wanting to escape from her own thoughts and afraid to look at the anxiety on his face she'd taken refuge in lengthy but fitful daytime sleeping, giving in to the dragging fatigue with its deceptive promise of oblivion gratefully. Alex had tucked her into the duvet and stayed beside her reading or working when she did that. He was always there when she woke up all sweat covered and foot-fumbling at the uncomfortably rucked up sheet beneath her as she fought her way out of bad dreams where work and her father and Lizzie on the stairs in drunken car-crash chaos spurted unwelcome from her subconscious.

During the nights, as Alex lay beside her she would cling to him in sudden wordless panic at her own worthlessness and stupidity and he had smoothed her hair and kissed her cheek. It was this self estimation that informed her life now, the terrifying knowledge of self humiliation and repeated failures and the appalling certainty of how her behaviour must have appeared to others. Sometimes she lay awake with her eyes closed, pretending to be asleep but with her so-unwelcome life raging in her head and the memories and bad thoughts crowding in one after another, and her interior dialogue screamed her own obscenities at her. She could barely eat and was glad that Alex seemed to understand. He'd brought her nice things, bowls of ice cream with ginger in them to stop her from feeling sick and chocolate to keep her sugar levels up. She knew all that, even understood the careful choice of food, but it only added to the guilt she already felt, and she couldn't bear to look at him or talk to him and knew she was a bitch and often wished he would go away. Then the sickness churned in her stomach as she remembered how only a few days ago she had been the handmaid of the Lord for Christ's sake, the saint who saw fucking snakes that weren't there, and she beat the pillow in rage and self-loathing and wriggled as far away from Alex as she could because she couldn't bear a kindness that seemed to her to be so desperately misplaced.

She thought about death a lot. It had to happen sometime after all. She imagined her funeral and wondered if Poppy would come. Jack probably would, it would be his style to act the gent even if his wife was playing up. Oh dear Jesus, what a fuck up, and she squeezed the sheet again as she remembered him and all her failure there, she could imagine how much it would drag it all up for him, and she wanted to scream out and turn time back to when the kids were small. But of course she couldn't have that and instead she would really like black plumed horses and a Mass in a decent mixture of Latin and English but she could never afford the undertaker's fees, and Father Malcolm was hardly the brightest or most educated bunny in the world. She would be lucky to get am MDF coffin, a couple of choruses of *Kum Ba Yah* and a mention in the following Sunday's newsletter. Probably only a handful of people would come anyway and oh, God she hadn't made a will, although she supposed everything would go to the children and maybe Jack would at least look after that, although she would like Alex to have something, but maybe that would have to be tough luck. Her mind played around the idea more, despair taking shape in the practicalities of pills and ropes and a risky gamble on the God thing. But maybe it really would be the best plan, there must be ways of doing it reasonably neatly, perhaps even painlessly if she did enough research on the Internet. There was a kind of brick wall of somebody having to find the body, though. Then there would be the inevitable post mortem and inquest with its terrible news for Davie and Lizzie, the sin against charity encoded in suicide against which her intellect and love rebelled. Maybe even for Alex too. She envied lorry drivers killed quickly at the wheel, even the patients in St. Francis's Hospice with their terminal illnesses. Once or twice she prayed for death, wondering if she were blaspheming but weeping for what she'd been told was the wholeness offered in Heaven.

On the morning of the third day after her arrest Laura woke up and gazed at the ceiling. She felt different, cold and ravenously hungry and desperate for a cigarette that she dared not have until she'd eaten because she knew it would make her feel more sick than she could bear. With ginger caution so as not to wake Alex she slipped from under the duvet and descended the stairs, taking her winter dressing gown from behind the bathroom door and slipping her feet into her warmest slippers, fur lined soft boot shapes her mother had given her last Christmas. It was raining outside. As she waited for her instant porridge cereal to ping finished in the microwave she watched the straggling roses outside the kitchen window whipping the garden fence, their leaves yellow-blighted and curling beneath petal-dropping dead heads. The cereal smelt great, the best thing ever, and she shoved sugar on the top and slopped milk over it to cool it down, blowing on it desperately as she carried it to the sofa and curled up with her legs tucked up beneath her, turning the television on low as she passed. She ate quickly, feeling the comforting childish pap coursing through her body until she lay back and gazed at the screen, waiting for the feeling of fullness to register properly. She started to notice the news. A BBC reporter had gone missing in the Middle East, which was bad, but it was slightly more cheering to learn that another peer had been caught with his hands in the till and the President of Venezuela was twisting the Republican Administration's tail. The weather, it appeared, was going to brighten up. She reached for the packet of tobacco Alex had left on the coffee table, digging around in the dark sweetness inside for papers, then rolled herself a cigarette. She'd not been smoking much while she'd been in bed and for a moment the unfiltered strength made her head buzz, but with the next more cautious drag her fingers tingled with pleasure and she wriggled her toes against the fleecy lining of her slippers and leant back into the cushions.

Alex had heard the ding of the microwave somewhere seeping inside his dream. He was on a steam ferry crossing the Wallet, anxious because he could see the paddle wheels churning up the sand over the side and a man was standing on a bank of it waving at them to keep clear. Alex kept trying to alert the other passengers but some claimed they couldn't see anyone there and others just laughed because the man was wearing theatre pyjamas and had a seabird standing on his head. One of the crew rang the ship's bell and Alex was on the sandbank taking Laura's hand, but she wasn't beside him in the bed and his fingers closed on the sheet. Fully awake now, he could hear the musical alert that announced the Headlines from downstairs, and there was a smell of porridge.

The bed felt luxurious as he stretched into the cool space left by Laura's body, and Alex allowed himself a few moments of solitude. Mid-way through a sumptuous yawn he wanted to grin, and when he'd finished he swung his legs over the side.

'Hi. Good to see you again.' Laura was just stubbing out a roll up, and as she turned to look at him he noted with satisfaction the creamily-smeared dirty spoon and empty bowl on the coffee table.

She smiled and said, 'Thanks. You've been brilliant.'

Alex waved it away, although actually he felt he'd been

pretty brilliant too, making arrangements at work and getting groceries delivered, carefully choosing things which might tempt her appetite and raise her mood. It hadn't been that easy missing out on the pub either, although he ruefully admitted that enforced abstinence had probably done him some good. He sat opposite her on the low, squidgy armchair and reached for his tobacco.

'You look a bit better.'

Laura tested the corners of her mind, pushing gently at the places where it hurt and finding that howling misery had given way to more bearable feelings of emptiness. She looked out of the window at the falling rain and reasoned that she had at last exhausted her arguments with herself and could no longer work things our on her own. The smoke from Alex's cigarette curled through the gap between them as though searching to join something together and she said, 'I think I am a bit.'

'Good.'

'Why am I like this?'

The unexpected question with its promise of getting straight to the point made him want to choke, and he had to let the lungful of smoke out very slowly, feeling the blood rushing to his head and pushing behind his eyes as he closed off the back of his throat with a small snorting sound until he could feel his ears beginning to pop. Unable to speak, he waved his hands at her and abandoned his roll-up in search of a glass of water.

'Sorry about that. Caught me unawares.'

'You OK? And me or the cigarette?'

He grinned. 'A bit of both. Do you want to talk?'

It occurred to Laura that this could be construed as a bloody daft question when they were holding a conversation already, but she decided to go easy on him.

'Sure. I think I owe it to you apart from anything else,'

she said. Alex was pleased to hear the laugh in her voice.

'OK. Tell me what you think has been going on then.'

'Well, I think I've been depressed.'

He risked a moment's light-heartedness. 'I think we could safely say that. You've had a very rough time.' It was interesting to see her insight groping around, the look of concentration on her face. He loved the way she frowned, the apparent obliviousness she had to her surroundings as she thought, almost as though you could see the damaged struggling brilliance passing across her mind.

'Since I got arrested you mean?'

'Uhuh.'

'But its not just that, though, is it? I mean, obviously anybody might feel down after that and I know I'm a depressive and everything so I probably would be expected to get it worse. But I thought the Prozac was meant to help with that. And it's not just getting arrested, is it? I mean, it was the things that led up to it.' She was frightened now, her lip trembling, thank God, thank God she hadn't actually had the time to tell Alex what she'd thought about his part in everything earlier when she was still like that. My God, what would he have thought? She wiped her cheek and Alex was sitting very quietly, just waiting for her, and she loved him for it. That was a bit strange really because it was exactly the same thing that Jean Tomlinson had done and she'd hated it then. But then Laura hadn't liked her and maybe really effective psychotherapy could only be done in a context of love. Ooooh, look, that was interesting, her brain had started working again, clever ideas had started to pop off in her head.

Alex watched her struggle towards her answers, trying to judge at what level of her dawning insight he should intervene. He was at once relieved and saddened, excited and trying to keep his distance.

'Do you want to talk about it?' he asked again.

He'd used those words hundreds of times with his patients, of course. But presumably he used them because he knew that they were effective, and she knew, she absolutely knew he was a brilliant mental health nurse. And she loved him and he obviously loved her, he'd said so enough times. So maybe there really was an opportunity here. She might not get one again. Perhaps there was a way of putting all this lot down, she was safe now. But to say it aloud would make it all seem so ridiculous, laughable, even with him. So did she want to talk about it or not? She sighed.

'I have a feeling I should,' she said, surprised to hear herself give a half laugh. She looked at up and Alex was grinning. He looked so handsome, and it had stopped raining and, Oh God how clichéd she could hardly believe, the rainclouds had gone and now the morning sun was behind him and making all the fluffy bits on his hair where he hadn't brushed it shine ridiculously. She laughed fully now and he looked astonished.

'I'm sorry, you should look at your hair.'

He grinned and flattened it, then ruffled it up to make her laugh more, wondering at the same time if this were her way of a distraction technique and that was enough for the time being.

'Do you want a cup of tea?' he asked.

'Mmmmm, yes please, but I want to go on talking though.'

He busied himself in the kitchen, pleased and increasingly encouraged by her responses. Laura watched him through the open door and somehow the informal domesticity of the scene and his physical distance made it easier to make the jump.

'Oh, God this is going to sound ridiculous...'

'I love ridiculous. I am the ridiculous merchant.' He was throwing away the used tea bags now.

'OK, oh fuck it, OK, I had this thing about being involved in some sort of a plan of God's. You were involved too, by the way.' She was glad she'd said it. It didn't seem so terrible now.

Alex nodded and picked up the chipped mugs. That was pretty much the confirmation he'd needed. It was interesting and touching to hear that he was involved himself. A bit of a first there.

'And you don't think so now? About God's plan for us, I mean?'

Laura was a bit surprised at this. Since her arrest she hadn't considered for a moment that Alex might be willing even to consider the possibility of her experiences to be coincidental with reality. For a moment she was filled with some hope that, apart from a boyfriend, she had at last found a mental health care professional who might actually take spiritual matters seriously. Then the thought occurred to her that of course it was really just his clever way of trying to gauge the state of her cognition. 'No, I don't think like that any more. But it seemed very real at the time, you know? I can understand why in New Testament times people thought the mentally ill were possessed. I felt like that, thinking about it, as though something was inside me that isn't there now, driving me on and making me all sort of buzzy. There was the most dreadful scene in Jack's house, you know.'

'He rang the other day while you were asleep. He seemed to be hinting that something had happened.'

'Yeah, well, I went mad. I reckon probably Poppy called the police and Jack must have talked them round because I only got done for D and D. It was kind of him I guess.'

Alex kept his thoughts about that to himself. Now was certainly not the time. Instead he said, 'That must have been terrible for you. I am so sorry.' And he was. Despite himself and all his professional reserve, like a priest at the funeral Mass of a friend, he felt himself wanting to cry. Grimly he forced the rebellious tears of empathy back.

'But that's not all, Alex. There's something else I want to tell you about.'

How was he to deal with this? He felt stretched out, at the very edge of his skills as they beat against his personal involvement, he must not mess it up now she had come so far. He bit back the jokey 'You mean it get's worse?' response that had first occurred to him and replaced it with, 'OK, go on if you want to.'

'I saw something I don't think was really there.'

Oh Christ, he wished he'd known about this sooner. He thought back to his first suspicions. Had he really acted quickly enough? In retrospect it seemed to him he could have been faster about moving on those drawings. But in other ways she had seemed so well and they'd been happy. So he'd thought that she'd been in the mild hypomania of love that he'd also been experiencing. Christ, he'd had no idea it was the beginnings of a full blown episode. He watched as Laura made herself another roll up, light it, and pick a thread of tobacco from her bottom lip.

'It was a snake,' she said. 'I thought it was the snake from the Garden of Eden, you know, the devil who tempted Eve.' She shrugged and tried to laugh, but he kept his face unmoving.

'OK. How do you feel about that now?'

281

'Well, I don't think it was real, not you know, in the sense of having any ontological reality. But it had tremendous existential reality for me. It informed my actions. And I guess that, thinking about it, because those actions ended me up in that business at Jack's house and then getting arrested and my subsequent depression, it didn't do me much good. I was exhibiting, what would you call it, unacceptable social behaviours.' She drew on her cigarette deeply, apparently lost in thought again. Then she added, 'That would be OK if they did any good. But they didn't. Instead I just hurt Jack and Lizzie, which was a pretty bad sin.'

Alex was getting used to this now, the way she wove her language about so that well read modern language and the terms of social science abutted the jargon of her childhood Catholicism. He'd read somewhere that the poetry of the ancient Near East worked like that, Babylonian and Hebrew scribes forming couplets where the meaning of the first line repeated the first's in different language. It was about the only thing he knew about the Psalms, and he made a mental note to show his knowledge off to Laura at some convenient date in the future. He was troubled by the word Sin, though. He was too good a socialist not to admit the existence of such a category, but had serious doubts as to whether it was helpful in Laura's case.

'You feel you've sinned?'

'I don't know, really. Of course if one could establish that one wasn't capable of making a conscious moral choice for some reason of course there would be no sin involved. Did you know that in some countries the mentally ill are called The Blessed Ones, because it's believed they can't sin and go straight to Heaven? I rather like that idea. But it seems like a bit of a get-out to me. I don't think there's really a distinction in these things. Do you remember the story of Jesus when he's criticized by the Pharisees for telling a paralysed guy his sins are forgiven? He just says, "Which is it easier to say, your sins are forgiven, or pick up your bed and walk?" That's what I want. Do you understand?"

He was struggling a bit, he had to admit it. Neither his NHS training nor his sympathetically critical attitude to Christianity had really prepared him for this sort of thing. In an acute hospital he would have been tempted to pass the buck along onto one of the chaplains, although of course they were always the ones to get first hit by budget cuts.

'OK. Look, I'm a bit out of my depth here,' he said. 'Maybe that's something we need to go back to. I'd love to explore it more with you. You've used the language of mental illness a lot as well as the language of your faith, though. That's really quite a brave thing. A lot of people try to run away from it.'

She threw the lighter at him in mock irritation at his patronizing tone. 'Oh, do me a favour, I may be mad but I'm not a moron.'

He laughed. 'OK, fair enough. You were asking what was wrong with you…'

'Yeah, OK, Nursey, give it your best shot,' she said, hanging her tension on flippancy.

'OK. I've felt for a while now that you've been misdiagnosed.' Laura felt a murmur of surprise at the idea she had been the object of his attention in that way, as though he'd somehow jumped the gun even though she'd asked him what he thought. How bloody long had he been looking at her like that, for Christ's sake? But of course that was unreasonable, of course he was going to, she had to accept that was what love did. She nodded at him.

'OK, go on.'

'Well, all the treatment you've had so far has been predicated on the idea that you are suffering from unipolar depression.'

'You mean the Prozac?'

'Yes, and not just that, but your initial treatment at Earl's Friary and your GP visits as well.'

'As long ago as that? But that would take me back to teaching, to when I was married to Jack and everything.'

'I know. And of course you lost your job.'

'No, but hang on, I think that was my fault, the job thing I mean. I mean, I just wasn't capable of dealing with it.'

Alex raised an eyebrow. 'Really? I don't expect so for one minute. Or at least there were reasons you weren't capable of dealing with it that nobody helped you with.'

Fuck this, she wanted to be in control now, this was scary. She rolled another cigarette, head bent over the coffee table. Alex watched her as she struggled with licking the paper and sticking it down in a rough cylinder, wondering to what extent her actions were being affected by interior processes. She wasn't usually this cack-handed. It was time to give her a pause.

'OK, let's leave that for a moment,' he said, and watched her smoke for a while in silence.

'So what's up with me?' she asked at length.

This was it, he was going to be allowed to tell her now. 'I think you're a manic depressive. We don't call it that these days, though. It's more politically correct to talk about bipolar disorder.'

Laura had heard of it, of course. It was one of those things she had vaguely thought she ought to know about, because she was socially aware and damn certain that the image presented of mental patients in the red-top newspapers and on the News wasn't the right one. Even so she had to admit that wasn't completely inoculated against that kind of influence herself, and what Alex had said was making her frightened as well as holding out the possibility of an answer.

'Are you sure about this?' she asked.

'As sure as I can be. I've seen a lot of bipolar patients and your symptoms and self-description are pretty classic.'

'Bloody hell.'

'Bloody hell, indeed.'

'How bad am I?'

'Well, there are two types of bipolar disorder. In both you get periods of deep depression followed by highs when you feel terrific. Sometimes there are gaps of normality in between. In some people the highs spiral out of control and can become dangerous, for the patient or for people around, and in rare cases you can get hallucinations as well. That's called Bipolar One Disorder, and that's the sort I think you've got. Bipolar Two is when you get milder mania.'

'Wow, bummer.' But actually Laura was astonished to find that what Alex was saying was cheering her up immensely, and that as he talked each description clicked in her mind with the events of her life, as though she were looking in a mirror which was showing a reflection of astonishing and novel clarity. Oh My God, she thought, that explains that then, and that, and that. She looked at him and managed a grin.

'Tell me more. I am fascinated by conversation which has me as the main topic.'

Alex laughed aloud. The sun had come out fully now and he got up to open the windows, leaning out slightly into the fresh air and enjoying a sense of thankfulness and relief that seemed to begin somewhere in the back of his neck and stretched right the way across to his smile muscles.

'Well, there are some peripheral things as well. It tends to affect high achieving, creative types, which fits of course.'

'Well, thanks.' She remembered something. 'Hey, yes, Didn't Van Gogh and Byron have it, and loads of other artists and scientists too?'

'Yeah, so they reckon, but there's always the proviso that it's difficult to diagnose somebody at that kind of a distance. And don't start thinking that just because you're bipolar you're a bloody genius, you'll become more insufferable than ever.'

'Oh, pooh. What about a cure?'

'There isn't one, although there's quite a lot of evidence that it burns itself out as you get older. But it can be managed with drugs. Usually people need some support from counselling as well. That's partly because they often have some issues about the damage they've done or that people have done to them while they've been ill, and because the process of actually being well again can be quite a peculiar experience. A very large number of patients only present with bipolar after they've been treated wrongly for a long time for something else, so they will have been ill for a while, sometimes years. I'm afraid you're not alone in that.'

'How much older do I have to get then?'

'Well, it depends. Quite lot older, actually.'

'So it's unlikely I'll still be a manic depressive by the time I have Alzheimer's? Wow, thanks. That thing about people not getting help sooner is pretty terrible, isn't it?'

'Yes, it is. It's partly because people usually go to their GPs when they are in a depressed rather than a manic state. After all, nobody goes to see the doctor when they feel fantastic. Unless the GP is really hot on mental health and asks the right questions people get handed antidepressants for the immediately presenting problem. So nothing happens until there is a real crisis, when the police or emergency services often get involved and we try to pick up the pieces. And ironically there are some antidepressants which can sometimes make people worse because they can push them into mania. It's often only after a crisis like the one you've had that people get a proper diagnosis. Unless of course they end up in jail, when it all becomes much more difficult.'

'You mean my Prozac might have made me worse? Should I stop taking it?'

'No, for God's sake don't do that. You'll risk destabilizing yourself. Brain chemistry is not something to be buggered about with lightly.'

'What about that poor boy?'

'Who?' Alex's mind had been so concentrated on his job that for a moment he could not understand what Laura was talking about.

'You mentioned prison. I was wondering about Andrew Halloran, the boy who killed George Brightly. What's happened to him, do you know?'

'He's on remand. It was on the News while you were ill.'

'Oh, OK.' She gazed out of the window for a long time. 'That was what the Plan was about, you know.'

'I know. I read your notes, remember? I'm sorry.' But sorry for what he didn't know. Still sorry that he had invaded her privacy, perhaps, or sorry that she was being forced to face a humiliating obsession, or sorry for her pain for the boy and for the boy's pain itself.

'Tell me something,' she said. 'Do you think that the

insights given in mania can ever correspond to or illuminate what you might call reality, or do you think that they should be discounted absolutely?'

'Oh, that's easy,' he said, all unaware of the trap she was laying for him. 'During hypomania, the first, slightly raised phase which can either go away or turn into a full blown episode, loads of people say they do their best work. You've mentioned people like Van Gogh yourself, and he may be a typical example.'

'Good,' she said, and again he watched her think in silence for a while. At length she spoke. 'OK, brainbox, you've convinced me. Tell me what you think we ought to do.' He liked the 'We.'

'Really?'

'Yup, there's no point in messing about, is there? I want to be guided by you, you're the expert.'

'OK, I think we should make an appointment for you at the GP's surgery with a view to getting you a referral to David Owens. He's a really top notch bloke and has done a great deal for the Trust, for bipolar patients in particular. I'll come to the surgery with you if you'll let me. It might make things easier for you. David will know what to do, but I expect he'll put you on either Lithium or Sodium Valproate, and fiddle around with your antidepressants. Then we can talk about counselling if you want it. How does that sound?'

'OK, let's go for it,' said Laura. 'We'll ring the surgery today.' She felt strangely elated, unburdened as though by giving her condition a proper title had at last enabled her to get a hold on it, as Christ too had asked the demons' names in the Gospel stories. 'And today I think we should go out for a boozy lunch and you can take me home and make love to me.'

'Sounds great to me,' said Alex. 'Are you sure you're up

to it though?'

'Absolutely,' said Laura. 'I've had enough of frowsting around and being miserable. There's one condition though.'

'What's that?'

'That you come with me to the police station first.'

They had argued a little about it at first, sitting nursing unusually chaste coffees at the café across the street from where Dominic McGahan was sitting contemplating a letter in front of him with satisfaction. Alex was concerned about Laura's possible reaction to revisiting the place, but she'd been adamant that she wanted to, saying it wouldn't make sense to leave it all unfinished and needed to rescue the best bits before she would be able to put a lid on the thing. Eventually he'd had to give in good-humouredly, and in this way he'd come to be standing with her talking to a pleasant looking woman constable. Of the brutal git they had seen before there was no sign so far, though he was tense about it and was wondering how Laura was feeling.

'Just take a seat, Mrs. Morton, and I'll see if he's available. Sir, are you with this lady?'

'Yes, I…'

'…this is my partner,' said Laura.

Gosh, that was intriguing, thought Jane Roberts. Events had already put her in a good mood, and now she smiled as she closed the interior door and crossed over to the stairs. She reproved herself for a girly love of romance, but couldn't help dwelling on the look of astonishment followed by completely soppy love which had come over that bloke's face when Laura Morton said the 'partner'. The poor little puppy hadn't seen that one coming. She giggled as she knocked on the door.

'Blue skies over Mootborough, eh Jane?' Dom said. 'I can tell from your face that you are not unmoved by our glad tidings, which have no doubt been round the entire constabulary already.' He rubbed his hands together and laughed, and Jane thought she had never seen him in such high spirits.

'I shouldn't say it, Guv, but yes, I'm very pleased.'

'Balls, Jane, say it, go on. The man's a nightmare. A total nightmare.' He wagged his finger at her and the comic gesture made her laugh. 'Not that one should say it about somebody who is still strictly speaking a serving fellow officer of course.' He was pretending to be pompous now, doing his impersonation of the Chief Superintendent, and then changed to a mock theatrical mode. 'But be not alarmed, Jane of my heart. I have so arranged things that the awful visage of the abhorrent Constable Wright shall no longer infest our nick even as he serves his last few weeks. Such is the privilege of rank. He has gone, he has gone, and our infection has been cured.'

'Yes, Guv. Thank you, Guv.' She was pleased he was this easy with her, it confirmed what she'd thought, that they could be really good friends if she wasn't still so junior. Privately she wanted to lay a bet with him on how long Mick Earl would last, but knew she couldn't go that far, so she said, 'Actually there's something else. It's quite interesting actually. That Mrs. Morton Darren arrested for D. and D. after the domestic with her ex is downstairs. She says she wants to talk to you about the Halloran case.'

'Really?' He wondered what on earth that was all about, how the two things could possibly tie up, and searched his mind briefly for what he'd planned to do that morning. The in-tray, of course. There was no contest.

'OK, show them up, Jane. Thanks.'

'Drew can't possibly have been alone in it.' They'd been in there for about twenty minutes, sun-struck dust fairies rising and falling above the institutional fitted carpet and bouncing onto the cheaply faked antique furniture. 'I absolutely know the other boys were involved.'

Laura watched as the Inspector turned her list over thoughtfully and placed it on the leatherette thing on his desk. She was pitifully aware of how thin her evidence must have seemed to him although she'd done her best with it.

Dom pulled a piece of paper from his briefcase and looked at his own list, the boys who had been talked to because they'd been sailing with Brightly. He frowned and placed it beside the one Mrs. Morton had brought with its identical names and describing her disturbingly likely conclusions. From what she had said her ideas seem to have sprung *ex nihilo*, and in her written comments she was way ahead of him. He couldn't quite grasp what was happening, could not account for it, and he thought hard before saying, 'Thank you Mrs. Morton. Would you excuse me a moment? I'll be back in just a minute.'

Dom emptied his bladder in a kind of Pavlovian trance brought on by the surroundings he'd sought to give himself some pause for reflection. His conscious mind was whirring with some uncomfortable ethical stuff while deeper down there was a sense of being spooked. There was no question of re-opening the case just on this, of course, but what she'd said was disturbing from someone who was after all, an intelligent professional woman with some connection to the case. He'd recognized her as the one who'd been on the Prom that day as soon as she'd walked in, and as he washed his hands he considered whether her prettiness made it more likely for him to take her seriously. He hoped not. The chap with her was no fool either. Dom had met him a couple of times at joint NHS and police force things. Of course that bastard Wright was good looking, too. A disturbing thought. You can't judge a book by its cover, and all that sort of balls. But as a matter of fact a lot of people did, otherwise publishers wouldn't spend so much time worrying about design.

'Sorry to keep you waiting,' he said, sitting down and assuming what he thought of as his 'I have made a Decision' posture, hands clasped in front of him as he sat square to the desk.

'Mrs. Morton, you must understand that a list of names like this is hardly enough for us to reopen enquiries at this stage. For reasons I can't tell you we know that nobody else was involved in the crime.' He knew he wasn't going to get away with that, she was far too shrewd, but it was worth a try and in any case he was duty bound to say it.

'You mean Drew told you he did it on his own, don't you?' Laura said. 'But you know there could be a hundred reasons for that. Loyalty, friendship, fear, a pre-agreed pact he's sticking too, and that's without thinking.'

Dom smiled, shook his head and held his hand up. 'OK. Look, I really am grateful for you coming to see me and I won't deny that what you've said has been extremely interesting. To be honest I'm worried about the possible welfare of the boys you have named. I think your partner works in that field and I'm sure he'll agree with me.' He nodded at Alex, who grunted in agreement through his surprise at suddenly being included. 'But look here,' the Inspector went on, 'Suppose that you're right. Suppose I go round these boys' houses and we question them?' He jabbed his finger on the table. 'We know that nobody else was on the boat when Brightly was murdered. Drew Halloran has confessed. It really is up to the lawyers now. Look, draw your own conclusions but I'm really not supposed to tell you all that.' He really didn't know why he was taking such a ridiculous risk but it was done now.

'What will happen to the boy?' Alex asked.

'Drew? Oh God, if he's lucky he'll get a good lawyer and a sympathetic judge he'll be sent to a secure psychiatric hospital. Then if his treatment's successful and he's deemed safe he'll get out eventually. Probably not back here though. If he's unlucky he'll go to inside on a life sentence, and be stuck there for God knows how long.'

'Oh dear God,' said Laura. 'So he might actually end up in a place where he'll be subjected to the same kind of abuse he's already suffered?'

Dom nodded. 'Again I shouldn't say this, but that's about it, yes.'

'Christ,' muttered Alex. He was going to need a drink after this.

'So,' said Laura slowly, 'are you saying that even if I'm right it's best to let sleeping dogs lie?'

Sleeping dogs, cans of worms, whatever. He wasn't going to answer. Instead he said, 'Not at all. I'm saying that nothing you've shown me or told me is enough evidence to suggest that any of the boys you have named had anything at all to do with Brightly's death. But I am concerned that, having had the kind of professional contact with them and Brightly you had, you have had serious concerns about the possibility of their having been abused. I shall take advice on what to do about that, I promise you. It will be done.'

Laura looked at Alex briefly and they agreed with wordless nods that this was it. Alex rose to his feet as Laura picked up her bag. Another of her mother's presents, this time a Holy Medal of Our Lady of Ransom, dangled from the strap. 'You've been terribly kind with your time, Inspector, but there was just one another thing.'

'Of course.' Dom smiled at her, though he could do with a cup of coffee now.

'Well, it's a bit embarrassing really, but I was arrested for drunk and disorderly the other day. All this murder business has got on top of me rather and I haven't been very well, as Alex could tell you. Anyway I was in a bit of a state and I'm afraid I behaved rather badly. But the policeman who arrested me was unbelievably rough, as though he was enjoying it. I was terrified. Do they really have to be like that?'

No they bloody don't, thought Dom, seething with anger at Wright and thanking God that he could still tell him exactly what he thought of him.

'I can only apologize, Mrs. Morton. In fact I am aware of the incident you mention and you may be interested to learn that the officer in question has handed in his resignation. You may, of course, lodge an official complaint which I should be very happy to forward to the appropriate authorities.'

Laura stood up and shook his hand.

'Thank you very much, Inspector. I'll think about it.' They said their polite goodbyes, but Laura turned back to speak to Dom just as he was leading them out.

'What about Justice, Mr. McGahan?'

He smiled.

'Well, to be honest, I think human justice is often pretty awful. It's one of the major reasons to believe in God.' He saw the astonishment behind her eyes, pointed at her medal, and laughed. 'Oh, I'm one too. Couldn't be anything else with my name, could I? Other parish though. You mind how you go, and as you love me, don't talk to any reporters.'

Thirty

4th July 2017

Dear Laura,

I got your letter Thursday. Thanks very much. I am pretty alright and glad you are too. As you know I am moving to a half way house soon and I'm very excited about that. It will be ever so good to get out of here at last. But I am nervous too. You will keep writing to me won't you? I keep remembering when you and Alex came up to see me and how happy I was that day. It was lovely to meet Davie and his girlfriend too. Perhaps one day I might get to meet Lizzie too, that would be nice.

You'll be pleased, I am going to Mass. A lot of us go to chapel just for something different to do but now it seems to mean a lot more to me. There were a lot of bad memories at first because of George and everything but I talked about them to Father Tim, he's our priest. He is really cool and has helped me a lot. I can think about it all now and pray about it and even for George without getting ill. I would like a lot more priests like him, they don't seem to understand people like me on the outside.

It's great you are so much better. I was really interested about what you told me and I am so glad you have Alex and a good doctor. It's great the pills work, mine too. I wish they could find something like that for Mum's Alzheimer's, it's awful being in here and knowing about all of that, and sometimes it makes me feel very guilty though Father Tim says I mustn't.

A bit of a scary thing happened last week. Some new screws arrived and one of them was that copper who arrested me. I recognized him immediately and it gave me a bit of a shock, I can tell you. He didn't know who I was though, I expect because of my beard, and I've put on a lot of weight. I bet he'll be one of the really awful ones. Thank God I shall be out of here soon.

Anyway, that's all for now. Thanks ever so much for your letter.

Your friend

Drew.

Alex handed the sheet of lined paper back to his wife and cuddled her closer to him. The low-skied sun was lighting up the Estuary, and through the picture window they were watching one of the barges haul herself round on her anchor chain. The ginger cat was purring on Laura's knees.

'Nice letter,' he said, and kissed her on the top of her head. 'Weird about the copper thing, though, isn't it? Poor old Drew, as if he hasn't had enough. What time's Lizzie arriving?'

Laura glanced at the clock. 'We've got a while yet. She said she'd be here at four.'

'It'll be good to see her and the baby.'

'Martin. He does have a name.'

'OK, Martin then.' They always played that game. She looked up at him and said:

'And yes, you're right. I so hope he doesn't cause Drew trouble. By the way, I didn't tell you about my dream.'

'No you didn't. Go on then. Do I have to be concerned?'

'Bastard.' She hit him with a cushion. 'I may have been a bit up again, it's true. And I had been thinking about things before I went to sleep to do with next Sunday's service and that.'

'OK.'

'OK, I dreamt I saw the Blessed Virgin, you know, like at Lourdes, and she was pointing to Christ nailed to the cross, then I kind of zoomed in on the wounds in his hand and instead of a nail there was a pill with Medication written on it, and on the other hand there was written, Love. It was nice. Do you think that's silly?'

Alex didn't think it was silly at all. He'd wondered for a while whether she'd been right all along, but she'd only seen the Drew business when she'd been so acutely ill. The plan had been one of healing, and He'd brought them together for that. Bonkers though she was, he kissed his wife again.

'I think it's cool. When you talk like that you bring love to the chained man among the tombs, and the pigs of ignorance and stigma run down the hill. How's that for a metaphor?' He was rather pleased at how he was progressing.

'Oooooh, great. I shall use that one at the Mental Health Conference next month. Another opportunity to play tame loony to a bunch of clerics and health workers.'

Years later, on what was to be the last Sunday before she died, Laura shuffled to a votive stand and lit a candle for Alex, asking again that what had happened to her could be set beside his pains in Purgatory. She couldn't genuflect any more, so she sort of nodded her old lady nod. As she raised her head up her glance was caught by the stained glass of the Virgin, crushing the serpent under her feet.